DEDICATED ANGEL

DEDICATED ANGEL

Before Herbert Shaffer died, he had dedicated his latest book to Agnes, although she soon realised the dedication must not appear in the book—in case her husband were to read it. However, Herbert's literary agent, Josephine Long, who had also loved him, is happy to agree to have the dedication made out to her instead. The only cloud on the horizon is the dead man's angry wife. When the truth behind the dedication falls into desperate hands, Agnes finds herself subjected to a blackmail attempt. However, little does the blackmailer realise that crossing Agnes endangers your health.

DEDICATED ANGEL

by
Anthea Cohen

Dales Large Print Books
Long Preston, North Yorkshire,
England.

British Library Cataloguing in Publication Data.

Cohen, Anthea
   Dedicated angel.

   A catalogue record for this book is
available from the British Library

   ISBN 1-85389-911-9 pbk

First published in Great Britain by Constable & Co.,
Ltd., 1997

Copyright © 1997 by Anthea Cohen

Published in Large Print 1998 by arrangement with Constable
Publishers Ltd.

Dales Large Print is an imprint of
Library Magna Books Ltd.
Printed and bound in Great Britain by
T.J. International Ltd., Cornwall, PL28 8RW.

Agnes took a sip of the white wine that she had just taken from a tray being handed around by a rather tired-looking waitress. The wine was sour—cheap? Couldn't surely be cheap at such a gathering!

The gathering was the launching of her husband Bill's new book. Since her marriage to Bill Turner much water had flowed under the bridge of their lives together. Bill had gone from strength to strength. Instead of grinding out detective stories—books for small advances as he had during their time in the Isle of Wight—they had suddenly seemed to flow and two had been serialized on television and the latest one was being seriously considered for a film.

Agnes picked up a small square of toast on which rested a piece of smoked salmon—she looked at it without enthusiasm. Then the people in front of her shifted their position and revealed Bill talking to a tall, slim, stunning girl. The girl was looking at him in that admiring way Bill loved, giving him her entire attention, her eyes never leaving his face. She was slightly taller than Bill. She had been introduced to Agnes as 'a banker from Sweden, my dear. Have you ever seen such a beautiful banker?' Agnes had said something appropriate—what does one say after such a remark?—and then the men had almost immediately clustered round her and Agnes had left the group.

She bit viciously into the salmon on its rather soggy piece of toast. It was not Scotch salmon, it was Pacific and she registered the fault. She would like to go home and get away from the wash of conversation around her. 'How are you darling? That beastly man, that chap in the *Guardian*, giving you such a review, I hope you didn't let it get you down.' 'Oh, not at all, I always ignore bad reviews.' And so on, and so on. Writers were bores, even Bill said that and she certainly agreed. She put her glass down on the table with a little bang. 'Rather have a gin and tonic Mrs Turner?'

Agnes jumped, her thoughts had been so far away, as she turned she did not smile at the speaker. 'Sorry, did I interrupt, are you just in the middle of a novel—or a writer's block?' Then Agnes' mouth did become a little more relaxed.

'I would love a gin and tonic and I'm not a writer, just a wife of one, Agnes Turner.'

The man turned his eyes up towards the ceiling. 'Oh the wife of the Lion of the Evening. Ice and lemon?'

'Please.' Agnes looked round for a chair, there were none available. There was a small settee in the corner occupied by three ladies of varying ages between thirty and sixty. They were chatting, gesticulating and occasionally taking a sip of wine. 'Writers, journalists or authors' Agnes said quietly to herself. A little distance from the settee was a cane-backed chair occupied by a morose-looking man in a crumpled suit. At his neck an equally crumpled coloured shirt protruded from a suit jacket which did not match his trousers. He was gazing into space, frowning.

Her gin and tonic arrived. The Swedish banker was still talking to Bill. Agnes wondered what on earth they could be talking about that engendered the girl's attention. Then a guess, the rapt attention was probably part of the girl's act. Another catty thought, she admitted.

'Ice and lemon.' Now Agnes was

9

less preoccupied, she noticed the man handing her the glass was bronzed, handsome, perfectly suited, a publisher she guessed—could be an editorial director. Agnes was beginning to recognize the various species. Agents, especially women, were so often called Elizabeth, Vanessa, Claire. The male agents, Timothy, Patrick.

'Let's go and talk to that stranded individual in the chair. My name's Miles, by the way.'

'Publisher?' Agnes asked.

He nodded and they approached the man, who immediately got up as if to make an escape. 'Woe, woe!'

'We're not writers. We don't want to talk about plots, books, television, films, copyright, public lending rights, we were just going to offer you a drink.'

The man paused, ran his hand through his already untidy, curly greying hair. 'OK, but I'd like a beer.'

'Very well, I'll go and see what I can do.'

Agnes was left with a now standing man, hands in pockets. He put a lower lip forward, which made him look younger. 'Mind if I smoke?' he asked.

Agnes shook her head, expecting him to

10

bring out a packet of cigarettes, she was wrong. He drew a covered cigar from his breast pocket, took the plastic cover off, looked round helplessly then put the cover back in his pocket. 'Hate these affairs,' he said, feeling around the rest of his pocket for a light.

'Why do you come, then?' Agnes said and realized her remark was brusque.

'Have to, bloody agent, frightened to death of her.'

'Where is she?' Agnes asked, looking round to see if she could guess who the woman was.

'There by the table.' He pointed to a tall woman with short grey hair in an immaculate black suit. As if she knew she was being indicated, she looked straight across, drew on a cigarette and nodded to her author. She looked fairly formidable.

'I'm Agnes Turner, I don't think I know ...' Agnes felt embarrassed. Her embarrassment was increased when her companion, by now clouded in cigar smoke, said 'Herbert Shaffer'. Agnes almost took a step back in her surprise. *Glass Diamonds*. I love that book! *Forbidden Fruit*. I like that too.'

He grinned. 'Probably the only person

who's read my book in the whole damn room.' The end of his cigar was now sodden and repulsive looking but again Agnes, rather to her surprise was not repulsed.

'Rubbish, your books are well liked in this country, as well as America.'

'Bollocks!' he said, running his hand through his hair. Agnes was slightly shocked by the word but nevertheless could not keep the smile from bending her lips again. She looked over to where Bill was still talking to the Swedish girl but he had now been joined by several more men. That, for some reason, relieved Agnes.

The hotel in which the launch was taking place was one of the largest in London. Bill had been pleased and anxious about it, had even been ready early. Agnes had bought a very expensive dress for the occasion, pale grey, beautifully cut, the small gold and diamond necklace surrounding her throat a present from Bill. She felt good and knew she looked good, too. She was not twenty-five but fifty-three.

'Are you married, Mr Shaffer?'

He interrupted her. 'Herbert, please,' he

said. 'Yes, I'm married. I'm a bugger to live with.'

The handsome publisher rejoined them again. 'Here you are, beer. Obtained with difficulty and perseverance.'

Agnes' former companion handed Herbert Shaffer a glass of beer. 'Thanks.' He took a long pull at the liquid as if it was something he was used to. 'Ah, that's good. Hate these short drinks. I drink when I'm thirsty and that wine gives you heartburn.'

'Oh, Miles, come right along with me. I want you to meet ...' A writer Agnes knew slightly grabbed Miles' arm and tugged him off.

'Popular chap that, isn't he?' Herbert Shaffer drained his glass. 'I believe he's a publisher.'

Agnes was peering round trying to locate Bill. The Swedish banker was now listening intently to a much older man with a thick grey moustache and long hair. He was much shorter than the girl, who had to bend over slightly to maintain her intense listening attitude. Agnes felt a great feeling of pleasure at this and realized she was jealous of the girl. She hated the feeling. She remembered only too well how vulnerable jealousy makes you. In the past it had caused her to do things she would rather forget.

'I must go and find my husband.'

She was conscious of the smell of beer on the man's breath. 'Don't go, come and sit down a minute. Those harpies have gone. Look.' He motioned towards the settee which was empty, Agnes had not seen the women leave it. Her eyes went round the room once more looking for Bill but she could not see him, so she followed the man across to the settee. 'Do you like these launches?' Herbert Shaffer did not look at her as he asked the question but gazed at his watch. Agnes laughed. 'I detest them, but it is my husband's launch so I feel a good wife should show up.'

'What, *The Bald-Headed Killer?*' He looked incredulous.

'Why not? They think it will make a good film.' Agnes' voice was defensive.

'OK, OK. Good for him, I haven't met him.'

'Why do you come?' Agnes' voice was slightly sharp.

'I told you, my agent, maybe if she sees me sitting talking to you she will think you are a writer.'

14

Agnes laughed. 'Otherwise she will be dragging me around introducing me to new publishers. I don't know why.' Agnes laughed again and relaxed. 'Is that why you are talking to me?' Agnes had a feeling of amusement bubbling up in her that she was unused to. She had just seen Bill talking to a grey-haired and bearded man and felt ashamed of her relief. 'I might be a writer for Mills and Boon.'

He laughed then. 'Not wearing a dress like that and using that perfume.'

Agnes felt herself blushing, got up abruptly. 'Come and meet Bill, my husband.'

Herbert got up, stretched and gave a huge yawn. 'Could do with another beer,' he said and followed her across the room to Bill.

Bill, momentarily deserted, smiled at Agnes and kissed her on the cheek. 'Enjoying it, darling?' he asked.

'This is Herbert Shaffer.'

Bill held out his hand. *'Glass Diamonds,'* he said with enthusiasm and much to Agnes' relief. He had tried to read the book before he returned it to the friend from whom she had borrowed it but he couldn't, said it was too deep for him.

15

Bill was not a reader, he was a writer and Agnes was or had been surprised to learn that it was quite a common thing amongst writers that they didn't read. Bill didn't even read his own books. Agnes corrected the proofs for him and enjoyed doing it. He took a glass of wine from a proffered tray and offered it to Agnes, who waved it away.

'Don't drink that, it's gut-rot. Stay right there.' Shaffer ambled off.

'Snazzy dresser,' Bill said smiling.

Agnes laughed. 'You wait, Bill, he'll come back with two G and Ts and a beer.'

A few minutes passed and Herbert appeared. Behind him, a smiling waitress with a tray on which were two fizzy drinks, the G and T's and a large glass of beer—a pint at least.

'Going to make a film of your book, then, Turner?'

''Fraid so.'

'Well, good luck.' Herbert downed a quarter of his pint glass.

'Doing *Glass Diamonds* in the States.' Bill sipped his drink but his sipping was arrested by Herbert's remark.

'Are you doing the script?' Herbert

16

Shaffer shook his head. 'No, can't stand the heat, keep out of the kitchen, that's what I say.' His smile was sweet, genuine, Agnes thought.

'I'm having a go at it. I want to see how it's done.'

Agnes, quick now to know her husband's feelings without words, felt he was defending his actions. Perhaps the party, the launch, the involvement with the film, perhaps he was defending it all. 'I agree with Bill. I think making a film must be fascinating.'

Herbert Shaffer drank more beer then looked at Agnes, then at Bill. 'Well, it isn't.' He poured the beer into his mouth. Agnes had heard somewhere that people can pour beer straight down their throats without actually swallowing. Herbert's drinking almost proved it. He turned round and waved his hand to his agent, who was talking to another woman about six feet away, gave a little bow said, 'Mrs Turner—Turner,' and made for the door, placing the glass on a small side table as he left. 'He makes me feel uncomfortable,' Bill said.

At home in their flat in Rutland Gate Bill regained his normal cheery manner. Agnes went through to the bedroom and changed her shoes. She looked in the mirror; her lipstick had remained immaculate for some reason, she felt pleased about this. Herbert Shaffer had liked her perfume, that might mean he often bought it for someone, perhaps his wife. She picked up the atomizer and sprayed a touch more on her neck. She couldn't forget the way the beer had passed his rather full lips, and she shivered. 'Want a snifter, darling?' Bill called from the sitting room. Agnes didn't answer. As she passed him he was mixing another gin and tonic.

'I'm rather hungry,' he said.

'Scrambled eggs?'

'Yes, nice.'

Agnes went into the kitchen.

At the meal, eaten on their laps in front of the television, Agnes mentioned the girl.

'Yes, she was Swedish, Gerta something. Egbury? I think that was it. Stunning-looking girl.'

Agnes agreed.

'Read some of my books too.'

'Oh, so she said, dear.'

Bill looked up at this remark.

'I think she had, she knew the titles.'

His eyes gazed past his wife into the distance. 'She was a beautiful girl, whether she had really read any of them or not.' His eyes refocused and he grinned at Agnes. 'Makes you realize how old you are getting.'

For some reason this made Agnes irritated. She gathered the plates and carried them out to the kitchen and on the way back caught sight of herself in the hall mirror; she looked old. Her lips after eating now looked slightly blue. It's different for men, she thought, women just get old, men seem to get more distinguished and young women seem drawn to them for some reason. As she walked back into the sitting room she determined to go to Elizabeth Arden's salon for a facial tomorrow.

Some days after the launch party for Bill's book, Agnes stood waiting for him in the flat in Rutland Gate. She had waited impatiently because they were going out, but he had just telephoned to say he wouldn't be able to go with her to the theatre that evening. As she had waited she had suspected he would do this, he would call, almost hoping it would happen so that she could be as angry as she wanted to be.

Whether Bill was really unfaithful to her she was not sure. He was easily flattered, easily a prey to admiration. Sexual infidelity was not uppermost in Agnes' mind. An admiring young female hanging on his every word could hardly be called sexual, but he would enjoy it almost as much. The excuses were coming more often, working late on the script with old so-and-so. He was not particularly good at excuses, so perhaps they were real. On the whole she felt Bill was a sincere man but vulnerable and she resented this vulnerability, or rather resented the people who took advantage of it.

She gazed out over London, their top-floor flat gave a wonderful view. Lights below her trembled and flashed. The red tail lights of cars leaving the city trailed in lines, looking like a large dragon, moving slowly because of their numbers. A few headlights into London flashed their message of crowding and impatience. The red lights were on vehicles heading home to the dormitory towns and villages, to stockbroker-London mansions and converted cottages. The ones coming

20

into London were probably coming to concerts, theatres, clubs, dinners, functions of all sorts and descriptions. Agnes felt suspended above it all. She felt that she was not sure, not quite certain, whether she was coming or going, coming or going where? Was Bill just a man with fantasies or was he devious? She didn't know, could not make up her mind, and if there was one thing she hated all her life as Agnes Carmichael and now as Agnes Turner, it was not knowing—not being sure—not being in the know. It seemed to sap away all her power and destroy her sense of well-being and confidence. She took one long last look, the Post Office Tower loomed high and black, cutting the scene in half, its blue lights relieving a little of its darkness. She turned away from the window. It was too late now to telephone a friend and say she had a spare ticket for the theatre—for the play *Maybe Maybe*.

The tickets had been hard to get, the play was extremely funny, or so friends had said who had seen it, and the reviews had said the same. Agnes was well aware that her sense of humour was not well developed and seeing the play alone with a vacant seat beside her was daunting. On the other hand, she did not look forward to a night here trying not to wonder about Bill, faithful or otherwise. She would go by herself, to hell with it. Probably it would make Bill feel worse, more guilty, if she went alone. He would probably think she would not go. She went to the wardrobe and took out the same dress she had worn at the book launch, decided against it, and as she hooked it back a faint smell of cigar smoke made her think of ... what was his name? Herbert Shaffer. She took the dress out and hung it outside the wardrobe and chose another, slipped it over her head, switched out the bedroom light. She was still a little early to set off. She checked her make-up and wondered idly, or was it idly? Picked up the telephone directory, looked through the Shaffers, no H, either he had another first name or he was ex-directory. She was faintly surprised at her reaction but smiled to herself, picked up her car keys and left the flat.

The play was not as good, or as funny, at least to Agnes, as the reviews had read. After the first and second acts the interval seemed welcome to quite a crowd of people. Agnes joined the throng, jostled a little now and then by people anxious to get to the downstairs bar. Agnes, being alone, was able to get through the crowd more easily and reach the lower bar. Two barmen and a pretty young blonde girl. (Was every pretty girl blonde these days? Agnes thought with a slight feeling of irritation.)

She was one of the first to be served and backed away from the bar holding her drink a little above shoulder height to avoid the milling crowd bumping into her and spilling it. They were shouting their orders and waving their money in the air as she drew back. The familiar smell of a cigar folded round her, the same aroma that had invaded her wardrobe as she had prepared to select a dress to come to the theatre that evening. The crowd grew thick as the theatregoers succeeded in buying their drinks, chatting and laughing, repeating snippets of the play. Some were delighted with it, some disappointed, arguing among themselves about the performances of the various actors. Agnes sipped her drink and rather wished she had not come.

'Not as funny as the reviews gave us to believe, Mrs Turner?'

The voice came from slightly behind Agnes and to her left. She turned, there was Herbert Shaffer. He looked rather as he had at Bill's launching party, a darker suit—perhaps his theatre suit, it looked as if he had slept in it—and a rather frightful salmon-coloured shirt that also looked innocent of the iron sprouting out round his neck, no tie. Perhaps because she was alone and off guard Agnes could feel herself looking pleased to see him among this crowd of unknown people. She could feel her smile becoming warmer and welcoming, almost as if her face was out of control, it was so pleasant to find a familiar face.

'No, indeed,' she said. She could think of nothing else to say, she felt girlish. The theatre bell rang. Agnes finished her drink. He took the glass. 'We'd better get back,' she said, conscious that she was sorry to lose a companion.

He waved a rather fat white hairy hand, 'Don't hurry, I've got a box, join me, if you will. Where's your husband?'

'At a script meeting,' she said, her voice perhaps a tiny touch crisp.

'They always are,' he said looking at her directly and grinning. They were still pinned in by people around them but he led the way through. She had time to look at him. He was not handsome. his face round and rather pale, his nose blunt and ill shaped, his mouth red and moist like a baby's mouth. His greying hair was slightly curly and she could see from where she was behind him that it was growing a little thin on top and a small patch of white skin shone in the bar lights. Almost every other man round them was in a dark suit and a grey suit or some in dinner jackets. One or two were in jeans and trainers, the clothes of the young, but no one matched her escort, his attire was entirely his own. She followed him up red-carpeted stairs to a small corridor, the third door he opened. Four chairs were grouped, backed by a red curtain which fell to as they entered.

Agnes had never been in a theatre box before and looked down at the rows of stalls and up at the balcony. She watched the returning crowds edging their way along the upturned seats and sitting down and settling. She turned and seated herself on one of the comfortable gold chairs. Herbert Shaffer sat down next to her. 'Mind if I go on smoking?' he said. 'Not allowed in this theatre but until someone sees me.' He looked at her and smiled again, she was beginning to like that smile. He leaned forward over the edge and pointed down to the stalls. 'Those your seats?'

Two vacant seats remained. 'They could be. Do you always have a box?' she asked and felt curiously childish as she asked the question.

'Yes, usually, if I'm bringing someone with me.'

Agnes turned her eyes away from his face and looked at the still curtained stage. She was aware that her companion was gazing at her with amusement.

'You don't ask questions, Mrs Turner. I brought a woman with me to see this play with me this evening but we had a goddam row at the end of the first act and she stormed off.' He took a last pull at his cigar and stubbed it out.

'How unfortunate,' Agnes said stiffly.

He let out a throaty and chuckling laugh. 'Agnes Turner, you are the ultimate. Any other woman—may I call you Agnes?' he said. Agnes nodded. She had never met a man like this, never. The curtains rose on the last act which, to Agnes, was very little better than the first two, though Herbert a couple of times let out his throaty burst of laughter. Once or twice she stole a glance at him, he looked totally relaxed, his hands clasped over his ever so slightly protruding belly. Agnes thought of the beer. His socks were crumpled around his ankles but his shoes were beautifully polished and obviously handmade. Once, he caught her looking at him, just as the curtain was closing for the fourth and Agnes felt undeserved round of applause.

'Bit of a slob, aren't I?' he said affably and as she stood he helped Agnes on with her light coat.

'Yes, a bit of a one,' Agnes said gravely.

He laughed again. 'Well and justly answered.' They left the box.

In the foyer a man came up to them as they were halfway over the red carpet and making for the exit. 'Excuse me, sir, are you not Herbert Shaffer?' His foreign voice was pleasant.

Herbert nodded, already lighting another cigar. 'I am.'

The foreigner held out his hand. 'I'd like to shake your hand and congratulate you on *Glass Diamonds*—a great, great book. I'm David Usher of *Time and Events,* New York. Just reviewed your book.'

Shaffer's face hardly changed. 'Thank you. May I introduce Mrs Agnes Turner.'

27

The man bowed. There was a woman with him, a pretty, well-made-up blonde—again! Hair curling round her head, face slightly too old for the hairstyle, but wearing well. She looked with interest at Agnes' dress and coat. For some reason Agnes was glad she was wearing a Susan Muir outfit, flattering and beautifully cut. More pleasantries and they parted.

Herbert Shaffer glanced at Agnes sideways, a look of mischief in his eyes, which Agnes noticed for the first time were hazel, in fact almost yellow.

'That bitch had a camera. Do you mind?' he asked.

'Why should I?' Agnes asked.

'No reason, but that woman, I expect, knew that I came in with one woman and left with another. Newspaper people are eternally curious.'

Agnes felt suddenly uneasy. 'I must go, my car is just round the corner.'

'I'll walk with you.' He guided her out of the crowd. At the bottom of the steps a slight mist of rain blew in their faces. They quickened their pace. At Agnes' car he watched her press the control and heard the door locks click open. 'Porsche,' he said.

'Yes, I've had a Porsche for years.' Agnes was glad to be able to say this but could not think quite why, she was not a woman who liked to make an impression.

'Not this, though, this is a new one,' he said, opening the door for her and slamming it shut when he saw she was safely in. He turned away then with a wave of his hand and a little smile on his lips. Agnes looked up, waved and slid away from him. She turned the corner and saw Herbert Shaffer walking back towards a Rolls. 'He would, wouldn't he,' she muttered to herself and wondered at her own feelings. Did she resent the Rolls or the fact they were parting?

Agnes drove home, concentrating on Bill's being there. Should she mention her meeting with Herbert Shaffer, yes, of course, why not? It was just after eleven when she arrived back at Rutland Gate. Bill was not in. The empty flat was still smelling of cigar smoke, or was it just her imagination? She went across, picked up a photograph of Bill she had had framed. It was one he had had taken for a book jacket, his face not handsome but reliable looking. He was a good husband. His sex was not exciting but was that his fault or

29

hers? She was not sure for some reason she could not explain. As she looked at Bill's face it was obscured by that other face, full lower lip and yellow eyes—Herbert Shaffer. She couldn't understand herself, he was such a ... such a what: *uncouth* was a word she tended to use about him. But it didn't fit. With Bill there was always a little anxiety, Bill cared what people thought about his books, about himself. At parties he was careful to say the right thing, often incensed her with sentences like, 'He's an important publisher, Agnes, or producer, or director, or editor, or TV channel manager,' as if he was nervous something might be said to offend the important man or woman. But with Herbert Shaffer, Agnes sensed a complete indifference. Take it or leave it.

She thought of his book, at least the last book that she had read, it meant a lot to her, *Glass Diamonds,* before she had met the author. Agnes put the photograph down and tried to dismiss the man from her thoughts. Stop seeing his face.

As she went through to her bedroom the closing of the front door announced Bill's return home. Agnes glanced at her watch, a quarter to midnight.

'Hello, darling. It's me.'

Agnes went into the hall and greeted him with a kiss.

'All right, dear?' she asked.

He nodded. 'Tired though,' he said. He looked tired.

'Everybody pleased with everything?' Agnes knew that there was more than a hint of sarcasm in her voice, but Bill obviously did not notice it.

'So-so. They're a tough lot, darling.'

'I can imagine.' Agnes knew her reply too was tinged with a little irony. For once, Bill seemed conscious of it. He came over and put his arm round Agnes' shoulders.

'Anything the matter, darling?'

'No, why should there be?'

Bill squeezed her shoulder. 'I'm sorry about the play. I just couldn't get away.'

'It's all right, Bill. I met that man'—she pretended to hesitate on the name (the first deception?)—'Herbert Shaffer, so we joined up—met in the bar. It was rather better than being alone.'

'Play good?'

Agnes shook her head.

'Shaffer like it?' he asked.

Again, Agnes shook her head. 'I don't think so. We met in the bar at the interval.'

She did not mention the box nor the editor they had met in the foyer of the theatre. She was conscious there was a reticence growing between them that she could not understand, let alone banish.

Josephine Long sat in her office just off Fleet Street waiting for her client, Herbert Shaffer. His appointment with her was for three o'clock and it was now quarter past. The telephone went in her small outer office and her secretary answered it, she could hear her murmuring into the receiver. A car hooted four or five times in the street outside her window. She got up and looked out. A long silver-grey Honda was stuck behind a taxi from which an elderly lady was emerging. The young man in the Honda hooted again and Josephine could just see his hands, the fingers extended, the palms of his hands beating on the steering wheel.

The woman paying the taxi glanced towards the hooting car without apparently feeling any need to hurry her actions. She took the change, handed some money back to the cabby. He drove off and the Honda started jerkily. More traffic followed on.

Josephine's door opened. 'Mr Shaffer

says he's sorry, he'll be a bit late, he sounded as if ...' She hesitated.

'I'm sure he did, Amy. I'm sure he did.'

Josephine returned to her desk and sat down. One of Herbert's long lunches, probably. She knew exactly what her secretary meant by 'he sounded as if'. Damn the man, she thought, pulling a thick manuscript towards her and starting to read. But she couldn't concentrate, got up and went to the window again. 'Herbert Shaffer is an inconsiderate bastard!' she said to herself, but had it all been her fault, had he meant too much to her, and she too little to him? She had slept with him, years ago. The first time had been wonderful, his lovemaking at first gentle yet satisfying. Her reactions to him had been powerful—that was the first time. The second time he had nearly brought her to climax then suddenly said he was too tired, rolled over and slept soundly all night. She had felt this was enough to make her hate him—yet was it? She knew only too well that sexual act, or lack of it, was to show her she was not for him. Since then he had treated her solely as his agent and had never referred to their affair, if one could call it that. She had wondered if he would leave her, find another agent. Any agent would be glad to get him on his or her books. This liaison had happened three years ago and since they had developed a totally different relationship. He had not left her, she could boss him about, demand he would hand the manuscript over when she said so—he usually obeyed. He looked amused when she was bossy with him but he did what she said, probably realising she was a good agent. She knew he represented her to friends and acquaintances as a Gorgon, a Medusa among women.

Her tardy client arrived at twenty to four carrying an untidy parcel, his new novel. Word processors were not for Herbert Shaffer. He typed his own manuscripts on an ancient typewriter.

'Finished the bugger. It's good, very good.'

'Modest, as usual,' she replied. There was no animosity between them. Now she supposed the ashes were cold, with him anyway. Maybe she had concluded he wanted to sleep with every woman he came into fairly close contact with. The starlets who she imagined must flock round him in the USA might have been used by him. But for some reason he hated going to America. His film, *Glass Diamonds,* had caused almost a riot in the cinemas. He knew the producer, director and cast had received Oscars and had to take one for him because he wouldn't go to the ceremony. It seemed to inflame his anger; he had signed their contract, had gone out to the States and come home telling her, 'They can get on with making a balls of it, I'm getting on with my next book.' This was the manuscript he now dumped on her desk. Part of it spilled out and she saw the title *A Cold Night in a Hot Country.*

'Rather a long title, isn't it, Herbert?' she suggested, pushing a large ashtray reserved almost solely for him across the desk towards him as he sat down and drew out the inevitable cigar.

'Long or short, dear, that's it,' he said.

Josephine smiled, a touch frostily. 'And that will probably be it, Herbert,' she said, pushed the other manuscript away to the side of her desk and removed the rest from its tattered parcel and placed it in front of her. He did not get up but drew on his cigar and looked at his shoes then he looked up, his eyes met hers.

'Heard of the Turner feller, murder chap, any good?'

Josephine shook her head. 'I haven't read one of his. I think his agent is Goldstein Burke.'

He dropped the ash off his cigar neatly into the ashtray. 'She drives a Porsche,' he said.

'They live in Rutland Gate too.' Josephine added this snippet of information while running her slender white fingers backwards and forwards on a yellow biro. 'Why the interest, Herbert?' she asked.

'Ah, this and that.' He suddenly got up and left in a cloud of cigar smoke.

Josephine sat after the door had slammed behind him. She heard him say, 'Take care, girl, watch out for seducers,' and a returning giggle from her secretary. Josephine looked at the first page of the manuscript now in front of her. Why the question about Turner? She tried to remember, had he a young nubile wife? But as far as she could remember she had just glimpsed Mrs Turner, beautifully dressed, austere looking, cold, not Herbert's cup of tea, fifty if she was a day. She felt relieved then laughed inwardly at her own stupidity. What was it to do with her anyway? But always after dealings with him, seeing him, after hearing his name, she felt disturbed, knowing he only had to raise a finger—beckon and she would follow him anywhere.

In Rutland Gate lights from the upper flats beamed out from the windows where the curtains need not be drawn, nobody could see in. An elderly lady came out of number 47, walked carefully with the aid of a stick down the six front steps. The dog, a West Highland terrier on a long nylon leash, came down the steps behind her. As she crossed the road towards the central railed gardens, the private property of those who lived in flats or houses in the square, she fumbled in her coat pocket and brought out the key of the gate, inserted it with difficulty and went in. The dog cocked its leg on the nearest shrub and a bright stream shone in the lamplight as it relieved its small self. Its owner waited for the animal to finish then went on up the path, the dog's long lead enabling it to run around a little, now and again it gave a short sharp yap.

Although it was nine o'clock the old lady had not locked the gate behind her; rather asking for trouble, Agnes thought, looking down on the scene, anybody could come in and hit her over the head and grab whatever jewellery she had on—the woman was not carrying a handbag. However, after ten minutes or so she turned, the dog lead shortened, she came out, relocked the gate and made her careful way across the road. As she negotiated the path Agnes could see that her ankles were slim and the shoes she was wearing were high heeled; elegant feet, Agnes thought. And the heels, for some reason, started a train of thought in Agnes' mind about the progress ahead of her own life. She was fifty-three now, just over half a century old. She was here alone in the rather smart London flat—a good address. From a downtrodden staff nurse she had arrived at her present position. A fastidious, well-dressed, not bad-looking, slim, middle-aged woman. Married to a man who she had felt, up till now, had been the ideal husband for her later years—was he? Did she still feel the same? (He had telephoned her earlier in the evening, he always phoned to say he would be late home.)

Agnes wondered what was the matter with her. The woman's high heels had filled her with an odd feeling—the feet, so neat, so perfect, like her own, but the woman with the little dog was old, completely belying the appearance of the shoes. Was that how it would be with her? Agnes Carmichael now Agnes Turner, old, walking carefully, gingerly, on high heels. Bill liked high heels. On the very few occasions when she had been wearing flatties, Bill had said, 'What funny shoes, darling, not like you at all, they make you look shorter and you don't walk as elegantly.' She had remembered the remark and bought her shoes accordingly, after all it was her first marriage and she wanted to please Bill. He liked things 'just so' his way, neat, but then so did she. Why then, why, did she continually, since she had met him, think of Herbert Shaffer with his crumpled clothes, his ill-pressed shirt (if pressed at all), his indifference to opinion, his carelessness? The little time she had spent with him had been such a relief, such a holiday from her own perception of—what? What was she aiming at? Her neat clothes, her neat hair, neat neat neat.

Agnes wondered if he had a neat wife or partner, was he promiscuous—using women when he wanted them? Who was the quarrelsome lady who had accompanied him to the play and then disappeared? But most of all, and this question puzzled her greatly, why was she standing here in her own flat thinking of him? Perhaps the book, *Glass Diamonds,* had influenced her. It was based on values men put on things that turned out to be valueless, but to some that difference, that valuelessness, persisted until they died. Were they the lucky ones, or were the ones that learned what a thing was worth while they were still alive, were they the lucky ones? Was she still believing in the diamond and not yet seeing the glass, not yet seeing the true worth of anything—and yet of course she was. She had Bill, she had this nice flat, she had the Porsche. Oh God, then was Herbert Shaffer the diamond or the glass? Would she ever know, would she ever be allowed to know? Somewhere in the back of her mind she desperately wanted to know.

The familiar, 'It's me, darling.' Bill was home. As usual she met him in the hall. 'Gee, I'm ravenous, sweetie, we didn't have time for a bite even.'

Agnes smiled. 'I've got something ready for you, darling, won't be a moment, get yourself a drink.' She went through into the kitchen. At least he hadn't dined with anyone, she thought, although he smelled of someone's perfume.

As she turned on the electric stove that thought was followed by another. I could smell perfume, well of course he'd smell of perfume, he's surrounded by these youngsters trying to get close to him because he's the writer I expect, and after all why should I feel suspicious about that? She thought how that faint smell of cigar smoke on her dress had affected her. What was happening to them both? Suddenly she felt excited, intrigued, shaken out of vague boredom.

That evening Agnes sat close to Bill on the settee. She felt slightly guilty but what had she to feel guilty about? She couldn't think. He wanted to pour out his problems, the day's problems. Basically, Bill was a simple, uncomplicated man, lovable and loving. The deviousness of some of those in the film-making business appalled him, he couldn't handle it. Not all of them, but many.

'They're frightened, Agnes, I suppose, frightened of losing their parts, their jobs, that makes them a bit bitchy to each other.

41

Sometimes when I suggest cutting one of their lines, they look at me as if they could kill me. You can almost feel their need for reassurance, for help, praise.' Bill was smoking again now more than usual. He'd stopped smoking but had resumed since the film had started.

'No more,' Agnes said firmly as he reached for another cigarette, 'I don't like you smelling of tobacco, darling.'

He had relaxed since eating, drinking a couple of glasses of wine, now he turned to her, smiling, not minding her denying him another cigarette. 'No, you're right, besides I want to make love to you.' They watched the news, then went upstairs and afterwards as Agnes lay beside him and he kissed her goodnight she had to put out of her mind again the thought how different was the smell of cigar smoke to cigarette. The cigar smoke was sweet and perfumed compared with the bitter smell of cigarette tobacco.

Helen Ashley lived in the same block of flats as Agnes. She was a good-looking stylish divorcee, about Agnes' age, although she only admitted to forty-five. Agnes had formed a friendship with her. When she and

Bill had arrived in Rutland Gate she had asked them to drinks and later to a slightly larger gathering including her man friend, David. The couples had dined together several times at various restaurants. David was a rather brainless man whom Agnes really could not understand Helen being so intimate with—but as she often said, 'it takes all sorts'. Helen knew her way round London better than Agnes and knew exactly what shops to go to for hats, stockings, costume jewellery, anything, so they had had several shopping sprees together. Helen admired and trusted Agnes' taste. She was dark haired with almost Italian-looking dark eyes and a beautiful magnolia-like skin. She was vivacious and outgoing, Agnes' natural reserve gave way to her easy laughter and wit.

Helen knew little or nothing about authors or making films, or television series or their problems, but read Bill's books with enjoyment. Indeed detective novels were really her sole reading matter. Her ex-husband had been a banker and a big bore, according to Helen. Her present lover, David, was a golf professional, not really in Helen's orbit as far as money or social position—but he had looks, youth, and according to Helen was 'major in bed'. David was rather brusque but he got on very well with Bill, and if Bill occasionally said he was fed up with something in his book being altered to suit the TV people or the film people, David's reply was normally something like, 'Oh, tell the bastards to go stuff themselves.' This usually made Bill laugh and relieved his tension. David was trying to persuade Bill to play more golf, Agnes felt he didn't get enough exercise but Bill was always—according to him—too busy. Agnes recognized the thought was probably wrong—Bill was busy and totally taken up with his success.

This afternoon however they were all four on the course, and David was doing his professional best with their swing. Helen was quite good, Bill's swing needed a good deal of attention from David, Agnes had not played before. The sun shone warmly; it was midsummer. The film was shaping up, the contracts safely signed. Agnes looked at Bill with affection. He really was trying hard, he looked good too. He was keeping his figure, partly due, she felt, to her care with his diet but he was out so often she couldn't oversee what he ate quite as much as she would have liked these days.

'Well done, Bill.' David's remark caused Bill to smile widely, loosen his hold on his club and pat himself on the shoulder, striking an attitude for Agnes' and Helen's benefit. A voice called 'Fore' and a figure appeared over the brow of the hill following the ball that had soared over their heads.

Agnes was truly astonished by her own reaction. Herbert Shaffer walked up to them, said, 'David,' went a little further then gave a small formal bow to Bill and Agnes and walked on. Agnes felt her heart hammering. She knew her cheeks had flushed. He had passed so carelessly. Had his eyes met hers for a second longer than the others?

'Come on, darling, your turn.'

Agnes felt herself come back from a long way away. 'Right—right,' she said but her mind was given over entirely to the man who had just passed them. He looked a little tidier, his white short-sleeved shirt, the collar of which looked slightly less crumpled than usual, stuck out from a rather hideous waistcoat-type woolly. His arms were hairy, and he was pulling a trolley, one hand slightly behind him. On his head a white baseball cap, PEPSI printed on the upturned white visor.

Bill suddenly spoke. 'Wasn't that what's-his-name, Shaffer?' he asked, not directing the question at anyone in particular.

'Shaffer, yes. Decent golfer, fourteen handicap, won't listen to advice, though. Could learn a bit from me if he would.'

Agnes could just imagine him saying with impatience, 'I'll do it my way.' She wished he had stopped—spoken.

They finished playing about six and went to the bar for a drink. Agnes could not understand why she was feeling as she was. She had met this man twice, talked to him twice, yet she was almost afraid to enter the club house in case he would be there—or he would not be there. He was not there. She was relieved and she was disappointed.

'What will you have, Agnes?' David was getting a round in.

'Oh, brandy and ginger ale, please, David.' She felt she needed the brandy.

Bill's hand was resting on the bar counter

beside her. His short-sleeved golf jacket showed his arm brown and hairless. She disliked hairy men. Agnes put her hand over his. He looked at her, smiled and gave her a quick peck on the cheek as he so often did. It comforted her but it did not explain or expel her feelings and she wished that she had never met Herbert Shaffer at all, ever. But she had and she could not conceal even from herself that she felt affronted by the fact that he had just walked by her with hardly a word, hardly a glance, but she asked herself again, had his eyes lingered?

'Oh, don't be so stupid.' She didn't realize she had said this in an audible whisper.

Helen beside her said, 'What did you say, Agnes?'

'Nothing, Helen.' Agnes accepted Bill's offer of another brandy and ginger ale. She had downed the first one rather quicker than she usually did.

As she sipped the second drink and the conversation flowed round her she was recognizing the feeling of her own weakness. She disliked immensely another human being able to influence her, have an effect on her. Agnes knew she liked power more than anything in the world. She knew she was stronger than Bill, stronger than his daughter and son-in-law, whose lives she had been able to influence and manipulate. But this man Herbert Shaffer was manipulating her; at least, after their meeting, she felt manipulated. How could she stop this feeling of—anxiety, almost? Find out something about him, something detrimental. But why bother—she had to bother. Knowledge was always power, gave you power over the other person, that she had known all her life. David quite suddenly played into her hands.

'Funny feller, that bloke who went through us this evening, Shaffer his name is.' Agnes felt her whole body stiffen with anticipation. 'Yes, we met him at a party, didn't we darling?' Agnes only nodded. 'I gave his wife a few lessons, if it was his wife. He paid me but he never asked how she was getting on.'

'What happened to her?' Agnes felt the question forced out of her.

'Don't know. She stopped coming. Common dame. Wore a hell of a lot of jewellery, even on the course.' David downed his drink. 'Takes all sorts,' he said.

'He wasn't very attractive, if you mean that fat man who passed us,' Helen said. She had a way of pouting as if an unattractive man was somehow an insult to her.

David, tall, young, bronzed, handsome, grinned at her. They looked at each other like conspirators and, for some reason, Agnes envied them.

Meanwhile, she was thinking of the mentioned wife or mistress. Did she go by the name of Mrs Shaffer, was she well dressed, how old—she sounded in bad taste but she said nothing and soon the party broke up.

'Do you like this, Agnes?' Helen's voice was slightly loud because it was the second time she had walked to and fro in front of the foot mirror in her pale fawn Delman shoes.

Agnes was tired. When Helen suggested a day shopping she always agreed mainly because she had probably spent several boring days alone and she liked clothes and she liked Helen. However, by about teatime she always became a trace bored and therefore, tired. She roused herself and looked at the shoes, they were pretty and suited Helen's slim feet and ankles. 'Yes, they look very nice, Helen.' She smiled up at her friend. 'Are you having them?'

'Yes, I think so.' Helen walked by the floor mirror once more then stepped out of the shoes, picked them up and handed them to the assistant. 'Agnes, you've hardly bought anything, only gloves and one blouse.' She sat down beside Agnes and got out her credit card. 'We'll go and have a lovely cup of tea, my treat because I've dragged you round Harrods where I know you never buy anything.'

Agnes laughed. 'Helen, I buy quite a lot there, underclothes but not dresses ...' She was about to go on but the assistant appeared again with the shoes in Delman's distinctive bag. Agnes was longing for the promised cup of tea, did not pursue the matter.

She led the way out of the shop into Bond Street, not quite as busy as it would be in about half an hour when people started the rush for home, catching buses and crowding round the underground, honking taxis—

'Come on, it's only a little way up. Has lovely cakes.' Helen took the lead now. It was then that Agnes saw Bill across the street a few shops further up Bond Street. He was just emerging from a café, by his side was Greta Ekburg, the girl he had pronounced 'stunning' when describing her to Agnes after their return from his launch party. Bill was talking to the girl earnestly and she was looking at him rather as she had at the party. Bill had an arm around the girl's waist, guiding her to a taxi which he had obviously just hailed. The girl got in. Agnes could just see that he spoke to the driver and handed him some money, raised a hand as the cab drew away, then stood for a moment watching its departure before he turned on his heel and made his way up Bond Street towards Oxford Street. He walked rather jauntily.

'Agnes, Agnes.' Helen had gone into the café on their side of the road and was calling her from the door. Agnes had been about to pass through after her but what she had seen had stopped her.

'Sorry Helen, I didn't see you go in.' She followed Helen into the smart tearoom, buzzing with female conversation and smelling of perfume and cream cakes.

Had she got the girl's name right? Yes, Greta Ekburg. That was it. She was almost sure, or perhaps Gerta something? What was Bill doing shepherding the girl into a taxi, his arm encircling her waist—no, she was exaggerating. He had only had his hand across the girl's back, just seeing her through the crowd.

'China or Indian, Agnes, wake up, dear.'

Agnes started, switched on a smile and answered, 'Oh, I don't mind, truly.'

Helen ordered China tea from the waitress who Agnes hadn't even noticed had come up to their table. 'Nice place,' she said, looking round the flower-festooned café. Small white tableclothed tables, nearly all full at the moment. She noticed the expensive logos on the carriers leaning against the chairs beside the women eating cakes and drinking tea.

Their tea arrived. She drank it gratefully. Bill, what was he doing with that girl? As far as she remembered she was a Swedish girl, hadn't Bill said she was a banker, was that it? Nothing to do with film making or television or writers. Still she had been at the party, for what reason?

'I've tired you out, Agnes.' Helen poured

herself a second cup of tea and took Agnes' cup to refill.

'No, no of course you haven't, I was just wondering if I should have bought that dress at Monsieur Maurice. I don't like his clothes usually but that rather tempted me.'

'It suited you, Agnes.'

'Yes, but Bill hates red so it's probably a good thing I resisted.' Agnes sounded as preoccupied as she felt. She was trying to banish the picture of Bill and the girl. It was difficult. Her husband in a tea shop seemed so unlikely, still he would be bound to tell her about it that evening, it was in all probability accidental, just a chance meeting. He had, she suddenly remembered again, pronounced the girl 'stunning' and she had also remembered that Bill had said that she had read his books, or at least one of them.

Surely Bill wouldn't have— Finally she managed to put the scene and speculations out of her mind and after insisting on paying the bill they emerged into Bond Street. Managed, with difficulty, to get a taxi and even Helen burdened with shopping sank back into the taxi with a sigh of relief.

'Going out to dinner with David tonight?'

'Think I'll put him off. He's beginning to bore me a bit.'

Agnes nodded but felt there was no direct answer needed. The next remark her friend made however made her interest revive.

'The Shaffer fellow, a queer fish, isn't he? David knows him quite well, thinks he's gross. Well, he is in a way, rich though, so David says.'

'How does David know about his finances?' Agnes felt her interest at the mere mention of Herbert Shaffer's name block out, or almost block out for the moment, the shock of Bill and the girl.

'He belongs to the club, don't you remember, we saw him there. He has a BMW, a Rolls, dresses like a slob, I mean it follows, doesn't it?'

While Agnes was digesting that remark Helen went to sleep. Agnes had to wake her when they arrived at Rutland Gate.

Bill was in and called out that he was in the kitchen. Agnes went through. He was standing at the kitchen sink, a J-cloth in his hand rubbing at a mark on his lapel.

'What's that, darling?' Agnes came up to him and took the cloth from his hand and remoistened it and rubbed the small white mark. 'What did you spill?' she asked.

'I think it's cream,' Bill said. He hated marks on his clothes. When sitting at his desk writing he was usually in pretty casual clothes, jeans and T-shirt or white open-necked shirt if it was warm.

'Cream?' There was a question in Agnes' voice and she found her heart quicken a little, now was his chance to tell her about the girl.

'Yes, I know it's cholesterol—forbidden —but one of the girls brought in some éclairs and I couldn't resist one.' He said it easily, the lie if it was one, but kept his eyes downcast on the spot that Agnes had by now almost completely removed.

The answer upset her. She threw the J-cloth almost violently into the sink. 'I should keep off the cream, Bill,' she said and left the kitchen. She was hurt but probably the greatest feeling was disappointment. It was a small lie, she supposed, something one might expect but they had only been married for such a short time. 'I'll go and change,' Bill called out and at that moment the telephone rang. At another time, perhaps even the next day or later that evening her answer to that telephone call would have been different but at that moment ... It was Herbert Shaffer.

'Mrs Turner, Agnes, Shaffer here.'

Agnes felt almost abnormally pleased to hear his voice and her slightly disgruntled feeling as to his behaviour on the golf course lessened. She had to answer keeping the warmth she felt out of her voice.

'Hello, Herbert, yes it's Agnes Turner. Did you want to speak to Bill?'

There was a tiny pause. 'I was hoping you could both dine with me on Thursday, Claridge's?'

Agnes paused, then: 'I'm sure we both would like that. Will you excuse me, I think Bill is in the shower.' Agnes covered the receiver with her hand and stood thinking, plotting, then, 'Yes, that would be pleasant. Seven thirty?'

'A bit later, I thought, if you don't mind; say eight thirty, yes?' Another pause. 'I'm bringing along another guest who Bill might like to meet, Neil West, another crime writer. They like to get together, don't they?'

Agnes felt a quick flash of annoyance but agreed.

'Bye-bye, then. Nice to speak to you again.' He was the first to ring off.

Bill came downstairs, he had changed. 'Who was that, darling?' he asked.

'Helen, suggesting a dinner date with David and you and me.'

Bill did not look particularly pleased. 'Did you accept?'

'No. David bores me, Bill, and truly I think he's beginning to bore Helen too. You didn't particularly want to go, did you? I said we were booked.'

'No, I don't really. Anyway I probably will be working late, that's the way it seems to be at the moment.'

The fact that Bill did not mention the girl in Bond Street irritated Agnes. When she brought in the coffee after their meal she placed it on the little coffee table in front of the settee with a small bang and the rattle of the coffee cups made Bill look up.

'How long will you have to work late on this wretched film, Bill?' Agnes went and sat down in the armchair opposite

57

him leaving him to pour the coffee. 'Only until it gets to the studios and locations, I suppose.'

Agnes nodded then picked up the television remote control, not to put on the set, she just held the little black object in her hand, watching Bill adding sugar to her cup before he handed it to her. 'Thank you.' She played with the TV control. 'Meet anyone exciting today, Bill?' she asked.

Bill stirred his coffee. 'Not really, on the whole they're a pretty ordinary lot.'

'All men?' Agnes asked.

Bill shook his head—then amended the negative he had indicated. 'Well, one—I don't quite know what she is, deputy producer, I don't know?'

'Pretty, young?' Agnes was aware she was pressuring him but he seemed not to notice, willing him to tell her about the girl, but she failed.

'No, she's terribly fat.' Bill laughed. 'Really huge but nice, lovely speaking voice.' He sipped his coffee. 'Perhaps she was an actress—or actor I should call them now,' he added, 'but she's the only one.'

Agnes felt she had given him his chance. Now she felt justified, she felt pleased she had given herself what she could call 'an out'. Why Herbert Shaffer? She tried to picture his face, not as he had appeared on the golf course but as he had looked sitting beside her in the theatre box.

'Can you switch on the news, dear?' Bill's voice came through to her as if from a long way away. 'Oh yes, sorry.' She pushed the button, the news was just beginning. Bill leaned back to watch it. He looked calm, relaxed, less tired than he had when she had come in. It was obvious that he was not going to mention Greta, or whatever her name was. Could it be that the incident was so unimportant that Bill had forgotten it? She could not sell herself that idea. She watched as the news droned on. She would like to talk to someone about the incident—Helen, no, she would make light of it and she felt a sense of loyalty to Bill. It had to be considered, husbands, wives. Then another feeling came back to her, an old feeling she recognized that had followed her almost all through her life, she knew something that no one else knew, except Bill. Knowledge was power, she could hold the incident over him if necessary. All her life her paramount motivation was knowing what someone else didn't know, she knew. Bill might be unfaithful to her but if he was she knew it and he did not know she knew it, that thought and the anticipation of Thursday comforted her and before the news finished her complacency had returned.

Agnes' affair with Herbert Shaffer appeared blessed from the start, from the first dinner, that wonderful four or five hours they had spent together. Of course Bill had been working late and anyway had not been aware she was dining with Herbert but, because of her deception, thought that it was David and Helen who had asked them out. There had been no sign of the crime writer, indeed Herbert had not even mentioned him or perhaps it had been a her, she could not remember precisely what Herbert had said.

Bill went to Scotland with a location crew. He had suggested Agnes come with him but had quite understood when she had demurred and said he would be so busy and she would be bored. Bill's visit to the Highlands had resulted in Agnes' first weekend with her lover. It had been wonderful. They had gone to a hotel in

Wales—three wonderful, wonderful nights, how many times could she use that word? Without doubt, Herbert was the most hairy man she had ever seen and long, long ago she had seen and nursed and cared for many naked men. Her monkey man, she called him and loved his almost brutal lovemaking.

'What made you fall for me, Agnes?' he had asked her one night.

'The long hairs on your back,' she had answered.

'Liar,' he had replied. 'You fell for me at the lousy party of your husband's, so you didn't know I had a hairy back.'

Which had been true. Agnes admitted she had not been able to stop thinking of him after the first time she had met him, the very first time.

More weekends followed, more stolen nights. When they met, as they did at several literary parties, they greeted each other distantly and politely. Agnes wondered, did his heart beat as rapidly as hers when this happened? Sometimes she thought not. They, when alone together, never mentioned, or hardly ever mentioned, Bill or Sylvia his wife. Agnes had seen a studio portrait of Sylvia in his flat, alone in profile, she had beautiful bone structure—aristocratic. The slightly arrogant tilt of the chin, long slender neck, Sylvia—a suitable name for her, 'Sylvia'. Agnes tried not to hate her for the times she had spent with Herbert. Once she had mentioned this—they had just made love and were lying side by side—he had turned quickly to her. 'Envy.' He laughed. 'That bitch, do me a favour, darling.' This had pleased Agnes and she had not mentioned her again. Sylvia was in Los Angeles, another blessing heaped down on their affair. Herbert did not mention when she might return and Agnes did not ask.

It was a strange time in Agnes' life, the excitement, the passion of her time with Herbert and the tender, loving behaviour of Bill, almost apologetic because he was away from her so much and valuing her understanding and support. Did she enjoy having two lovers so different they could not even be compared? Herbert, during the rare times he mentioned Bill and his books, was almost derogatory, whereas Bill when he talked of Herbert, again very rarely, admired and respected him. He had recently read Herbert's latest book and his remarks had thrown Agnes into a strange mixture, almost a turmoil of reaction—his admiration for Herbert in his remark, 'He's so much more able to cope with these film people, he has the strength to leave them to it, or to ignore them, let them interpret his work how they damn well want and not resent or regret it. Why can't I be like that?'

They, Agnes and Herbert, went where they wished, to Wales, to Cornwall. His large car met her well away from Rutland Gate whenever Bill was away and sometimes even when he wasn't. Agnes invented a friend in the Isle of Wight whom she visited. Herbert was intrigued by the Island. He had never been there before, he laughed at it, the smallness, the slowness. He never seemed to her to have the slightest fear of them being seen together. 'Supposing Bill found out?' Agnes said once and only once. He rather jeered at her remark—the very idea of it. 'Poor old Bill,' he said. 'What would he do, challenge me to a duel?' Agnes hated him at that moment for the remark, but only for a moment then she was mad for him again, he was like an addiction, she needed him like a drug.

Their meetings went on and on. It

seemed so long to Agnes that she could hardly remember when there had not been a Herbert Shaffer, no meetings, no lovemaking, no walking in the rain talking about his next novel, his passion against cruelty. Once they had stopped and had beer in the sunshine outside a little pub, a black and white cat had walked out of the front door across the grass to the wooden trestle-table where they were sitting. Agnes had called it, made chirruping noises to it, she adored cats, but it had jumped on Herbert's knees and sipped the beer from his glass. He had been delighted at this and when the cat jumped down and began to wash its face he picked up the glass and drank, laughing at Agnes' surprise that he had not asked for another pint of beer. 'Rather drink after that animal than many humans,' he had said, wiping his lips with his hand. On and on, days turned into weeks, weeks to months. Agnes felt it would never end, but it did, suddenly and disastrously.

It was their last completely uninterrupted weekend together. Sylvia had telephoned to say she had had enough of Los Angeles and would be flying home on Tuesday, arriving at Heathrow in the evening and would he meet her at about six. Bill was going to Holland and he was as delighted as a boy because there was a rumour, more than a rumour, that his next book, which was set in Amsterdam, would be added to the TV series. 'Darling, do you mind?' He had stopped to ask if she wanted to go with him. 'I seem to be neglecting you, leaving you so often but if you don't want to come?' Agnes had difficulty in concealing her delight and assured him that his success made her so happy and of course she did not feel neglected.

Herbert had had a fairly hectic week and said he felt tired, it was so unlike him that it took Agnes by surprise. Then, 'Look, darling, I feel a bit punk, let's spend the weekend at the flat.' Their flat was in The Boltons. 'I can tell Marie'—Marie was their help—'to come in on Monday and rev up the flat and get provisions in.'

Agnes hated spending time in the flat where he and his wife had slept together, indeed she'd only consented to do it once before and that early in their relationship. She agreed. 'Herbert, my love, that means we will only have Friday and Saturday night together. If we went to the Conway Hotel—?'

But Herbert sounded slightly irritated. 'No, it's a long drive and, as I say, I've had a hell of a week, Agnes, and I don't feel like that journey and no one will know that you are here with me.'

Agnes had given in, usually he spoiled her and did what she wanted. There was something repugnant to her sleeping in the marital bed, she had said this to Herbert the one and only time they had done so but he had laughed at her. 'Such delicate feelings, dear one,' he had said and because of her objection they had not made love that night.

Rather the same thing happened on this Friday night. Bill had departed for Amsterdam, the night before he had taken Agnes to dinner at the Hilton and during coffee had passed over the table a long black velvet-covered box, it had contained a delicate filigree gold bracelet, each link set with a diamond.

'Bill!' Agnes was really astonished at the gift. Bill was usually rather bad at choosing gifts, but this was exquisite.

'Do you like it?' He took the bracelet out of the box and fastened it round her wrist. 'It is so beautiful, Bill.' She looked up into his anxious eyes as they met hers, so open, so loving. 'I can't take all the credit for choosing it, darling, I was going into Cartier's with very little idea in my head, I just wanted to get something you would really love, and your taste is so good, so much better than mine.' He pressed her hand as she withdrew it. 'Anyway, who do you think I bumped into, almost on the doorstep of Cartier's?' Agnes shook her head. 'That fellow Herbert Shaffer. He greeted me like a long-lost friend, then he came into the jeweller's and helped me choose that for you.' He beamed at Agnes. 'He's a nice chap,' he said.

Agnes touched the bracelet with her fingertip. 'Anyway, it's lovely,' she said but she was aware that her voice shook. The thought of Herbert choosing or even helping to choose the gift made it a greater pleasure. What had happened to her conscience, she wondered? It had never been particularly active, she realized, but looking at Bill's face ... yet the very thought of ceasing the affair with her lover filled her with such a feeling of desolation and loss it made her feel physically sick. She could not bear to think like that, she was looking forward to a weekend—to two days and nights—with her beloved.

They met at Herbert's flat, it was nearly dark and he opened the door to her. Agnes found the flat claustrophobic, it was almost as small as Rutland Gate. Herbert and Sylvia owned a larger house in the West Country and an apartment in New York. Agnes had never been to the country house, it had always been hotels. As to the apartment in New York, Herbert said Sylvia detested it. Agnes had had the old dream that if Herbert left, divorced Sylvia and she Bill, that was where she would like to go, to the country house in Cornwall and to New York. They sounded strange and anonymous places but she would like to see them. But this, she almost knew, was only a dream. She felt the relationship between her and Herbert was too febrile, too consuming to ever last. She felt and dreaded the feeling that it would one day burn itself out.

That evening they drank red wine and ate Camembert cheese and buttered biscuits. Herbert looked tired and was quieter than usual.

'How can I cope with Sylvia, Agnes?' he said suddenly. 'These months without her and months with you have made me love the peace, the ...'

Agnes glanced immediately at the photograph of his wife. 'What it is that destroys the peace, Herbert?' He laughed. They were sitting together, side by side on the overstuffed settee, very close Agnes could feel the beating of his heart, slow and measured. 'What destroys the peace—my mode of dress, my hairy belly, my inability to feel flattered when an earl or even a duchess compliments me on my latest book, my complete inability to mix with the great?'

Agnes sighed. 'It's strange that I have never seen her, she looks ...' Agnes hesitated then went on, 'aristocratic.'

He laughed again. 'That's the word. I don't know why we married. A racehorse married to a milk-round horse, or perhaps a carthorse?'

Agnes put her arm through his, he had taken off his jacket, she pressed his arm and leant forward and kissed his cheek. 'Why did you marry, Herbert, why not just ...?'

Herbert leant back on the couch. He was breathing deeply as if he was relaxing. He took a long time. 'She didn't like living together, she thought it was—' he looked at her and grinned, "unaristocratic," perhaps.

Why indeed, Agnes? Well, it's really over now, in a way but we trundle on.'

'Will you ever end it, Herbert?' Agnes asked the question with beating heart.

'End it, divorce? I couldn't go through with that, Agnes. If I had met you first, that would be different. But we're too old, we're too welded together with something or other.'

Agnes felt her heart sink.

It was the quietest and yet perhaps the most wonderful weekend they had spent together. They didn't leave the flat. Friday from about eight, the whole of Saturday drifted by like a boat on coloured water, talking, listening, caressing with quiet tenderness but no lovemaking.

On Saturday night Agnes could feel the approach of the end of their idyll. 'Don't worry, sweetheart, we'll find a way to be together. For ever, perhaps—if that's what you want.'

'Of course it's what I want.' Agnes' heart rose again. Even as she said it she knew she was thinking of Bill though, dear, tolerant, dull Bill.

Herbert got up. 'I'm so tired, darling, I don't know what's the matter with me.' He rubbed his eyes. 'Perhaps it's the thought of Sylvia coming back, usually I couldn't care less but now—-' He bent and kissed Agnes. 'I'm going to bed.'

Agnes felt slightly worried and stayed behind as he left the room. She sat gazing at the blank TV screen, her mind running this way and that. Herbert, he consumed her, his idiosyncrasies, his eccentricities, his mind. It enclosed her so much, his contempt for human behaviour which so matched her own. After a time she got up, switched off the lights but before she did so she looked over again at Sylvia's photograph. The face, rather beautiful in its way, made her feel cold, she shivered, went into the bedroom and got into bed beside the already sleeping Herbert.

It was about five o'clock, or just before, when Agnes woke, the light was slanting through the curtains dimly. What had been a sunny day yesterday had totally changed, a drizzling mist was almost obscuring the houses opposite. Agnes parted the curtain a little and looked out, then turned, the room seemed unusually chilly. She went back to the bed. She was not sure what had disturbed her but as she went back the sound of a milk bottle rattling on the doorstep seemed to solve the problem and bring the memory of her waking to life.

Herbert was still in the same position as when she had come to bed. She approached closer, touched his shoulder, bare above the sheet, it was cold. She had only to look at his face turned on one side on the pillow to see he was dead. Alas, she had seen too many deaths, too many times, to be deceived into thinking that he was asleep although his eyes were closed. The skin of his face and neck was livid and stained. Even so she put her hand on his neck to find the artery, there was nothing. She must have slept all night beside him without knowing. She heard herself say, 'Herbert, my love, come back.' She heard herself utter the words and yet it didn't sound as if it were her, it sounded as if it were someone else in the room uttering the words. Then she sank down by the bed on her knees, her face buried in the pillow beside him. She was glad that he had not moved and that his eyes were closed, he looked peaceful. She prayed that he had felt nothing, no fear, no discomfort. She got up—as she did so she thought of the current book. That at least was finished.

Then a practical thought galvanized her into action. Bill. Bill must be protected.

Now there was no Herbert, he had gone, only Bill to think of. He would be back the next day. She put on her watch, ten past five. She dressed. hastily but carefully. Packed her small bag, gathered the few things from the dressing table, collected what she had left in the bathroom, even fetched a clean pillowcase from the linen cupboard and changed it. The one she had slept on, just in case it should smell of Joy— She left the room, at the door she turned backward and looked, wanting yet not wanting the picture of this memory.

She left the flat, no one—the road deserted. At the end of The Boltons a slowly cruising taxi took her back to Rutland Gate. There she saw no one. Once in the flat she got into the bath to try and warm her shivering body. Then she went to bed, lay back, the bedroom curtains pulled against the day. She lay there no longer than half an hour when she heard the flat door open and close and Bill's familiar voice say softly, 'Are you awake, darling? It's only me.'

He had returned a day early. Herbert had died just in time. This affair, this encounter, this love was still their own, still blessed, still guarded. She turned away from the door and buried her face in her own pillow and let a single sob escape from her chest, then she turned.

'I'm not asleep, Bill. I didn't expect you until tomorrow.'

'No. I managed—' He saw Agnes' face, even in the dim light she looked white. 'What's the matter my darling, you don't look well?'

Agnes lay back on the pillow. 'No, I don't feel very well, I think I've got a virus or flu or something.' But her heart was crying the words Bill would never hear, 'He is no longer in this world. He is gone.'

Agnes did not get up the next day, Bill would not let her although she constantly insisted she was better, perfectly all right and only wanted to rest. All she really needed was to grieve but Bill continually came in and out of the room, asking her if he could get her anything, did she feel like having something to eat—should he get the doctor? She could not even cry. Bill, she felt so strange, so frozen that she doubted, even if he had not been there, that she would have cried, been able to cry. The day dragged by and the following day the announcement of Herbert Shaffer's sudden death was in *The Times*. That morning Agnes got up and dressed and joined Bill at the breakfast table in the kitchen.

'You don't look well, darling, you're still very pale.' She assured him again for the hundredth time that she was all right. Then he read the piece about Herbert Shaffer. 'Good God.' Agnes knew exactly what was coming, even what were to be his next words and she braced herself. 'Herbert Shaffer died at the weekend, I can't believe it, he was only fifty-two.'

Agnes tried to speak, to say something appropriate, she had to clear her throat twice and still couldn't get any words out but then at last, 'How dreadful,' she managed to say.

'There will be more about him tomorrow I expect, he was so well known, particularly in the States.'

Agnes nodded, finished her coffee and got up. 'Do you feel well enough to go to the Hansons' for drinks tonight, darling, or shall I ring up and say we won't come?'

Agnes hesitated.

'We needn't stay long.'

She nodded again. She was finding speaking almost an impossibility.

'Wear your bracelet tonight, darling, I

haven't seen you with it on.'

Agnes managed a rather choked, 'Of course darling,' and left the kitchen. Back in the bedroom she sat down for a moment on the still unmade bed. She closed her eyes, she allowed herself the brief indulgence of imagining sitting again with her lover on that big settee in his flat. Their loving words, their touching, kissing, before he got up and walked to the bedroom to die. She had got to stop this thinking. Bill—he must never know.

The thought of his remark about the bracelet struck her. It was true, she couldn't remember when she'd had it on, the box was on her dressing table, she opened it—empty. She put her hand to her forehead, she felt confused, she was trying to remember what was the day, today—Monday—it was Friday she was at—Thursday night Bill had given her the bracelet when they were out having dinner at the Hilton, he had put it on her wrist, Herbert had helped him choose it, he had told her that, had she worn it home? Yes, she surely would not have taken it off that night. In bed with Bill, had she had it on then, he'd been so loving, had they made love? So much had happened, Friday, Saturday, Sunday. Bill had left for Holland on Friday, she remembered kissing him goodbye. Yes, she had been wearing the bracelet then she remembered Bill touching it on her wrist and smiling. Had she taken it off before she met Herbert? She couldn't remember, but if she had where was it now? She opened her wardrobe and put her hand into the pocket of the light fawn coat that she had been wearing that evening with Herbert—nothing, no bracelet. Then she tried the small breast pocket of her dress, again nothing. She was beginning to feel panic, for Bill's sake, she couldn't lose the bracelet, have to tell him that she had mislaid it, his gift he had taken such pleasure in giving her.

Agnes stopped herself from tearing all the clothes out of her drawers and cupboards, she knew she was nearing hysteria, she must play Bill off, say she had taken the bracelet to be made a little smaller—or go to Cartier's and see if they had a similar bracelet and buy it. She made the bed carefully, smoothing the covers, as if she were trying to smooth away her own problems, but she was trembling.

Some days later, Bill surprised her.

77

'Shaffer's funeral, his cremation, is on Friday, I'd like to go, I liked him.'

Agnes put her arms round him, she did not kiss him, just held him close. 'Yes, dear,' she whispered, 'I liked him too, I'll come with you.'

As Agnes said this she thought that her heart would break, did hearts break? She knew now at least what it meant when it said in the romantic novel that 'her heart was broken'.

She had been to cremations before, but those coffins that she had witnessed gliding out of sight had been sad but not taking her life with them. But she willed herself to do it, she owed Bill so much. As she drew away from embracing him, he said something that nearly cut her to pieces again, maybe he said it without knowing to punish her. 'It's so wonderful to have you always supporting me. How lucky I am!' She felt how little she had supported him lately.

Agnes watched the coffin trundling away through the purple curtains. The wheels, or rails or whatever it was on which the casket travelled, made a strange, nightmarish noise which did not fit into the scene. The purple curtains, the polished wood, the flowers, the black and red tiles of the aisle that separated the two blocks of pews, the smell of the flowers and death.

Agnes and Bill sat right at the back. The pews were full, mostly men. Agnes could see a woman, sitting in the front, dressed in grey. The large circle of her straw hat hid her face, even the back of her neck and no glimpse of even her hair was visible. As the coffin disappeared, the music swelled and a man, dark-suited, solemn, appeared from the side door at the left by the pulpit and spoke softly to the people in the front pew. They rose and followed him out through the door. Agnes saw Sylvia's face, just the profile, almost the same picture she had seen in the photograph. Then she disappeared followed by the four or five people from the front row. Another woman, perhaps her sister, Agnes had no idea. Then everyone began emerging from the other seats and following slowly. Bill and Agnes were almost at the back, behind everyone. They walked slowly—Bill took Agnes' hand in his.

As they came out into the air, the sickly smell of picked flowers twisted into wreaths and crosses and sheaths. They wandered slowly down the covered way, looking, in Agnes' case without interest, at the various flowers. There were many. She saw their own sheaf of flowers that Bill had organized, for some reason yellow and white, and she read the card, *From Bill and Agnes Turner*. She felt a pang that made her lurch a little against Bill, she clasped his arm more firmly. 'You all right, darling?' He looked at her anxiously. If he knew, she thought, hers would not be the only heart to break. He trusted her so implicitly but Herbert, Herbert, if only you were here and those lies and deceits could have gone on and we could have been, at least sometimes, together.

Slowly they moved down further and further, nearer and nearer the way out. When they reached the end of the depressing mounds of flowers Agnes came face to face with Sylvia. Their eyes met. Sylvia's were large and very pale blue, almost ice-blue. They held Agnes' gaze. 'Thank you for coming, Mrs Turner,' she said. There was a slight hesitation before the name, as if she had to search her memory. She shook hands with Agnes then Bill. Her handshake was not firm but rather limp and her hand was cold.

Agnes dropped her eyes, not wishing to hold Sylvia's look. The hand holding hers gripped a little tighter and then they parted, and Sylvia turned away to deal with the next couple. Agnes felt Bill take her arm, she felt physically sick. Then she heard Bill's voice saying, 'The car's over here, darling.'

'Thank you so much for coming ...' The words, much the same as she had uttered to them were being said to the people behind, hanging in the air.

The car seemed miles away. Bill opened the door for her. They had come in her Porsche but Agnes made no effort to get into the driving seat. The coldness of Herbert's wife's face had been so apparent, so uncaring, so composed, how could she act like that with Herbert dead such a short time?

'What did you say?' She turned, Bill had said something to her as she got into the car and she wondered for a brief second if he felt the same about the recently bereaved wife, but no—

'Poor chap,' he was saying. 'His wife seemed very controlled, didn't she? Very self-possessed.'

Agnes opened her bag, took out a

81

handkerchief and put it to her lips. Joy, her lovely perfume, wafted round inside the car, for some reason it comforted her and brought Herbert nearer, he had loved her perfume. 'Yes, she did seem very, very controlled.' She had almost been tempted to say cold, but somehow she thought that was unwise. They drove out of the crematorium area and started home.

Helen telephoned the next day and asked Agnes to come to have lunch with her. It was the last thing Agnes felt like doing but she realized she'd got to put on a front for Bill's sake and to help keep her secret intact.

They lunched at a quiet little Italian restaurant in Knightsbridge. They had scarcely met when Agnes realized that Helen's purpose for the invitation was to unburden her troubles. 'I don't know how to get out of it, Agnes. David is just a big boy at heart, he relies on me, Agnes, he thinks—I don't know whether he's really in love with me, he says he is.' Had Agnes herself not been feeling so miserable she would have laughed—David, who had the pick of all the women at the golf club, well, most of them, and as far as she had heard took advantage of it, well at least for a night's enjoyment. She sympathized with her friend however and even suggested she had a talk with David and told him the relationship was over. Agnes was not even sure Helen was being truthful with herself, was it really David who was getting bored with Helen and wanting out rather than she with him? People lied so easily, not always to deceive others but often to deceive themselves ... She knew she herself fitted into that category, as to deceiving, but try as she would she could not compare her relationship with Herbert to Helen's with David. But did everyone feel like that? She herself had felt that her feeling for Herbert, and maybe his for her, had been the ultimate, perfect feeling. To her embarrassment she felt her eyes fill with tears. Thankfully Helen was so self-centred about her problems that she didn't notice.

Whatever she was feeling, Helen ate her meal with appetite. Agnes could hardly swallow a bite, did that mean anything? She felt totally confused.

Helen broke into her thoughts again. 'Yes, you are absolutely right, Agnes, I must tell him it's all over, no matter how he takes it, he has got to be told.'

Agnes looked across at Helen, she seemed to be looking at her friend through the microscope of her own grief, the small tell-tale lines round Helen's eyes, the lids of those eyes, carefully made up but the make-up not quite hiding the slight crêpiness. The droop of her lips, the deeper lines each side of her mouth—Helen had no one, she had Bill. How could she have risked losing him? Were women all so stupid—yet had she had any choice, Herbert had drawn her to him, like a pin to a magnet. After all she hadn't asked to meet him, chance had done that. The old cliché crossed her mind but it didn't sound so much of a cliché now, after what she had been through she wondered at that saying, that cliché, 'This is bigger than both of us.' And it was, it had been.

Helen was choosing a sweet from the sweet trolley, Agnes waved it away. 'You need a husband, Helen,' she said suddenly. The remark came out without thought.

Helen looked up, her eyes a little wide. 'I've tried that, I've had two,' she said, looking with appreciation at the profiteroles the waitress had put in front of her. Agnes suddenly smiled. Helen's relationships were probably simple—maybe not very deep, and she shed them like taking off a coat and putting on another. Was this a preferable way to live?

They finished lunch, did some shopping. 'You're such a help, Agnes, there's no one else I can talk to like you.' Agnes pressed her hand and left her and went into her own flat.

As she passed the hall mirror she stopped, turned and looked at herself. 'Agony Aunt, that's what you've turned into,' she said aloud, referring to Helen's confidences and her remark about how wonderful it was to be able to talk to her. But there was no one who could act as her Agony Aunt. Her agony was too real, too piercing. She went through into the kitchen wondering would Bill be home for dinner.

Agnes decided to prepare a meal, it would be there whether he came or not—but why did everything, everything return her mind to Herbert, remind her of Herbert? The red wine, as she drew the cork it came back to her, sitting on the sofa that last evening, sipping the wine while she buttered biscuits for him, his favourite dry water biscuits, his favourite. It was like having two pictures in your mind at the same time, seeing him, hearing him, with Bill underneath looking with those tired anxious eyes at her, through the picture of her lover. 'I feel so tired, Agnes,' Herbert said again to her memory, as she took place mats through to the dining room. 'It's been a hell of day.' Would he still be here had she gone through to the bedroom with him then, undressed, got into bed, perhaps held him in her arms—would it have been different? She wondered if the thought of him would gradually fade, if it didn't she felt she didn't wish to live without him.

When they ate their meal together Agnes could sense Bill's anxiety about her, he was so gentle, talked only a little about the film and the next television series and then only to tell her amusing things that had happened to make her smile—dear Bill. Agnes decided there and then making a vow that no matter what, no matter how, by fair means or foul, she would never, never let him find out that she had been unfaithful to him.

Josephine Long sat at her office desk staring in front of her at nothing. The death of her client, the death of Herbert Shaffer, had affected her much more than she liked to be affected by anything. The thought of their love affair would not be banished as all thoughts of it had been before his death. They came back to her strongly. The feel of his arms around her, his smell, the abrupt way he had of withdrawing, selfishly withdrawing when she wanted him to remain in her. The feelings were so strong she had cried all last night and in consequence had a nagging headache this morning. She had taken two aspirins and the taste of them lingered in her mouth and she felt altogether upset, out of sorts, old.

The typescript of his last novel, *A Cold Night in a Hot Country*, lay in front of her on her desk. She had read it now and though there were one or two things she would have liked to have him alter, to have talked over with him, now he never would, never could. It was nevertheless brilliant, thoughtful, robust, all the words which would be used in the crits, she knew it would be received well, she was a good agent, she knew her work, knew exactly what the publisher wanted and knew that he could supply it, he who would supply no more, but one thing worried her. She turned the pages back to the beginning of the book and read again for the hundredth time the dedication. There in the middle of the white page alone, the sentence and the top copy typed ready for the publisher, and underneath it not a copy but written in Herbert's own hand the same dedication. Why had he done that? It had been perhaps to tell Josephine—or perhaps he had intended to give the written page to Agnes but had forgotten and left it there.

For Agnes, who is my for ever.

If only it had been for her, that dedication. She was aware, as she was aware of most things, what went on around her, particularly about those for whom she was working, fixing contracts, editing, talking to, she could tell. She had known Herbert was sleeping, or copulating would be a better word, with Maria, Sylvia's daily. She knew he had tried to extricate himself from a relationship with a young lady with whom he had been sleeping while he was sleeping with Josephine herself, she had known that. He talked about it—pillow talk. He had told her at the time that the girl was a nuisance, becoming a nuisance, was a good lay but—and then he would make love to her. She knew she had to restrain herself from tearing out this dedication page and crushing it between her long painted nails and throwing it in the wastepaper-basket and forgetting it, pretending there had been no dedication, and yet she couldn't do that. Somehow it seemed wrong, wrong to do it to him, even now she felt that, although he was despicable, despicable—

There again her thoughts turned to him with kindness, he had never hidden what he was. 'I'm a behaviourist, Josephine also I have no conscience, no scruples, so expect nothing.' At least there had been honesty there, as well as cruelty. Two warm tears ran down her cheeks. A small radio by her desk played gently an oldie, why were the oldies so popular, was it a sentimental time? 'Make the world go away, take this weight off my shoulders.' She slammed her hand on the radio to silence it then began to think about Sylvia.

What was she to do about the dedication as far as Sylvia was concerned? Josephine knew who Agnes was, the Turners had been at the funeral, she had seen the flowers from Bill and Agnes Turner. She remembered Agnes, frozen-faced, she remembered seeing Herbert talking to Agnes at some party or other, he must have liked that elegant, middle-aged woman who looked passionless—cold—but that dedication was a contradiction of her looks. What a storm it would create with Sylvia, with Agnes' husband. Sylvia would be humiliated.

Josephine sitting there, hating and envying Sylvia—she would let it through, let the publishers have it, imagine Sylvia's face when she opened the book! It would be worth the storm. Could one sue for a dedication? How she would love to substitute *Josephine* for *Agnes,* after all Sylvia had not seen it yet, but her hard-headed commonsense ruled that out. Everybody knew, even her secretary, the office cleaner, how he had dropped her, dumped her, they knew everything and Sylvia too probably. But supposing she lied, said it had started again?

Josephine picked up the telephone—she must of course discuss this with Sylvia—a little smile replaced her tearfulness. Sylvia would be furious, she thought a lot of herself, Sylvia was very self-admiring. This should pull her down a little. With a trace of relish Josephine dialled the Shaffers' number.

Josephine's telephone call was not well received.

'What do you want to see me about, Miss Long?'

Josephine noted the 'Miss Long'. Sylvia Shaffer had called her 'Josephine' before Herbert's death, obviously she was now demoted to Herbert Shaffer's agent, not a friend or even an acquaintance.

'It's rather difficult, Mrs Shaffer.' It was 'Mrs Shaffer' now too, not 'Sylvia', as had been allowed, but Josephine secure in the effect the bombshell of the dedication and the effect it would have, kept her voice like honey. 'I'm so sorry to have to wish this on you.'

There was a riffle of pages, as if Mrs Shaffer was consulting her diary. 'Well, I could manage tomorrow morning about eleven on my way to Lady Mel's drinks party, Miss Long, otherwise I can't.'

'That will be perfect.' Josephine put the phone down.

Josephine sat for minutes looking at the dedication. Her heart was full of envy for this Agnes. Suddenly she sat bolt upright in her swivel chair. Why Agnes, why show bloody Sylvia the 'Agnes' dedication? The only one who had seen it was her secretary and she valued her job. She threaded an A4 piece of paper into her typewriter and retyped the dedication. There it was in the middle of the paper, clear and precise in its central presentation and it read, TO JOSEPHINE WHO IS MY FOR EVER. She took the paper out, placed it in its correct place in the beginning of the manuscript, opened the drawer below and put in the true dedication carefully flat inside. She knew now in a flood of inspiration what she would do. She closed the folder of *A Cold Night in a Hot Country*, put it to one side, then rested her hands on the blotter in front of her, it was not true, if only it was—The tears pricked her eyelids again. She got abruptly to her feet. 'I'm going home, Amy, you can go too.'

The girl sitting at the desk outside looked up surprised. 'Right, see you tomorrow,' she said, putting away some papers and closing her desk drawer. About ten minutes later Josephine Long passed through the office, banging the door behind her, the girl followed, stopping to lock the door.

She stared down the stairs watching her employer leave, it was unusual for her to go early, very unusual, she looked a bit odd too. 'Wonder who rattled her cage?' she muttered and followed more nimbly than her employer, but then she was young.

Josephine did not sleep that night.

The next morning Sylvia Shaffer arrived promptly at eleven, Josephine had to admit she looked sensational. The death of her husband appeared to have left very little mark on her. She sat down in the chair Josephine had placed for her, crossed her legs, inclined her head to thank Josephine for the ashtray. Sylvia had opened her handbag and withdrawn a packet of cigarettes from a gold case and, refusing Josephine's offered light, tapped the cigarette daintily on the case, lit it with a gold lighter. Josephine looked at her with grudging admiration. Her coolness looked unassailable. 'What was it you wanted to see me about, Miss Long? Is there something you want me to do?'

'Oh, nothing for you to do, Mrs Shaffer, it's just this.' She turned the typewritten novel and pushed it across the desk. The result was not quite as dramatic as she had fantasized. Sylvia rested her cigarette carefully on the ashtray, opened her bag, got out a pair of gold-rimmed glasses, put these on, again carefully so as not to disturb her hair, then as her eyes focused on the dedication the drama of the situation did at last materialize.

'How dare you show me this.' She snatched off the glasses.

'Well, I felt I had to, Mrs Shaffer. Herbert and I were very much in love. I didn't know he was going to do this, I assure you. And also, I rather presumed you knew.'

'Very much in love!' Sylvia's voice rose to a scream.

Josephine got up and crossed and closed the office door on a wide-eyed Amy. She sat down again. 'You know and I know that you and my husband had a brief, sordid affair and he quickly tired of you. He told me all about it.'

Josephine shook her head quietly to and fro. 'No, I'm afraid that's not so, Mrs Shaffer.'

'Do you mean you've still been sleeping with my husband?' Fuming, Sylvia stood up, paced the floor a few steps. 'Were you there the night he ...'

Josephine covered her eyes with her hand and let that signify her reply. 'You bitch! You bitch! This must be yours, then. This common-looking bauble.' She snatched a bracelet from her bag and threw it across the desk towards Josephine 'This sordid dedication must be stopped.' She seized the paper and was about to rip the page to shreds when the quiet voice of the woman opposite stopped her.

'I'm afraid that's impossible, Mrs Shaffer, he had already sent the book with the dedication to his publisher.'

'Then alert them. Say if they include this dedication I shall forbid the publication of the book. Do that, do that. Get on the telephone.' She picked up the receiver on the desk and waved it menacingly in Josephine's face.

'Don't you think that would be rather unwise?' Josephine felt herself smiling. Sylvia's rage began to make Josephine feel that the dedication was really true. He had loved her. Well, once he had. On that, the dedication she had typed would cancel Agnes out.

'What do you mean, unwise?'

'Well, it would draw the publisher's notice even more to the name and Herbert

95

seldom dedicated his books to anyone.'

'Usually a famous author, not a trollop!'

That finished Josephine. She rose to her feet. She was considerably taller than Sylvia. 'Please leave my office, Mrs Shaffer. It is my responsibility to carry out what my client suggested.' She crossed the room, opened the door. 'Mrs Shaffer is leaving, Amy,' she said.

'I will consult my lawyer, Miss Long, believe me you haven't heard the last of this.'

Josephine closed the door behind her. Heard her slam the outer door. Sat for a moment then drew out the Agnes dedication, changed it for the Josephine one and put that carefully in the drawer and drew the telephone towards her again. She looked up the number and dialled. 'Ah, Mrs Turner, I wonder, would you do me a small favour—it's about Mr Herbert Shaffer's new book. I would like your advice about something.'

To say that Agnes was bewildered by Josephine's telephone call would be a large understatement. She had only seen Herbert's agent once, at Bill's book launch Herbert had mentioned her several times, not in particularly amiable terms. He admitted he had had a brief, very brief affair with her at one time, admitted freely that he thought she was an efficient woman and a first-class agent, and had even said at one time, Agnes remembered, that anyone who would put up with him as an author must either be in love with him or very short of cash. What the small favour was she could not imagine and Josephine Long had made no attempt to explain.

Agnes agreed to come to Josephine Long's office the next day.

She seemed to want the 'small favour' dealt with as soon as possible. Agnes was having a dress fitting in the morning so three thirty in the afternoon was decided on. Agnes realized, of course, that nothing must be said of this meeting to Bill. There could be no possible reason in his eyes that Herbert Shaffer's agent would want to see his wife. Now Herbert was gone Agnes felt more guilty in hiding anything from Bill but this had to be, she wanted all the deception to be over. Next day she was almost impatient at her dress fitting and after lunch took a taxi to the address Josephine Long had given her. The office was just off Fleet Street. Agnes was glad she had not come in her Porsche. The road was lined with cars, parked almost bumper to bumper. She found the block where Josephine had indicated, no lift, dark stairs, the indication on the door lintel read, JOSEPHINE LONG, LITERARY AGENT, SECOND FLOOR, OFFICE 8. It was two flights up. Agnes walked the last flight which ended in a small hall-like space. She paused for a second, thinking of the connection between Herbert and this place. The door, clearly plated with Josephine's name and business, Agnes knocked.

It was immediately opened by a girl with glasses rather low down on her nose, her brown eyes peered over the top of them. 'Mrs Turner,' she said and smiled. The smile completely changed her face from a blank enquiry to a welcome. 'Miss Long is expecting you.' She ushered her past a rather untidy, battered desk, some metal filing cabinets, a pretty table in the corner by another door. She opened this and announced, 'Mrs Turner, Miss Long.'

Agnes entered the room and immediately recognized the tall, rather angular woman with beautifully cut grey hair.

'Oh, good of you to come, Mrs Turner, please sit down.'

Agnes sat down, glancing round her with some interest. The room did not match the outer office, the desk was Chippendale, or Chippendale style, beautifully polished. A bureau bookcase behind and slightly to the agent's right was full of books in bright new covers behind the glass doors. The carpet too, was in good taste, French blue. The two long windows, looking out on Fleet Street, were flanked with terracotta velvet curtains, thought and taste were evident.

'This is a delicate matter, Mrs Turner.' Josephine Long was the first to speak. In that instant Agnes' heart quickened and she knew what she was about to hear was concerning Herbert but what it could be she could not imagine. The folder of typescript in front of the agent was reversed and pushed towards her. Much as it had been towards Sylvia the day before but not with the same dedication. Agnes read and it seemed as if instead of beating rapidly her heart stopped. TO AGNES WHO IS MY FOR EVER. They were the most beautiful, most poignant words Agnes had ever read. For a moment she was unconscious of anything around her. The man, their love, the words, seemed all there was, all that mattered, all that had ever mattered. Then the cold voice of reason came across the desk from Josephine Long.

'I did realize, Mrs Turner, what this dedication might do to your marriage and I felt it only fair to warn you. Did I do right?'

Agnes looked up. The woman opposite looked neither hostile nor was she smiling, she looked just interested. Perhaps there was a little concern just on the edge of the expression. Agnes encountered it, looked at her as if coming up from deep water. For a moment she could not speak, then 'You knew about this, you knew about us, Miss Long?' she asked.

'Josephine, please—yes, I guessed.' It was impossible to tell if this was a tactful lie or not, but Agnes' confused thoughts wondered why she should lie. 'I have thought of a way I can help you, Agnes, if I may call you that.' The agent opened the drawer in front of her and carefully drew out a sheet of paper, took the one from the typescript in front of Agnes and replaced it with the one from the drawer. As she was doing this, her eyes down, carefully so as not to crease the white sheet of paper, Agnes saw the bracelet on the desk. For a split second she could not believe her eyes. Sylvia had been here. She must have found it in The Boltons flat and thought it was Josephine's. She put her hand out and grabbed the bracelet and held it, her hand clenched.

Josephine aligned the new sheet on the typescript. 'Would that help you, Mrs Turner?' she asked. Now the dedication read, TO JOSEPHINE WHO IS MY FOR EVER. Agnes felt her whole being crying out, 'No, no, no it was me, it was me. It was me that he loved,' but she knew if the book was published dedicated to her Bill would know, he would be broken-hearted. He was kind and gentle, even perhaps forgiving, but would he ever be able to take the truth which she would have to tell him? Her feeling for Herbert would show through. She couldn't say, 'It was nothing, darling, just a fling, just an affair, nothing. He meant nothing to me.' She looked up at Josephine. Again her face was almost expressionless, neither calculating, eager, just waiting for Agnes' reply. 'Would you do this for me, but why?'

'I loved him always. Ours was just an affair as far as he was concerned, but I never stopped loving him, Agnes. I never stopped loving him.' The eyes that for the moment were not fixed on Agnes but were looking past her full of pain.

Agnes felt a wave of compassion, she got to her feet. 'Thank you,' she said. She felt she couldn't stay in the office any more. Josephine got up too and the two women looked at each other, eye to eye for a long moment. 'You were so lucky, Agnes, he really loved you.' Agnes walked towards the door leaving Josephine still standing behind her desk.

When Agnes got out through the second door into the little hall she opened her hand. The broken clasp of the bracelet had (Agnes had held the jewel so tightly) made a small puncture in her palm and a tiny drop of blood, no bigger than a pin's head, was just visible through the gold. I deserve more than that, she thought, but the broken clasp was one truth in the whole mass of deceit. She felt she could never wear Bill's gift again.

Outside she hailed a cab. 'Rutland Gate,' she said and got in, still clutching the bracelet as tightly as she had before. As they drove slowly through the heavily trafficked street towards home Agnes could imagine Sylvia throwing the bracelet on Josephine's desk. She must have been to see her husband's agent—thrown it at her—Agnes wondered what else had happened at that meeting. When she arrived home she thrust the bracelet in a drawer—at that moment she couldn't look at it, even feel it. It spoke too clearly of the last terrible night with her lover.

Sylvia lost no time in ridding the flat of all traces of Herbert. She felt his very name was synonymous with humiliation. Grief at his loss was there, since she liked basking in the fame of his books and plays. She had liked walking into a restaurant with him. Even, after a time, getting used to his eccentricities of dress, indeed, learned to smile acceptingly when he wore a plaid shirt when the other men were in dinner jackets. Even when he drank a little too much, or used extravagant language offensive to her fastidious taste, she always maintained her cool, always dressed with good taste herself.

No matter what she spent on clothes, and her taste was expensive, Herbert would never even remark at the bills, money came to him easily and flowed out at that same rate.

Sylvia hated and regretted the loss of her cool. She valued poise, a well-bred stance, keeping her emotions on a tight rein. She had a horror of losing face, giving way, and in that damned agent's office she had given way, exposed her feelings, shouted, behaved, in her own estimation, 'like a fishwife'.

By banishing all traces of Herbert, his suits, shirts, underclothes, shoes, she felt in some way she was restoring her own self-esteem. Maria, coming in every day to help with the clearance, shed, a few tears every time a box or suitcase was carted away. But this display filled Sylvia with contempt. Her own tears were few and those perhaps were more for her own loss, the fact that she was now a widow, than the loss of Herbert, of his death. It was his absence that was a nuisance.

The thought of the bracelet worried her mind more than once. When she had found it in the bed at first she had thought it was Maria's, she would watch the girl's reaction. There had been none. In Josephine's office when she had found out that it was Josephine's must be hers when she had seen the dedication, she wished that instead of flinging it in rage and fury and shouting abuse—flinging it across the desk—she wished she had behaved with more dignity, that was so uncouth, so common. She wished she had taken it from her handbag calmly and handed it to that bitch, perhaps saying, 'This must be yours, Miss Long, it must have come off during your acrobatics.'

She suddenly resolved to get in touch with Josephine and for her own benefit try to erase her behaviour and appear as her usual, controlled, poised self. How could she do it without appearing to patronize or placate Herbert's agent? She thought—why not perhaps ring her up and suggest another meeting. To talk again about the dedication, pay her to try and get the publishers to delete the words, *My for ever*. It was romantic, unlike Herbert. She waited a couple of days then telephoned Josephine and suggested they lunched and talked together. Josephine was cold in her reply and suggested if Sylvia wanted to see her she would prefer it to be in her office. Sylvia persisted and eventually Josephine capitulated and Sylvia mentioned twelve

105

forty-five at Claridge's Buttery. When she put the phone down she wondered what her plan of campaign would be, it was *non est.* at the moment, but she knew she would think of something in the forty-eight hours before they met, and she did. The idea, she felt, was so fitting, the lie so disastrous for her husband's paramour, and for anyone else who had had sex with him, and she was pretty certain that his 'for ever' in the dedication would not have meant complete faithfulness to any lover.

Josephine Long was nearly a quarter of an hour late for the lunch date, she had not intended to be but a phone call and visit from a promising young novelist had delayed her. She apologized, not profusely, but she did apologize to Sylvia, who received the apology with a calm and grave smile. 'What would you like for an aperitif, Miss Long?' she asked. She herself was sipping what looked like a gin and tonic but could, Josephine thought, be just tonic. 'I would suggest a double brandy, I have something rather disturbing to tell you.'

'No, just a gin and tonic, if I may, thank you. What is it you have to say, to tell me?'

'Please don't hurry me. Let's be civilized and have lunch first. I feel I behaved rather badly in your office, I would like to erase my behaviour.'

Both women ordered a light lunch. Josephine felt they were watching each other like two cats on a wall. 'Rather disturbing', Josephine felt, was a curious remark, a curious way to put it. Her immediate suspicion was that she had found out about her lie and knew that there had been no affair, at least not lately. They ate, almost in silence. 'Sweet?' Sylvia asked at last as the waiter removed their plates. Josephine shook her head and Sylvia looked up at the waiter. 'Just coffee.' She was silent after that, gently taking the petals off one of the roses in the silver vase on the middle of the table. One by one and letting them fall onto the cloth. The coffee came and the waiter withdrew. 'Josephine.'—the 'Miss Long' was dropped—'This is difficult for me but I feel you should be told.' Sylvia obviously had some difficulty in continuing. The difficulty was real, the plan, the plot she had conceived in those forty-eight hours was, even to her, so horrific that she had to force herself to speak. She had ordered liqueurs with the coffee, rather unusual at lunch, but she had waved aside Josephine's reluctance and the two small glasses of kümmel stood beside the coffee cups. At last Sylvia looked up, met Josephine's eyes squarely and then dropped her bombshell. 'Herbert was HIV positive Josephine, I am so sorry to have to tell you this.'

Josephine did not appear to take in the remark for several seconds then, 'That's not true, it's a lie, you're just saying that to frighten me because you are jealous.'

'Please keep your voice down, we don't want a scene, please, Josephine.'

'But how do you know, how—'

Sylvia interrupted her, 'He told me, of course, we have not had sex for years. We lived our own lives. I was tested, just routine, but of course I was negative.'

'But when did—who was—'

Again Sylvia interrupted her, 'My dear Josephine, how would I know that, he was so promiscuous. You may have been under the impression that you were his great love.' She laughed sarcastically, lighted a cigarette and then sipped her coffee, her other hand twisting the liqueur glass round and round with her beautifully manicured fingers. She then put the glass to her lips, her ice-blue eyes watching Josephine with a wide calculating stare. She went on, 'By the dedication you may well have been his last love but you may have paid a great cost.'

Such a torrent of thoughts was pouring through Josephine's head she could not answer. The affair, the brief affair with Herbert had been so long ago, had he been infected even then? And Agnes Turner, what of her and her husband? Good God, what a mass of tragedy could have been let loose.

Sylvia leant back in her chair. She looked relaxed, she was not actually smiling but the look on her face was complacent; as if she was feeling that the people, the women who had taken the risk must take what that risk entailed, it was nothing to do with her. For a second Josephine was almost tempted to tell her about Agnes but pride prevailed. HIV positive or not, she had loved Herbert and never stopped loving him. The thought that he had died loving her, or the pretence that he had, was better than him not loving her at all.

Sylvia was still watching her, now she was smiling a slightly wider smile. 'Have I worried you? I'm sorry if I have, but I felt it was safer to tell you, I mean you can—'

'Get myself tested?' Josephine stood up. 'Thank you for the lunch, Mrs Shaffer.' She was unaware that her voice shook, she was aware though that she was desperately frightened. Outside, the world, the pavement, seemed thronged with people, busy going somewhere, untroubled, calm, some even laughing. In the taxi Josephine leaned back in the near darkness, closed her eyes, AIDS seemed printed on the inside of her lids. The cab smelled slightly acrid, maybe of last night's vomit. She shuddered. A test, that must be done, but Agnes Turner, what to do about her?

The cab stopped, held up by the traffic. Josephine glanced out of the window, a car very close had drawn up beside the taxi, a man sitting waiting for the cars in front of him to move had spread *The Times* over the steering wheel and was reading, he too appeared resigned, placid but then he was probably well, healthy.

Josephine was conscious of a terrible feeling of loneliness, there was no one she dare tell, no one. If the test was positive she must go on working as if nothing was the matter, her only hope was that her affair had taken place too long ago—When to go for the test, where to go, ask her doctor? Oh God. 'How much?' she asked the cabby, who had already told her. He shouted the amount loudly as if she was deaf, he probably thought she was. She tipped him heavily and he looked at her with less irritation. 'Ta,' he said and swung the cab away from the kerb, then stopped as another fare hailed him, slammed the door and he was away, leaving Josephine horribly conscious of the complete change in her outlook and her life from when she had got into a taxi to take her to meet Sylvia Shaffer.

Josephine let herself into her flat when she arrived home, picked up some mail, felt no curiosity about it, anyway mostly circulars came to her home, she had few friends, so very few personal letters came for her, her family too were not good letter writers.

Her thoughts were still going round and round in chaos. Was Sylvia a liar, if what she said about Herbert was true she might have been terrified, Josephine supposed, of being herself HIV positive but now all the problem had fallen on her shoulders, Josephine Long, his agent.

Agnes and Bill Turner, God what a mess! She poured herself a stiff whisky and dialled her doctor's receptionist, she had to talk to someone. Even if her test was negative she still felt she must tell Agnes. What little she had seen of her she had not particularly liked but still in all fairness she felt she had got to tell her the risks she had run and the consequences she might have to face. Then again, her thoughts went off at another tangent, another part of her felt what was the point in letting Agnes know, what was the point in telling her, if she was positive, she was, if she wasn't, she wasn't, but then her husband Bill Turner, if he was not yet infected he could protect himself but how could Agnes tell him—warn him—it would mean confessing to the affair with Herbert. How would Bill take that? The marriage would perhaps break up inevitably. She debated and argued. with herself for days, and days turned into weeks and weeks went by and she couldn't make up her mind what to do, she knew by leaving it she was running risks for perhaps both of them or perhaps none at all. At last, at long last, she decided what was to be done, and done it was.

The Horton-Wyles lived in the next flat to Agnes and Bill, above the elderly lady whom Agnes often saw taking her little dog to the Rutland Gate gardens. They were fat, rather stolid people. Agnes could not quite remember how their rather nebulous friendship had started. But she and Bill had taken them out to dinner and had been asked back for a very pleasant meal in their flat. Another dinner—this time given by Agnes and Bill—the relationship had grown into a rather pingpong effort. Bill sometimes played golf with Horton-Wyles and said he was quite a good player. Agnes, who was, rather reluctantly, being talked into learning to play bridge, met Linda Horton-Wyles once or twice at bridge parties. So they were not surprised when she telephoned and suggested they had dinner together at the 'new' little restaurant she had discovered in Knightsbridge. Bill was not very easy about dining out, indeed he seldom enjoyed it, but Agnes felt dining with people who were not mixed up in any way with writing, television or films was probably good for him. Charles Horton-Wyles was some kind of financial adviser, seldom talked about his work and was golf crazy. A jovial, rather overweight man of about fifty-five, he loved food and wine and seemed quite oblivious to cholesterol problems or indeed anything to do with his health or figure.

This evening the restaurant turned out to be Italian, rather dark, the food was excellent. Agnes was pleased to see the laughter coming from Bill at Charles' remarks and jokes. The wine flowed, it was no cause for worry as Charles had ordered a car to take them home. The only remarks about TV were the soaps, it seemed that they were avid watchers. This suited Agnes, the talk wandered round the various characters that both subscribed to and were interested in.

Another thing came up that also interested Agnes, the People's Dispensary for Sick Animals, the Royal Society for Prevention of Cruelty to Animals, the Brook Horses, all dear to Agnes' heart. This led on to a mention of the old lady in the flat below, who according to Linda was also a great animal-lover. 'It's tragic, Agnes, she's going into a home, and that little dog has to be put down. Her beastly son won't give it a home. She's afraid it will be ill-treated if she sends it to a dogs' home and they—' Agnes was listening with great sympathy to this and was about to reply when she was stopped midsentence, she saw Josephine Long entering the restaurant talking animatedly with a young man accompanying her. Her eyes met Agnes' and she stopped in her tracks. 'Good evening, Mrs Turner. How nice to see you.' She passed on. Agnes felt her heart pounding. The sight of that tall, grey-haired woman brought everything back to her, the dedication—everything.

'Are you all right, Agnes. Who was that?' Bill, talking with Charles, had not noticed Josephine, or if he had, he had not registered who she was, the question came from Linda. Agnes drank some wine and smiled reassuringly at her. 'Yes, yes, I'm fine. I just—' She stopped.

Linda went on with the sad story of the little white dog and Agnes dragged her mind back from the sudden sharp, hurtful memories of Herbert and tried to give her entire attention to what Linda was saying. 'So she's heart-broken. I think she had a slight stroke. She's got a girl to take the dog out twice a day and she's trying to look after him but she doesn't trust the girl with the dog, but then she wouldn't, would she? She can't get down the stairs herself, poor old thing.'

Agnes realized she had not seen the old lady for a few days, maybe weeks, she couldn't remember. The vision, the very face of Herbert was beginning to blur in her mind. The wish to hold him there was still as great, try as she would, sometimes it all felt like a dream. The sight of Josephine Long however had brought it back with such clarity she felt she must run away, disappear to somewhere dark and remote where the joy of being in his arms would come back. She looked across the table at Bill and felt torn apart—Why did life expose you to such a coincidence, why should Herbert's agent choose the same place to dine, was fate that cruel, malicious?

'We can't have it, Charles is allergic to animal hair, why don't you take him, Agnes, you love animals?'

Bill broke in, 'Have what, Linda?' he asked.

'Lady Hanson's wee dog, Bill.' Linda related the whole sad story again.

'Oh, that's the little white dog, I didn't know Lady Hanson was ill. What a shame, he is a friendly little chap, that dog.'

Agnes had not even known that he had noticed the dog and his next remark surprised her. 'Couldn't we give it a home, darling? I would take it out to the gardens at night, like she used to do.'

'With a pooper-scooper, Bill?' Charles said laughing and downing another half-glass of wine. He always became more expansive and uninhibited as he downed his wine.

Agnes thought of the dog, of the old lady. 'I'd love it, Bill,' she said and put a hand over his.

'Right, call and see her, dear.'

Perhaps, Agnes thought, this good deed might do a little to push away, to banish the evil she had done him. A ridiculous thought, she knew, but it came and stayed in her mind all the same.

They were driven home about eleven. Agnes did not look towards Josephine Long's table, so she did not even see her again, the thought of her was upsetting, even though she might well have saved her marriage by putting her name in Agnes' place in the dedication. She was aware though that Josephine cast several glances towards their table.

The next day Agnes called on Lady Hanson. Her help was packing a suitcase, the dog, McDougall, was lying in front of the imitation-log fire, which although the day was warm was switched on. He looked up as Agnes was announced, she had already telephoned. Lady Hanson was seated in a winged chair, one arm was supported on a cushion, her mouth was slightly askew, her words were slurred but Agnes could understand everything she said. Old memories of nursing and cases like this came tumbling back into her mind. She sat down.

'Lady Hanson, I'm so sorry.'

'I don't mind going into a home. I'm eighty-eight, Mrs Turner. What can one expect? But it's only'—she looked at the dog—'he's only four.'

'You may recover quite a lot of your movements and speech.'

'Maybe, but I don't think somehow that I'll ever be quite the person I was. It was nice of you to call though.' Lady Hanson dabbed at her mouth where a small drop of saliva was slowly seeping down her chin.

'I'm not just calling, Lady Hanson,' Agnes said, 'I've come to ask you if you would trust us, my husband and me, to

118

give McDougall a home with us. Our flat
is similar to this and maybe he would
...' The old lady did not answer for a
moment, just looked at Agnes. She had
grey eyes with dark lashes, as if they were
mascaraed, which Agnes was sure they
weren't. She must have been so pretty,
Agnes thought, and suddenly the thought
of the woman opposite her with great age
and now great infirmity, the thought that
she must leave this charming and tasteful
flat overwhelmed her. Oh, no doubt she
had the money to go to some expensive
and luxurious home but it would not be
the same, no longer those small careful
walks round the little garden outside. 'My
name is Ursula ... Do you mean what you
say, Mrs Turner?'

'Agnes, please, and yes I do. He would
have the same little garden to walk in and
if we go to the country, our house in
Hampshire, he would surely come too.'

Lady Hanson, Ursula, was so pleased, so
relieved, so happy, she started to weep very
gently and Agnes put her arms round her.
It was a strange relationship, both women
hardly knew each other and yet—As Agnes
left her, promising to call for the little dog
and all his belongings the next day, before

his owner would leave the flat, they parted. Agnes fondled and played with the dog so that he would be familiar with her, he seemed friendly and ready to accept anybody who was nice to him, saying as she did so, 'I will call in again this evening and take him into the gardens.'

The help looked relieved. 'Yes, it's just so that he can make himself comfortable.' Delicately put, Agnes thought.

It was a sunny day and Agnes walked the few steps back to her own flat. The old lady's condition and fears for the only creature who seemed dear to her put her own preoccupations a little more into perspective. Yes, Herbert had been the love of her life and always would be, had blotted out everything else, just to get to him and spend time with him had been the one object of her life. She had pushed aside everything else, Bill, her bouts of anxiety, even Helen's silly little problems, perhaps not so silly to Helen though.

This slightly chastened mood continued as she let herself into the front door, crossed the hall, taking a look at the shelf where the mail lay, picked up a letter for Bill and continued on across the hall. The lights above the lift, rather an old-fashioned one, slow and creaking, showed it was coming down. Agnes had just time to think it would be nice to own an animal again when the lift arrived at the ground floor. Agnes stepped back a little to allow room for the person inside to step out.

The doors slid apart revealing Josephine Long. 'Oh, please, I want to see you urgently.' Her face was serious, her demeanour almost pleading.

'Very well, Miss Long.' Agnes stepped into the lift with the agent. The doors closed the lift started upward. Neither woman spoke on the way up, or even when they crossed the hall and Agnes unlocked the flat door. 'Please come in.' Agnes indicated the sitting room, she took off her cardigan and threw it over a hall chair.

In the sitting room Josephine sat down. She looked tense and did not lean back but sat bolt upright on the edge of the chair.

There was a moment's silence. Agnes chose, at first, not to break it and watched Josephine twisting a ring round and round her finger. At last Agnes broke the silence. 'Can I get you anything?' She looked at her watch, four o'clock. 'Can I get you some tea?' she suggested. Josephine looked up into Agnes' face and blurted out, 'Sylvia has told me Herbert was HIV positive. I felt it only fair to tell you, I couldn't at first.'

For a couple of seconds Agnes looked at her, then she said quietly, 'She's a liar.'

'You mean—' Josephine gripped the arm of the chair until her knuckles gleamed white.

Agnes repeated, 'I mean she's a liar. Did you believe her?'

Josephine nodded. 'Why shouldn't I?' she said. 'I had an affair with him, slept with him. I've been tested.'

'And you're negative.' There was a touch of contempt in Agnes' voice.

'Yes, but that was a long time ago, when we, since then ...' She tailed off.

'The dedication triggered this off, didn't it, Josephine?'

'Perhaps, but supposing it's true. He did sleep around.'

'You think I should be tested too because of Bill?' Agnes got up and walked slowly to and fro, from the fireplace across to the window and back again. 'I don't believe her,' she said again.

Josephine was silent then got up. 'I'll go now. You must do as you think fit,' she said and walked across out of the sitting room, through the hall. Agnes called out to her as she went, 'Oh, I will, Miss Long, I certainly will.' She heard the front door slam behind Josephine Long and she sat down, gazing in front of her without seeing anything she was looking at. Sex with Herbert had been unprotected. 'He would never have done this to me, never,' she said aloud. Her voice sounded strange in the empty room.

The next day Agnes went to collect McDougall. Ursula Hanson was packed, her suitcases behind her chair. She was sitting quietly at the window looking down into the square, McDougall at her feet. He had on a thin tartan collar, obviously new, and the lead attached to it led up to the old lady's hand, it was clawlike and brown-spotted. She looked away from the window and up at Agnes. 'Bit strange when a small creature like this,' she pointed at her dog, 'is really all you regret leaving—you will be good to him, won't you?'

Agnes sat down beside her and took her hand. 'I want you to let me have the address of where you're going and the telephone number. Mac and I will come and see you, I promise.'

'Will you pass me that pen?' She motioned towards a small table almost beside her. She gave the pen to Agnes and dictated the address of the home that was in Sussex. Agnes slipped the piece of paper into her bag, turned to put the pen back on the table. On the table lay a thick, shiny, hard-backed book, *Glass Diamonds,* and staring up at her the photograph, large below the title, the beloved face, beloved eyes looking out at her from the pale-blue surround of the dust cover. Agnes picked the book up.

'Have you read *Glass Diamonds,* Agnes?' Agnes nodded. She had of course read the book but she could not speak of it. Ursula went on, 'I haven't read it yet, I bought it to take away with me. Harrods recommended one or two books, I felt I will want something to take my mind off being—' Ursula stopped, stooped and touched the dog's head, her eyes were so sad. The combination of the old lady's sadness and the eyes of her lover looking into hers from the cover of the book were almost too much for Agnes.

'Life is unkind, Lady Hanson,' she said bitterly.

'In later life it certainly appears to be but memories of good times come back, at least I've got to live on those and there are plenty.' Lady Hanson smiled up at her. 'I hope you have too, Agnes.'

Agnes put the book down, her fingers gently caressing the photograph as she did so. She felt suddenly ashamed. She was comparatively young, comparatively healthy, compared that is with Ursula Hanson. She had a loving husband, no money worries. There were people in the depths of despair, ill, old, poor—Her life was so good and yet that face looking at her from the cover of the book made her feel there was no more loving—at least no more loving like that, no joy to come in her own future. She wanted to go and buy the book, bring it home but she wouldn't because she couldn't bear to have him or the picture of him so near her. 'Come on, little one.' She took the lead from Ursula's hand.

'Thank you, thank you so much. I know I can trust you with him.'

McDougall trotted out of the flat briskly enough, looking back once. Agnes picked him up in the lift talking to the little animal. Up till now she had been a 'cat woman', this was her first dog. 'McDougall,' she said softly, his tail wagged against her hip. She realized that Ursula had not told her about his inoculation, when it was due, she must telephone her before she left. The thought of the inoculation suddenly reminded her—HIV positive, Josephine had said. She, Agnes, had been so adamant that Herbert would never have exposed her to such a risk. He loved her, he had loved her; he couldn't, wouldn't do such a thing. Suddenly she was full of doubt. Bill's car was there, he was home. Agnes couldn't go in, the garden key was in her handbag, hardly ever used but she kept it there. She unlocked the gate and walked round the small square. The trees rustled overhead. McDougall looked up at her, obligingly cocked his leg against a shrub. His bed, long lead and food were being brought round after Ursula had gone.

At last, Agnes plucked up enough courage to go into the flat and face Bill, who greeted the dog with delight and took his lead off. 'I'm just going to phone,' she said.

'Yes. McDougall's just had his jabs Mrs Turner, and his teeth scaled,' the help answered. 'I'll bring his certificate round when I bring his things. His basket and his blanket, Lady Hanson would like him to have that.' Agnes put the phone down and went in. McDougall was already sitting on the settee beside Bill.

That night the dog decided to be a bit of a pain. Agnes settled him in the kitchen with his basket, his blanket, bowl of water and even a small amount of munchies that Ursula Hanson had said were his midnight feast. Bill and Agnes could hear him padding round the kitchen, scratching at the door, whining, then giving small pleading barks. Bill cracked first. 'It's a new place, Agnes, he's only a dog, he doesn't understand where he is.' Into the bedroom—Bill moved his basket. No good, he won the battle and snuggled in between them in bed, his wet nose under Agnes' chin, in the crook of her arm. Bill leaned up and looked at her smiling and Agnes looking at him thought what a sweet smile he had. 'You see,' he said and gently stroked the small, contented creature. Suddenly another thought seemed to strike him. 'Would you have liked children, Agnes?' he asked.

She shook her head and thought of

her time as staff nurse on that terrible children's ward. Of the crying children and the wet nappies, of the night superintendent thrusting her hands into the cots to see if the babies needed changing. The cots, like little cages. 'No, I wouldn't, dear,' she said. 'I really don't like children much at all.'

Bill relaxed back on the pillow. 'Well, that's a comfort, darling,' he said then kissed her goodnight, and he and Mc-Dougall dropped off to sleep, but Agnes was the last to sleep and when she did her dreams were troubled.

The next morning Agnes took McDougall walking in the park then drove to Knightsbridge, to Harrods. She carried McDougall, she was not sure whether dogs were allowed in the store, but she managed to buy what she wanted in the Food Hall and sneak out without the little dog being challenged. She felt thirsty and went into the Fruit Bar and sat down at the table, placing McDougall underneath. He was tired after his walk and well trained, by the look of it, he lay down and immediately put his head on his paws and slept. Agnes had found that the acquiring of the dog, the visiting and sympathy she felt for his mistress, the getting of him settled in their own flat and watching Bill's evident pleasure in the little creature's antics and possession, had done a considerable amount to at least push to the back of her mind her lover's death, the funeral and Josephine's implication of his extreme thoughtlessness, and indeed wickedness, in exposing her to the HIV infection. Now she sat at the table in the rather crowded Fruit Bar, sipping mango juice, it all came back to her with a rush of feeling that was almost overwhelming.

She decided, or almost decided, to change her mind to go up to the Book Department and buy the book, but the fact that she had the dog with her decided her against it, besides she was not at all sure she could have it at home in her bookshelves, with the knowledge she had only got to get up and lift out the book and have her lover's eyes gazing at her again. She felt it would bring back the tension, the longing, sorrow, guilt that were only just a tiny fraction away. They would all rise again, make her remember what she was trying to forget, and yet fearful of forgetting. So cut off was she by these thoughts that she did not, at first, register the fact that someone was speaking to her, standing beside the table about to occupy the opposite chair. 'Mrs Turner, isn't it?' She looked up, it was Sylvia Shaffer.

'You were at Herbert's funeral. So kind of you to come. I believe your husband is an author too?' She moved the chair and sat down gracefully. 'May I join you, it's rather full this morning?'

Agnes answered, 'Yes, certainly,' though on looking round there were one or two other vacant seats but she supposed it was natural for Sylvia Shaffer to reintroduce herself to Agnes, after all she knew nothing and did not know, thanks to Josephine Long, or suspect Agnes of anything other than an acquaintance with her husband Herbert.

Agnes thought Sylvia looked as elegant and composed as she had in the photograph in Herbert's flat, that well-remembered photograph, and as she had looked at the funeral. Her very presence took away Agnes' power of speech.

'Perhaps you don't remember me, Mrs Turner, and indeed why should you?'

Agnes recovered herself. She was wearing a pale-fawn linen suit and as she put out her hand to pick up her glass the sleeve of her jacket slipped back, she was conscious that Sylvia's eyes became riveted on her wrist, the gold and diamond bracelet trembled and glittered in the Fruit Bar lights. She had retrieved the bracelet from the depths of her handbag during her visit to Harrods and they had relinked the broken clasp while she waited—for Bill's sake she had let the assistant put it on her wrist. Agnes guessed in a second what conclusions Sylvia would draw from the presence of the bracelet. The last time she had seen it was in Josephine's office. Surely she must know now that Josephine was not the woman in her husband's bed when he died. It must be the woman opposite her.

Agnes remained completely silent. She had finished her fruit juice and she felt herself smiling very slightly as she put up her hand and gently twisted the bracelet around her wrist causing the inset diamonds to flash and sparkle in the lights.

'What a charming bracelet.' Sylvia's voice was quiet, husky but controlled.

Agnes played for time. 'Thank you, it was a present from my husband, Mrs Shaffer.' Agnes felt slightly sick, she must know she must know. She had last seen the thing in Josephine Long's office, presumably she had taken it there.

Sylvia lit a cigarette, drew in the smoke and exhaled it in a white plume, someone at a nearby table coughed meaningfully. Sylvia turned her head and looked at the coughing woman coldly and drew again on her cigarette. There were ashtrays on the tables, smoking had not yet been forbidden here.

This little exchange gave Agnes time to recover as Sylvia's cold eyes returned to her. She knew the time for deceit had caught up with her again. This woman, this cool, well-dressed, poised woman, if she found out the truth could ruin her marriage, hurt her dear Bill. All she had to go on was the gold and diamond circle round her wrist that she had found on that fatal, fatal morning. Should she face her? Should she say, 'it was me and not Josephine, I was your husband's lover and he loved me too with all his heart'? No, she said nothing. She forced her eyes to meet Sylvia's squarely, calmly. The steady eyes and unruffled air, she could tell, made Sylvia back a little.

She looked down again at the bracelet.

'Yes, it's very pretty. Have you had it long?'

Agnes looked at the jewel with casual carelessness. 'This? Yes, my husband bought it for me a long time ago. I've worn it ever since.'

Sylvia's eyes meet Agnes' again. 'It's very pretty,' she said, but she said it rather lamely. 'I hope you never lose it.'

Agnes laughed with genuine amusement. 'I hope not. I don't think my husband would be best pleased.'

A tiny frown appeared on Sylvia's smooth brow, Agnes felt she was puzzled. 'Cartier's? I'm sure,' she said equally casually.

Agnes merely nodded agreement, then immediately wished she hadn't. She was certain Sylvia would find out the truth if she could. She closed her bag with a snap. 'Nice to have met you again, Mrs Turner.'

She suddenly saw McDougall. 'Oh, I didn't know the dog was there and I didn't know dogs were allowed,' she said.

'I don't believe they are, Mrs Shaffer,' Agnes replied almost humorously. As she left the table Sylvia turned her head and their eyes met again. 'Well, sometimes one

133

can get away with breaking the rules, Mrs Turner, but, alas, not very often.' She went to the desk and paid her bill and Agnes watched her walking across the store until she was out of sight.

'Come on, McDougall.' Agnes led him to the desk. As she passed the money across the counter to the pretty girl she tried to keep McDougall behind her but the girl peered over the desk. 'Oh, what a sweetie,' she said. Sometimes one can get away with breaking the rules, Agnes thought; what had Sylvia meant exactly?

The meeting made her anxious. There was something ruthless about Sylvia Shaffer. For the first time Agnes wondered, could Herbert have been just as ruthless? Her love for him had been so shattering, so all consuming, it had blinded her perhaps to what he was really capable of. Would he, could he really have known he was HIV positive and—no, no she must not even think that. If what she was letting herself think was possible, she and Bill—Oh God! Her trust in Herbert was leaking away from her, she must have the test for Bill's sake. Should she have the test? She shuddered at the thought. When Josephine Long had said he was HIV positive she had not even thought of believing her, he would never, never do that, not Herbert, not to her. It was just Sylvia's way of frightening Josephine. Never, never, she could not believe that of him. That's what she had thought then, now, due to what? Sylvia Shaffer, a change in her feelings about Herbert, Josephine Long, worry about dear Bill? She walked in the park carrying her shopping, McDougall on his extending lead frolicked about her. She sat down, looked across the river, broke a piece of French bread off the crusty piece jutting from her carrier and started to throw small pieces to the ducks. McDougall barked at them.

As she sat there Agnes began to see things more clearly. Began to see how much she had risked for Herbert. How much she had risked Bill's happiness. What would have come of it if he hadn't died? He had never talked of leaving Sylvia, never spoke of a permanent relationship. There was, of course, the dedication to her, 'My for ever', had that meant anything, anything at all? Had Bill read it he would have known. Herbert had not thought of that, or had he? Was that the way he intended to declare they were lovers for ever? No Sylvia, no Bill, just them.

It started to rain, a fine misty rain. Agnes got up and made her way back to the flat, wishing she had not met Sylvia Shaffer. The meeting seemed to have stirred up her thoughts like turning clear water into muddy water. She was usually so clear-headed, so sure of herself, after all that's how she had helped to sort out Bill's problems, his family, and then they had fallen in love and married, now she seemed muddled, stupid, unable to sort anything out. Unable to make up her mind whether Herbert's death had saved her from hell or denied her heaven.

Agnes dried McDougall. He grabbed the towel and shook it. His very presence was a relief to her. Someone to talk to.

That night in bed beside the peacefully sleeping Bill, listening to his regular breathing, Agnes tried to assess the reaction of the two women, Sylvia Shaffer and Josephine Long. Josephine knew of her affair with Herbert, as yet she felt Herbert's wife did not. But supposing she found out; found out the bracelet in the bed was hers. Was the same bracelet she had thrown across the desk, broken? Why had she mentioned it, at least agreed, that

136

it came from Cartier's? Would that make it possible for Sylvia to find out if it was the only such bracelet? No, she felt Cartier's were too diplomatic to say anything about a customer. But there were ways. No, she swung the other way again. Surely Cartier's would never give such information. She tossed and turned and longed for sleep. Josephine was no threat to her, after all she'd let her use the dedication, which was a lie. But Sylvia, that remark about 'breaking the rules' as she had left the Fruit Bar—menacing? Maybe the bracelet was unique, Sylvia would never believe there were two of them.

Bill woke up, her restlessness had wakened him. 'Not sleeping, darling?' he said. Agnes turned to him and cradled her head on his arm. He soon fell asleep again—he could, she thought, his conscience was clear. A sudden deep hatred for Sylvia Shaffer came over her. If she started prying, even bullying Josephine, she might learn enough to make the affair between her and Herbert public, delight in it in her cool poised way. Something had got to be done. McDougall shifted against her feet and gave a little snore. Agnes had felt hatred before and had always managed to do something about it. Drastic problems need sometimes drastic measures—this thought comforted her.

Sylvia left Harrods, the sweet taste of the pineapple juice still in her mouth, making her feel thirstier than before she had had the drink, she wished she could have rid it by having something sharper but the presence of Mrs Turner had made her leave without a second drink. Agnes, that was her name, wasn't it? How did she know that? The funeral, of course. The wreath or sheaf, or whatever they had sent, Agnes and Bill Turner. Meeting the woman had been interesting. Good clothes, Patou perfume—Joy or Sublime, she wasn't sure but she recognized it. Expensive haircut, not good-looking but passable. Nicely, discreetly made up, nice speaking voice. Amusing about the dog. Sylvia got into a taxi, leaned back and her thoughts went on.

The bracelet, that was mysterious, very mysterious. Cartier's, they wouldn't repeat a design, gold and diamonds, would they? How had it, or a similar one, been in the bed in which Herbert had died? Josephine's bracelet? How could it then appear on

Agnes' wrist? Weird! Sylvia was not easily put off, she would go to Cartier's and ask for a similar bracelet. A present for someone, a rather expensive one for a woman to buy but she could say it was for her godchild, something like that. She had been foolish when she had first found it, she was so enraged she had not examined it, thought it was costume jewellery. Yes, she had been foolish. She was ashamed too of her behaviour in Josephine's office, throwing it at her across the desk as she remembered, but now the facsimile was on Agnes Turner's wrist, which was strange, it was very, very odd, an amazing coincidence.

Sylvia was bored, she had sacked Maria, suspecting her of having a bit of a fling with Herbert. She hated the flat, wanted to go back to Los Angeles, but before she went she had got to unravel the tangle of Josephine Long and this Agnes woman. Telling Josephine that Herbert was HIV positive had been rather good; shaken the creature quite a bit. Untrue, of course. And Josephine wasn't likely to put the story about. She would get herself tested, suffer a bit waiting for the result. Sylvia tipped the cabby more lavishly than was normal for her. She felt elated, less bored, more alive. Tomorrow she would go to Cartier's' and pretend to want a bracelet as a present for a godchild. Yes, that was good, after all one did buy expensive things for one's godchild. not that she had got one, but still that was good. She could say that the godchild had seen a bracelet in filigree gold and diamonds and wanted one as like it as possible. She could see in her mind's eye the delicate pattern of the gold on Agnes Turner's wrist. After all she had seen the damn thing three times but not paid as much attention to it as she had in the Fruit Bar. She could find out perhaps if it were possible for both Josephine and Agnes to have identical ones.

She looked forward to the little piece of detective work. What good it would do her she wasn't sure. Perhaps she would write a book, short and sharp, *Living With an Unfaithful Author*. She knew quite a lot about Herbert's dalliances but his dedication to Josephine, 'for ever', certainly that word had been a surprise to her. Such a dedication would make her acquaintances snigger a little, she was sure, of course she would ignore them. But Sylvia was not entirely without emotion. She played the part of a sophisticated, modern, tolerant, understanding wife, not always an easy role to play, especially with that damned dedication pending. Surely there must be some way to stop it, alter it, discredit Josephine Long.

Cartier's assistant was charming, helpful. Sylvia described the bracelet in detail. Since she had seen it so plainly on Agnes Turner's wrist, the lights had illuminated the stones, highlighted the little squares of gold, dainty. She even asked for a paper and pencil and drew the shape of the filigree. She was seated in the private back room of Cartier's, the grey-haired, rather handsome man was giving her his undivided attention. As she handed him the little sketch he smiled gravely.

'Oh, yes, madam,' he said, 'I do remember the bracelet. It was made by a well-known French jeweller, very gifted man. I can show you other pieces of his work but not at the moment a bracelet of his.'

'How disappointing. I wonder who bought it?' Sylvia looked at him, her eyes wide, questioning, her lips curved in a charming smile. Useless, however,

141

Cartier's she knew never gave anything away. 'Who indeed, madam,' he said, 'whoever it was, however, has a lovely possession.' He absented himself for a moment, then returned with a charming necklet, half gold, half diamonds. 'This is by M. Phillipe. The same jeweller who made, I believe, the bracelet you describe, of course I cannot be absolutely sure.'

Sylvia left the jeweller's with no more satisfaction than when she had entered it. There must be some way of finding out why this bracelet had travelled from Herbert's bed to Josephine's desk to Agnes Turner's wrist. There must be two bracelets, even though Cartier's handsome assistant/salesman had assured her the French jeweller/designer would never repeat his work and the piece was unique. 'Of course,' he had amended the remark a little, 'he might produce several bracelets slightly similar.'

Sylvia was annoyed, too, that she could not talk and charm the man in Cartier's into even discussing to whom he had sold the trinket. As far as she could remember, Agnes' husband did not in any way resemble Herbert. Her husband, once seen, was not easily forgotten. Who had purchased the thing in the first place? Why did she feel so obsessed? Jealousy, now he had gone? She realized she was jealous and not sure of whom to be jealous. She wanted to vent her anger on someone. Josephine would find out she was not HIV positive and that little revenge for her affair with Herbert would fizzle out. But Agnes Turner, where did she fit into the strange muddle? Suddenly it occurred to her out of the blue: was it Agnes not Josephine that the dedication was meant for, and had Josephine been put just as a blind to cover the truth? Was it Agnes who had been having the affair with Herbert? If so, she too must be informed of Herbert's 'infection'. She resolved to ask Agnes and her husband to drinks, drop the facts to Agnes about her anxiety about her dead husband's complaint had he lived. If it was Agnes who had left the bracelet in Herbert's bed she would be frightened, more frightened than Josephine had been.

Sylvia could hardly wait to see if she was right. But she must wait a little, or was the meeting in the Fruit Bar an excuse to say she wished to know Agnes better? They might refuse, make some excuse, avoid the meeting. She telephoned and they did not make an excuse. Bill Turner answered the phone. Sylvia heard him turn away from the phone, presumably to consult his wife.

'How kind, we would love to. Six thirty? I was and still am a great admirer of your husband's work and so sorry about his death, Mrs Shaffer.'

'Thank you.'

Sylvia put down the phone and stood for a moment, she was looking forward to meeting them. She hoped she could at least send one of them away feeling more anxious and upset than when they arrived. She smiled, anxious and upset was surely an understatement. Agnes would not, Sylvia felt, be able to hide her fear, her horror—such a revelation would devastate her, no amount of self-control could hide such feelings.

Amy Robertson was bored with her job. When she had first been successful in getting it she had felt pleased, elated even—secretary to a literary agent sounded glamorous. She had imagined meeting Jackie Collins, Mary Wesley, Jilly Cooper, anyone might stroll in to see Miss Long. A year in the post had destroyed these illusions. The authors who came in were mostly ordinary men and women, boring most of them. A lot of them old, or at least what Amy thought of as old. Herbert Shaffer, he was old and fat but there was something about him, she had to admit that. He had made a few advances, he was quite famous—he usually tapped her on the bottom as she showed him into Miss Long's sanctuary but it had never got any further than that. She could see her boss fancied him, though—poor old girl, he kissed her when he went into her office, at least sometimes he did.

Amy had soon learned the drill, the pecking order of the people who came. Some authors who weren't famous at all got coffee and biscuits which she had to make and take in; the famous ones, or ones that sold a lot of books, got taken out to lunch. Herbert Shaffer usually made an excuse and Miss Long used to be bad-tempered after he left. Amy had got to know the signs.

At first she had had a crush on Josephine Long—well, she was short-haired, a bit masculine, a bit butch and anyway Amy was at that time fancying herself as a lesbian, a bit more trendy and interesting than being straight she thought at the time. Then she had fallen for Tom and decided she wasn't that way at all, so the crush had evaporated and the job had become even more boring and Miss Long a drag, Tom a bore too.

Now though, a tiny bit of interest had arisen when she had packed the new Shaffer book up for the publisher—the dedication TO JOSEPHINE WHO IS MY FOR EVER. After the poor man had died too. She had taken the page in to Miss Long and had asked her wasn't it wrong, shouldn't it be 'Mine for ever', she had wanted to see her boss's reaction to it anyway. She had never got shot out of the office quicker.

'That is correct, Amy, don't you think I know what it means?'

'Yes, sure, Miss Long.' She had beat a hasty retreat because the old girl had looked near to tears. 'MY FOR EVER', funny way of putting it, and she would never have dreamt Mr Shaffer would have fancied her boss, still Amy had repeated to herself what she always did on such occasions, 'it takes all sorts', and she had packed the manuscript and put it on the side of her desk ready to take to the post and that, for the moment had been that.

One author, a new one, had come to the office just once lately, Mrs Turner she had said her name was, Amy had hopes that she was famous, someone for her to boast about knowing when she was out with Tom and her mates. Her clothes, this Mrs Turner's, were super, not Amy's taste but she knew good clothes when she saw them—lovely shoes too and gloves, a real posh piece. Polite—her perfume, it just wafted after her like good scent should, not hit you in the nose the moment you met someone, she had been 'class'. Hadn't been back since but she had spent some time in the office, so maybe Josephine Long had become her agent and she'd be returning.

Mrs Turner, yes that was it, Mrs something Turner, well she might write under another name, of course, most of them did. There had been no letter dictated about her though and she hadn't been carrying a manuscript, so maybe there was nothing to it and she wasn't an author after all. Josephine had taken to leaving the office earlier these days, she would have a look round one evening and if Mrs Turner had left anything, might have had a couple of chapters and a synopsis in her handbag, she would look and see when she got the chance.

The following Tuesday a fairly important writer rang up and asked to speak to Miss Long. Amy listened. The writer had been contacted by a friend who had introduced her to a TV producer who had shown interest in her latest book. He was in London and was to meet the producer for dinner that night, he would like to talk to her agent—could she possibly manage lunch? Josephine could and left the office at twelve, warning Amy not to take a two-hour lunch herself. Amy promised she wouldn't, she was broke anyway, also slimming and had brought a yogurt with her. She watched from the window her boss get into the taxi then turned the key in the door, so that no one would come in and find her in the inner office.

Amy had never done this before and only boredom was motivating her now. She looked at the files neatly housed on the shelves without much interest, she knew what was in a lot of them, after all she had typed some of it. She pulled the drawer on the right-hand side of the desk, it was locked but in the keyhole of the left-hand drawer the keys dangled—Not like old Long, she thought, must have something on her mind—she unlocked the drawer. Surprise, there was a large cutting from a newspaper all about Mr Shaffer and a picture of him with his wife. She knew it was his wife because she had come to the office recently, another posh dresser but a bit catty looking. Voices had been raised on that day, Amy remembered, and her boss had shut the door on her so she hadn't been able to hear the conversation. Now she shut the door herself. Although the outer door was locked, she felt a bit sort of creepy, looking round like this. She opened the other drawer and on the top of a neat pile of manuscripts and envelopes and letters lay a sheet of paper, uncreased, a dedication which read 'TO AGNES WHO IS MY FOR EVER.' Amy took the paper out, laid it on the desk; this revealed another sheet, creased, handwritten in what she recognized as Herbert Shaffer's handwriting—the copy of the dedication, perfect proof. She took that out too, shut the drawer and left the keys dangling as they had been before. She sat down at the desk in her boss's chair, hands each side of the paper, not touching it and tried to work it out. Who was Agnes? And which was the real dedication? Some squirrel-like instinct made her suspect this piece of paper should not have been left, not in an unlocked drawer, it should not have been there.

Did it belong on Mr Shaffer's new novel, maybe? The words 'FOR EVER' were the same, what was going on? She made up her mind, folded the paper carefully into four pieces then leant back in the chair. 'Josephine, you old devil,' she said aloud, 'the book wasn't dedicated to you at all.' She laughed, she didn't want to keep her job that much but maybe the piece of paper might mean she could leave with a bit of a golden handshake. After all, if all she wanted was the book to be dedicated to her, to make the world think Herbert Shaffer died loving her, what did it matter, but Amy decided it was going to cost her. Meanwhile, she had got to find out who Agnes was. She drew the photograph out and looked at that, under it the caption said: 'The writer Herbert Shaffer with his wife Sylvia at the launch party for *Glass Diamonds,* which won him universal acclaim.'

Amy remembered that was his last book,

the one before the neatly packed one on her desk. Well, Sylvia certainly wasn't Agnes. Amy sat for some time, how much should she ask to keep quiet—how much was it worth? She suddenly felt hungry and went back to her own office and ate her yogurt.

It was quite by chance that Josephine herself gave her the answer as to who Agnes was. She walked through the office one morning a few days later, looking pleasant enough, but within minutes her office door was flung open. 'Amy, come in here,' she said. As Amy entered she saw both desk drawers were open. 'Have you taken anything from the office, any copy?' Her face looked white. 'Anything at all?'

Amy shook her head, her face a picture of puzzled innocence. 'What sort of thing, Miss Long? You didn't leave any post for me to take, did you?'

'Not post. It was just a—' She stopped. 'Has Mrs Turner been back to see me—Agnes Turner? You know, you remember her?'

Amy frowned in pretended concentration. 'Yes, I think I do. The nicely dressed one, fair. No, she hasn't been back, Miss Long. Did you expect her?'

'No, no of course not. I just—' She slammed the drawer shut. 'It's all right, Amy, I must have misplaced it. It was nothing important.'

Amy noticed Josephine's face, the anxiety. Amy guessed at once, one Josephine or two Agnes. One was the true dedication, and Amy guessed too that it was not Josephine. She had to smile as she had left the room. 'Serve her right.' Amy had asked for a rise two weeks ago and been refused. This would teach her.

Amy had been working long enough in publishing to realize that anyone could put a dedication on the front page of a typescript, pack it up and send it to the publishers. If the author received his proof back and saw the dedication was not to the person he or she had intended she would of course contact her publisher and correct or erase the dedication. But in this case the author was dead, so Amy guessed to herself Josephine had put her name in place of Agnes Turner. What a giggle, silly old trout. What to do though? Thank goodness she had not yet posted the manuscript.

She sat sucking the end of her pen, her chair tilted back. Supposing Agnes Turner was married, had called at the office, had she wanted that dedication kept quiet? 'To Agnes who is my for ever', pretty hot when you read it as it was. Had she asked Josephine to keep it quiet and Josephine Long had agreed but put herself in the place of Mrs Turner? Amy's eyes narrowed; supposing she went to her boss and said she knew the truth and would tell the publishers unless—unless what? No, Agnes Turner of the lovely clothes and the expensive perfume was the one to feel worried. Mrs Turner was the one to go and see. She checked the piece of white paper was safely in her bag, she would go and see Agnes Turner. Where did she live, though? That was easy, Josephine had her telephone number. A careful look down the long list of Turners in the directory—she remembered, how she couldn't recall, that Josephine had mentioned that she lived in Rutland Gate, a posh place, perhaps she had envied her. Well, she would go and see her. She might be good for a little present.

Amy shivered with a tremor of delight. Always, she thought, she had to economize, to think about how to spend her salary, eke it out, make it cover rent, food, heating, there was little left for clothes, make-up, none for perfume like Agnes Turner had been wearing. It wasn't fair. She hadn't been lucky; she was not pretty, she was short-sighted, rather fat, her ankles were thick too—it seemed to her she was deserving of a little, a little extra. As these thoughts filtered through her head she realized, she wasn't that foolish, she was justifying what she had in mind, which was blackmail. Well, so what.

Miss Long called her in for some letters. She didn't mention the missing paper again, just dictated in the low, difficult to hear voice she always did.

Two or three nights later Agnes took the lift down with Mac for his late-night walk. She carried the garden key in her hand. It was only ten fifteen, Mac seemed to manage well on this late walk till about seven the next morning. He was quite happy. It was a chore but Agnes adored the little creature and Bill too. Usually, Bill took him out at night but this evening he had warned her that there was to be a late script meeting. He worried about Agnes going out now in the evenings, now they were darker, and warned her again and again to lock the gate behind her so that no one could follow her in during her necessarily leisurely stroll round the gardens. Mac liked to take his time and sniff his way round the shrubs. Agnes rarely did lock the gate behind her, the place—Rutland Gate—was usually deserted in the late evening; people were at the theatre or dining out. She did not lock it behind her on this occasion. Mac cocked his short leg against one or two shrubs, chased a piece of paper, barked at a cat and romped around a little, unimpeded by his long nylon lead. Then, after a time, Agnes turned to retrace her steps to the gate, pausing for a second or two to encourage Mac to follow her. She heard the gate squeak and it startled her. Then she saw it was a short, plump girl. The street light had just come on and the girl's spectacles reflected it for a second before she lowered her head so the glasses were no longer visible.

'Mrs Turner?' The girl sounded slightly nervous and as she got closer Agnes realized that the round bespectacled face was vaguely familiar.

'Yes.' She reeled in Mac's lead so that he was closer to her, the girl did not

155

speak again but opened her handbag, took out a sheet of paper and handed it to Agnes. 'TO AGNES WHO IS MY FOR EVER.' Agnes looked up and met the girl's bespectacled brown eyes. 'Where did you get this?'

The girl's mouth twitched nervously. 'I work for Miss Long, I'm Amy Robertson.'

'Then you stole this?'

Amy nodded. 'I've got the same in Mr Shaffer's own hand, too, Mrs Turner.'

'What for? What did you intend to do with it?'

'Send it to the publisher and tell them the truth.'

Agnes felt angry but not particularly moved. 'And do you think they would take any notice of you, or this?'

The girl nodded. 'I do. I write lots of letters to them, particularly to Mr Shaffer's publisher and I use my own name, p.p. Miss Long. That's how they'll think what I say is true. Besides, the one Mr Shaffer wrote, they will believe that.' She stopped. There was not a sound in the immediate vicinity, only the rustle of the trees overhead and the distant hum of traffic passing the park at the far end of Rutland Gate. Then McDougall gave a short impatient bark.

Amy looked down at the dog. 'Nice little boy,' she said and leant down and stroked the dog's head. He responded by wagging his tail and giving the girl's hand a swift lick. Then her brown eyes met Agnes' again, this time almost with apology. 'I'm sorry, Mrs Turner but I'm sick of being poor and ugly. I want some money to keep quiet.'

'How much do you want for this?' Agnes said. She tried to suppress a slight feeling of sympathy. Through her mind flashed a picture of herself at this girl's age, scraggy hair, diffident to everyone, afraid of being found incompetent, afraid, even in those days, of any advance from a man, envious of those flirting nurses around her, who could say anything, do anything, knew what to do—there was something in this girl that reminded her of those days and herself. What had caused the low self-esteem? Money.

'Your husband wouldn't like it, Mrs Turner, I mean it's like romantic isn't it, and he didn't know he was going to die.' Agnes almost smiled. 'Could you afford £500?' Amy's brown eyes opened wider.

'What will you do with £500?'

The girl answered softly, almost in a whisper, 'Buy something—clothes, perfume like yours.'

'And how do I know you won't want more later?'

Amy was silent. 'I don't know, Mrs Turner, but I don't think I will.' Agnes hoped Amy was a better secretary than a blackmailer. Yet what she said was true, if Agnes' name did feature in the dedication what would Bill think of it? Should she, would she be able to make a full confession to him? Agnes knew she couldn't, he would never get over it.

This nondescript-looking girl had more power in her hands than she realized. Even as she stood there Agnes felt the old familiar sense of challenge growing in her. She would not, could not, let Bill be hurt. She would not let this stupid little fool ruin his life. How to prevent her, how to blot out her beastly little plan? Bill was out at the moment, it was safe to take her into the flat, give her the money. Agnes always kept ready a thousand pounds in notes—an old habit dating from the days when she had inherited her fortune and doubted banks.

She locked the gate and both women

and the little dog went up the steps, into the lift, up to the flat. She could sense Amy looking around her with envy. As she handed the money to the girl she looked at her with real curiosity. There was little reaction other than perhaps a slight look of surprise, possibly caused by the easy way Agnes had agreed, handed over the money. Again, Agnes almost smiled. She had an ally in Josephine, who would be as anxious to keep the dedication as she, Agnes, was to avoid it. Between them, this little brown-eyed insect could be exposed, obliterated and swept away. She would go and see Herbert's agent tomorrow, not in the office—a little plotting must be done. Josephine's secretary must not know they were meeting. Luckily, Herbert had told her where Josephine Long lived. Herbert—if only he was still alive. That dedication to her must have meant he expected to be with her for ever and she would have left Bill for him, left everything for him but it was no good thinking of that now.

Agnes felt her eyes fill with tears. She stood up and poured herself a drink. As she had closed the flat door on Amy Robertson she had felt a hatred that she had not felt for some years, not since that night in the darkness at the end of the pier. She experienced, almost lived again, the body hitting the water, the splash, the stillness from the water and the noise from the fireworks behind her. Well, she had been protecting Bill then, she must do it again. She sipped her brandy and ginger ale and a little thrill did something to dissipate the trace of boredom and the lack of action that had overtaken her since Herbert's death. She started to go through the telephone book. There were crowds of Longs but fewer J. Longs and she soon found the address that Herbert had mentioned.

Josephine herself answered the phone. 'Yes, Josephine Long.'

Agnes, her diary lodged on the phone table beside her, said, 'Josephine, it's Agnes. I think it's time we met.'

'Met, Mrs Turner?' Josephine's voice rose in surprise.

'Yes, Miss Long,' Agnes paused. 'Something rather interesting has come up.'

Amy Robertson felt terrified and yet self-admiring at what she had done. She had never held so much money in her whole life before. She had been a little surprised when Mrs Turner had produced the notes. She had gone into her bedroom and emerged with the money, five twenties, five times. Amy had felt curiously embarrassed as she had taken the money; not counted it, you couldn't do that with a woman like Mrs Turner—I mean you just couldn't, could you? She had been conscious too of the look of contempt that accompanied the giving of the money—nasty bitch. Five hundred meant as little to a woman like her as a fiver did to Amy. She had been surprised too that she had had that much money in the flat, she thought credit cards would be Mrs T.'s style; probably she gave the milkman five or ten pounds when she felt like it as a tip, or the plumber, or the dustman. She took out the notes from her handbag, they were all jumbled up and creased as she had thrust them in, almost without looking. She smoothed the notes out, one by one, on the table. What would she do with it; a frock, some jeans—good ones? It wouldn't go far. Still she remembered what Mrs T. had said, 'How do I know you won't want more?' Well, she didn't know. She smiled to herself. She had done it once, could

161

she do it again? She made the money into a neat pile, pushed it to one side of her and leant on the table, dreaming, then she put a little china pot on top of it, as if it might fly away. Then she took the two pieces of typing paper from her bag, one still fairly uncreased though folded into four, the other not so pristine, folded too but creased. This she realized was her trump card, her ace, written in Herbert Shaffer's own handwriting! She resolved to slip into the library tomorrow and get it photocopied, not do it in the office.

Amy knew she was not a bright girl, she knew her limitations, that she wasn't attractive. She had felt and hoped that she would be married by now; most girls 'trapped' men somehow. She sat there trying to make it out—TO JOSEPHINE WHO IS MY FOR EVER. Josephine? Miss Long had typed that, of course, on her old-fashioned typewriter, word processors gave her a migraine. How silly not to have destroyed the other one with Agnes on but perhaps she wanted to keep the bit with his handwriting, she loved him that much. A little flash of sympathy went through Amy but then she knew when the book came out Mrs Shaffer would believe the false dedication and would never find out about Agnes Turner. If she did then the fur would fly and Mrs Turner's husband would know and that might break up her marriage. Amy was sharp enough to realize that Mrs Turner didn't want that. There were two ways she could act—get some money from Miss Long, get that rise in salary perhaps? Amy felt the heat rising to her face, she had power over both of them. Fancy that old man, Herbert Shaffer, being able to turn both women on like that! Her face grew redder. And fancy her, overlooked, ugly Amy who only got a pat on the bottom from him, being the one who could mess up his memory and both of the women he turned on! She got up, she felt taller, slimmer, she looked in the mirror over the mantelpiece. She would buy that expensive new moisturizing cream—new lipstick that stayed on longer, have a hairdo at that expensive place in Bond Street. They would both have to pay if they didn't want a marriage to break up and Josephine didn't want the truth about her told and suffer the ultimate in humiliation and exposure of her lie.

There was a tap on her door and

163

Mrs Holmes stood outside. 'Rent due yesterday, dear,' she said, her tight perm and made-up face pushing itself through the door.

'Oh yes, of course.' Amy often had to put off paying the rent on the day and Mrs Holmes was always hovering. She backed into the room, turned her back on her landlady then turned round and handed her the notes. 'Keep the difference off next week, Mrs Holmes,' she said grandly. It was wonderful to have money, even her landlady's manner altered.

'Oh, doing well are we?' she said, pushing the money into her apron pocket.

'Very well, very well indeed, thank you, Mrs Holmes.' She shut the door and put her arms round herself and gave herself a big hug.

When should she approach Josephine Long for her rise? After all *she* didn't know she had approached Agnes Turner and she banked on the fact that probably Agnes would not tell Miss Long. If she did though, so what? She had the proof, she had the two sheets of paper, she had the dedication in Herbert Shaffer's writing and the typed copy. She had not yet posted off the novel, she must do that, covered as it was by Josephine's dedication to herself. The publisher might contact Josephine, ask her why the novel had not arrived, so she had better get it off. Amy savoured the fact that she, little nondescript Amy Robertson, held all the cards for the first time in her dull little life. She was in charge of dynamite and she was enjoying it—every bit of it.

'Slow up, Amy,' she said suddenly to herself. 'Slow up.' If Mrs Turner told Miss Long, Miss Long could sack her, but after all it was Mrs Long who had altered the dedication, it wouldn't pay her to sack Amy, would it? A little doubt crept in, then she regained her confidence; Herbert Shaffer's written copy. Oh no, there was no need to worry, not for a while anyway. For a minute Amy was frightened, really scared of what she was up to. It would be lovely to tell someone, consult someone, but of course she couldn't. Anyway she hadn't a best friend, not many friends at all. It was best to keep everything to herself—but sitting there, behind the locked door, the pile of money in front of her on the table, she felt very lonely.

The evening Sylvia Shaffer had asked them

to drinks, Bill arrived home early. 'Will I do?' He came out of the bedroom and presented himself to Agnes. She could see he had taken special care with his appearance. Usually he was neat and conservative in his dress but this evening he looked, for Bill, quite handsome. 'How about this tie, too much do you think?'

'No, darling, it's just right.' Agnes was quite surprised by his obvious wish to look his best. She knew he had only met Sylvia twice and that very briefly, once at the funeral and once—she tried to remember where the second time was. She wondered whether there was a snobbery among writers, he so admired Herbert Shaffer's books and had admired the man himself.

Agnes was dreading going to the flat, seeing again the place where Herbert had talked to her, caressed her, yet she had a conflicting feeling of longing to see it again. Would she be able to bear it, conceal her feelings, control the rush of remembering?

Sylvia greeted them courteously, but she looked slightly strained, tense. A new girl opened the door; Agnes had once seen Maria, she must have been sacked or maybe she had left after Herbert's death. The girl ushered them into the sitting room; the lights were on even though it was still daylight because the weather was stormy and overcast. The amber lights bathed the room with a golden glow Agnes so well remembered. The big settee, the long table on which the glass and wine and biscuits and the silver butter dish had all rested. Only one thing was not easy to remember without emotion overcoming her—her lover leaning back on the settee. He had looked so tired that night but seemed better after he had drunk some red wine. Agnes resolutely tried to turn her mind off, something she was good at and she addressed herself to Sylvia. She had imagined there were to be other people there but no one appeared and the three sat down after Sylvia had served them drinks from a bar cart, an American affair. Bill admired it and said so. He chose white wine, Agnes too. It was a delightful wine, perfectly chilled, not too cold.

In answer to Bill's polite remark about the flat Sylvia shrugged. 'It was too small for two people, I always thought, and an impossible place to pick up a taxi—and

167

I have a mistrust of minicabs, I don't know why.'

The conversation became boring, at least to Agnes—books, publishers, agents, though Josephine Long was not mentioned. Sylvia touched lightly on her husband's latest book. 'I suppose they will hurry up the publication a little because of Herbert's death,' she said. There was no emotion in her voice, she stated the fact as a fact. The conversation went on, Agnes trying to keep her mind closed and cold. The door to the bedroom in which Herbert had died was shut, she doubted that she could look at that bed again without losing her self-control. Then the talk was, for the moment, dominated by Bill and the subject drove anything about Herbert out of Agnes' mind. 'Yes, it's extraordinary, at least to me, how aspiring actors or actresses—though you are not supposed to call them that now, are you—are all over you if they think you can get them a part.' Sylvia lit still another cigarette. She appeared to be a chain-smoker and Agnes wondered perhaps if her determinedly calm and poised exterior could be a little suspect; why should she rely so much on tobacco?

'Yes, I'm afraid Herbert found that too.'

Bill then related a story that Agnes was very interested and relieved to hear and immediately felt guilty about her suspicions about him. 'I met this very pretty girl at my book launch.' He turned to Agnes. 'Do you remember, darling? Indeed, that is where I met your husband too. But this girl was introduced to me as a banker from Sweden.' He laughed as he said this and went on with the tale, making it short and amusing. 'She was like a little leech in the end. I took her out to tea, she was younger than my daughter and I really gave her a straight talking to.' He went on telling how he had at last convinced her that he could do nothing for her, careerwise. 'Banker from Sweden,' he ended up, 'actually, she confessed in the tea shop she had a bedsit in Battersea. Poor little creature—they do have to try, don't they? But I did manage to convince her that the writer has little or nothing to do with the casting.'

Sylvia refilled their glasses and fetched more olives from the kitchen. When she returned Agnes was conscious of a change in her. She spoke quickly and abruptly. 'Unfortunately, Herbert took advantage of these, what you called so compassionately

169

"poor little creatures". He slept with most of them.'

Bill looked embarrassed, indeed slightly shocked. Agnes tried to follow his lead and spoke for him, 'That must have been—'

Sylvia held up her hand. 'Don't worry, Herbert and I have long led absolutely separate lives, sexually and almost in every other way. His interests were not mine and mine not his. Unfortunately, he paid for his little follies.' She ceased speaking, waiting, Agnes felt, for them to lose their embarrassment as well as their shock. 'One of these little creatures,' Sylvia looked again at Agnes and took another cigarette from the silver box on the table and lit it. 'One of these little creatures was, unfortunately, HIV positive—poor Herbert. He suffered for it, he was very health conscious. There were rumours about the girl, so he had himself tested, that was that. He must have worried, not that it stopped the philandering.' She popped an olive into her mouth and bit it, her jaws moving. She suddenly looked older, vicious and strangely enough, unhappy. 'He never told me the result of his test.'

Agnes pitied poor Bill, he was speechless. He could only say, 'I'm so sorry.'

'Don't be. He got what he deserved, I think, and as far as I know none of the girls ever achieved anything from sleeping with him. He just used to use them—he had a name for them, "bed-bugs". He told me about them, I'm afraid by this time it was a joke to me too, how could anyone be so mindless as to trust him?'

After this the conversation turned to clothes then their meeting in Harrods and Bill remained almost totally silent. Soon Agnes got up. Usually she waited for Bill to signal when he wanted to leave but this time she took the initiative and they left. Agnes felt that Sylvia had got her message over and wanted to see the back of them anyway. Agnes could only think that she had a slight suspicion but was not sure the bracelet still was in her mind—was not sure that perhaps Agnes and Herbert—but Agnes could see she was not sure, perhaps she didn't suspect her at all but she wanted to spread the rumour around. Agnes still did not believe her.

In the car Bill was still silent for a long time. 'What kind of woman is that?' he said suddenly breaking his silence. 'His wife. She had no need to say anything, poor fellow.' Agnes could say nothing.

If she said she thought Sylvia was lying he would ask her why, why she thought that. Agnes' anxiety was taking another channel altogether than her husband's. Sylvia suspected her but was not sure? Agnes was certain it was only the bracelet that was making her suspicious. What a tangle. Amy, the only one in possession of the truth, so unstable and yet so powerful. Josephine wanting his apparent love to stand, not caring about anyone or anything, just as long as the literary world thought Herbert had loved her, and she, Agnes Turner, terrified that anyone would find out whom Herbert had really loved.

Quite suddenly a policeman stopped them. 'Sorry sir, you have to take the diversion, turn left, there has been an accident up ahead.' They could see the front of a crushed car, an ambulance. A quick glimpse and Agnes saw a stretcher being put into the ambulance, the stretcher completely covered.

'BID,' she said in a whisper.

'What, darling?' Bill asked. He was steering the car to the left and had not seen the drama up ahead.

'Nothing, I was just thinking.' Brought in dead, her old casualty nursing experience told her. She twisted the bracelet on her wrist and wished Amy was dead, indeed to get rid of the wretched little blackmailing creature seemed the only way out. That and to destroy the evidence she had. How to cope with it? She must find out from Josephine where she lived, what hobbies she had. To know more about a person always increased one's power.

'We're here, darling.' Bill had opened the car door for her, Agnes had been so preoccupied she had not realized that they were home. She smiled up at Bill, took his proffered hand and got out of the car.

'That little bitch! She asked me for a rise yesterday, but didn't say a word about—'

Agnes shook her head and sipped the bitter-tasting coffee. 'She wouldn't—you are not in such a vulnerable position as I am, she could ruin my marriage.'

Josephine added quickly, 'She did say, "A substantial rise, Miss Long, a substantial rise." She's not even particularly good, she's always forgetting things.'

The two women were seated at a wrought-iron, round, white-painted table outside the Serpentine Inn. For late summer the morning was warm and

173

sunny. For a moment they were silent. Agnes watched a wasp making its slow way across the lacy wrought iron. When she had told Josephine Long about her encounter with Amy Robertson in the Rutland Gate garden, Josephine had listened—almost open-mouthed.

'I can't believe it! And you gave her the money?'

'Well, of course, she meant business—but she will be back.' Agnes' eyes returned to the wasp, it nearly reached Josephine's side of the table then it flew away. 'She had copies—I suppose copies of the typed and the handwritten dedication. Why, why both?'

Josephine rubbed her forehead as if she had a headache. 'I don't know. When I knew he was dead I was so shocked—I changed the dedication, as you know, enclosed it with the publisher's copy, gave it to Amy to pack and post. Normally, he would have come and talked to me after I'd read it. Sometimes even altered things if I—he would sometimes take my advice. I remember—' Her eyelids reddened and she went on. 'He brought the novel, just the one copy, in for me to see. He didn't know he was going to—' She rubbed her forehead again. 'I said the title was too long but he said that was to be it, take it or leave it—something like that.'

'Was it carelessness that made him include the written one underneath the typed dedication—was that the reason?' Agnes asked.

The agent shook her head. 'No, sometimes he wrote whole pages in his own hand. "Inserts", he called them. I always retyped them for him and made it fit.'

Agnes thought of Bill's meticulous typed script, a mistake, even a small one, would worry him if he didn't retype the whole thing. As if reading her thoughts Josephine went on, 'He was so famous, you see, the publishers were waiting for the next novel. I think sometimes if he had written the whole book in longhand they would have put up with it.'

'Well, what is done, is done. That little insect secretary of yours must be dealt with. When will the book be published?'

Josephine shook her head. 'Hard to say. The film has got to be released then *Glass Diamonds* hasn't been out all that long—could be a year, could be six months, but more likely a year.'

Agnes tapped the teaspoon on the white-painted iron of the table, it made a dull sound, the thick white paint blocking the sound of the metal.

'I shall sack her, of course.'

Agnes looked up. 'Indeed not, Josephine! She will come back to see me for more money, I'm sure. £500 is little enough, you must give her the rise.'

'I can't do that, Agnes, I don't want her around me. She stole those pages from my drawer. I can sack her because of that.'

Agnes did not attempt to argue with the straight-backed woman in front of her, just looked and waited. Gradually she saw Josephine Long's expression change as she realized.

'Good God, she could wreck your marriage, Agnes, and my credibility as an agent. I can see what you mean, I can't sack her.'

'I'm glad you agree with me.' Agnes leaned back in her chair. 'No, we must find another way to deal with her, I won't have my husband hurt. Herbert is dead and I won't have Bill told of anything that will upset him. I don't intend to go on paying her either.'

'Well, what?'

Agnes smiled her tight smile. 'You want her out of your office, I want her out of my world, Josephine.' Agnes could see—was it a flash of fear come into her companion's widened eyes?

She stared at Agnes, her mouth drawn into a thin line. 'You don't intend to do anything too drastic Agnes, do you?'

'Too drastic, too drastic!' The wasp had come back and Agnes picked up the plastic menu and banged it down on the insect. Its squashed body lay between them. Agnes scraped at it and it went through one of the holes in the table onto the floor. 'What is too drastic when so much is at stake for me and for you?' She got up, picked up her handbag. 'Can I give you a lift?' she asked.

Josephine shook her head. 'No, I came in my car.'

Agnes was glad to be back in her car and to be alone. She felt the old feeling of purpose, of something to be done; no one crossed her, or anyone she loved, without paying dearly. Amy Robertson would regret the evening she had entered the little garden and accosted Agnes and flourished the two pieces of paper, demanding money. £500 meant very little to Agnes Turner, but she realized how much it would mean to that ugly little girl. The next sum would be bigger, it would mean a great deal, a great deal to the secretary but how to stop her?

According to Josephine they might have as long as a year, perhaps less but she had said probably a year. Well, she had always, or almost always, been able to let events take over, seize an opportunity when it came. She had got the girl's address from Josephine Long and her telephone number. It would be interesting to drive to where she lived and, what was the word, reconnoitre. A whirl of sheer pleasure swept over her, pleasure, too, that Bill was now uppermost in her mind. Her love for Herbert would never leave her, but it could be safely tucked into the back of her mind to fantasize over when boredom returned—to remember.

She wondered idly and without anxiety, should she be tested for HIV now—for Bill's sake more than her own? Driving home she decided she would, why not? She was sure Sylvia had wanted her to be worried, anxious out of sheer malice. Agnes wasn't particularly worried but she thought Herbert had had other women, she was sure, so maybe Agnes was rather horrified at the objectivity of her thoughts, not about the fact that Herbert had had other women, she had known that the whole time she had known him, what shocked her was the detached way she could now think of it, of him, of the relationship. She felt it was melting, like snow when the ground was too warm to hold it white and perfect. Was she—would she feel more comfortable when there was no snow, when the relationship was forgotten? But surely it never would be? She had been so sure it would last for ever. Would it last, would it have lasted if Herbert had lived?

Agnes had the test and it was negative. She felt now she had got that out of the way and Herbert was gone it was time to start on the next problem in her life which could spill over onto Bill if she did not deal with it and that problem was—Amy.

Amy Robertson knew her limitations, knew them only too well. She had always been weak, vacillating, silly, stupid, given to hero-worship—at school she'd hero-worshipped her best friend, Stella. At fifteen, Stella had been the leader, the one who dared. Now, when Amy had entered the darkening garden in Rutland Gate, terrified, to tackle Mrs Turner, her heart had been thumping in her throat. Mrs Turner was everything she Amy wasn't, certain of herself, had given her £500 almost with contempt. But Amy had come home, back to her bedsit, with a feeling of achievement, triumph. She had done it. As she had pushed open the gate and drawn nearer to the woman with the little white dog, she'd felt Stella, her best friend, pushing her, almost heard her voice as she had at school, the same, 'Don't be such a sissy, Amy, she won't eat you.' It had helped her, propelled her on, encouraged her, in some way she felt it was Stella not her who had crossed the road to the posh flat, taken the notes, walked out, 'Don't be such a sissy, Amy, she won't eat you.' She had heard Stella's voice all right. Stella the intrepid, the bold. Only the words in those days had not been quite the same, 'Don't be such a sissy, Amy, *he* won't eat you.' It had been he then, not she.

'He' had been the old man who kept the sweetshop near the entrance to the Convent, their school. He had been fat, with a white frill of hair round his bald head, a white bristly moustache. He used to put his hand up the girls' clothes, fondle them. Amy never let him go far, not even inside her knickers, so she only got a packet of Maltesers or a Fry's chocolate bar. But Stella! Stella would come out red-faced and giggling with a box of chocolates with a ribbon tied across it in a bow. Stella was not scared. 'Dirty old git,' she used to say. But she didn't share her chocolates. She ate half of Amy's Maltesers but she never opened her own boxes of chocolates or let anyone have one.

Amy did not think of Mrs Turner and her boss, or even Mrs Shaffer, as 'Stellas', but they had what Stella probably had now, they were strong and Amy knew she was nothing—or was that going to change? She had a year, perhaps, before the book came out to get more money but most of all she had a chance to prove she was as strong and as determined as her best friend had been long ago.

Paying her landlady with that little flourish had made her feel better, bigger. Asking for the rise, not successfully—but she had threatened, as Stella would have, and she would get that rise. She didn't use that word 'blackmail'—Stella wouldn't have. She wouldn't have said it was blackmail either, she would just have said, 'If they don't want people to know, let them pay for it.' Again, she could hear Stella's voice, though she had not seen her for years, or heard of her, or from her. She went to the little chest of drawers and took the money out from under her underclothes and fondled it—not much, but it was a start. Spend it or save it? She couldn't make up her mind. What would her best friend have done? After all she saved her chocolates.

Sitting there with the money in her hand, Amy remembered a cold day, walking to school with Stella carrying a big bag of books, heavy—Stella held one handle, she the other. As they reached the sweetshop Stella had said, 'Go on in, I'll wait.' Amy didn't go. She was frightened of the man—she wouldn't go. For once she had been firm in her refusal.

'No, I won't, I don't want to.'

They stood there, the two fifteen-year-olds, Stella with her long fair hair, loose and blowing in the breeze, in spite of the nuns' rules that it should be tied back or plaited—Stella had dropped the handle of the bag and flounced away towards the

182

Convent door. Amy had dropped her handle too and walked behind her. Stella had stamped away up the wooden-floored corridor and out of sight, but Amy had looked back at the heavy bag of books, lying there, handles upwards on the pavement.

She had wanted, oh how much she had wanted, to stamp up the corridor too, and leave the bag there where it was on the pavement opposite the sweetshop door, but she couldn't. She had gone back, picked up the bag by both handles, lugged the books into school, into the classroom. She couldn't even now forget Stella's smile. Triumphant. Stella hadn't said anything but the contempt was so like the contempt she had seen on Mrs Turner's face as she had handed her the money.

Amy stood up, went and looked at the head and shoulders mirrored in the glass over the gas fire. Fat, round face—her hair mousy and short, permed too often, split ends. Her glasses never fitted up to her eyes but seemed to slide halfway down her nose. A rush of feeling came over her as if she had taken a drug. 'No more, no more of that,' she said loudly to the mirror image. 'Stella, no more of that, I'm going to be different like you, strong. They've got to pay.' She thought of Herbert Shaffer, his thick body, his hairy hands—they had all three slept with him, his wife, Agnes Turner, and her boss. He hadn't asked her, no, not Amy. No one had even tried it with her, not once, not ever. They were all rich these women, that was the secret. Well, she could bank what she had got left of the £500, she felt filled with strength—money that's what it was all about. She would go and see Mrs Turner again soon, very soon. She would save the money she had got, like Stella had the chocolates. When she had enough—she was not quite sure what she would do but when she had enough she felt she would be transformed. Poor was poor and rich made you different, that was the secret and when you knew that you were on the way to being a 'Stella'.

Maybe, when she had more money, she would seek out Stella, probably she was married, had children—the thought made Amy feel lonely, neglected. She had tried with men, tried being a bit forward, come on a bit, but somehow it didn't work. Perhaps, she thought, it was the glasses or her figure or the way she dressed or just no sex appeal. Even boring Tom was nothing.

Next morning Josephine Long called Amy into her office and offered her a rise, surprising since she had totally refused one the day before. Amy sensed a change in her employer so she pressed for even more and got it! She left the office and went back to her desk, sensible again, with a rush of power—they were afraid of her and she must make the most of it.

After a week she decided to go to Rutland Gate again. Her courage was not sufficient to go the flat, anyway Mr Turner might be there; the gardens, that was the place. She would try the same ploy, even if necessary wait a little while for Agnes Turner and the little dog to appear, then approach her. Josephine Long's change of mind about her rise made her wonder if perhaps the two women had got together and talked about her. This made her feel important. No one, as far as she remembered, had ever felt her worthy of a mention, well, now all that had changed.

The square was darker than when she had last been there. The street lamp lighting up the little oblong garden made the leaves of the trees and shrubs look dusty, took away their greenness. Amy hovered by the gate, peered down the

185

path, no one there. She tried the latch of the gate, it squeaked. A man and woman walking by on the opposite path looked across then walked on. Amy hesitated, looked up at the window of the Turner flat, it was lighted, the curtains were not drawn. Was Mrs Turner in, Amy wondered, or was it perhaps her husband? She walked round the gardens wishing she could get in so as to take Mrs Turner by surprise. She had her speech, her demand already in her mind. It was to be a thousand pounds this time. 'I don't think I asked enough, Mrs Turner, last time. After all, it wouldn't do you any good, would it? I mean, your husband and the dedication.' She whispered the words as she walked, a little rehearsal which was rudely interrupted as she reached the gate again and tried the latch once more.

'I'm afraid you have to have a key, Amy.' She whirled round, frightened, at a disadvantage. Agnes Turner was standing there watching her, an amused expression on her face. Calmly she took the key from her handbag, unlocked the gate. 'Come in, I presume you want to talk to me.' She walked down the path, turned and brushed a few fallen leaves from the wooden seat almost at the end of the gardens. She sat down and patted the seat beside her. 'What is it you want now, Amy?' she said, 'I presume it's more money.'

Her poise, her complete mastery of the situation, made Amy feel as she had at school, as she had felt with Stella—inferior. Even the way she said her name, 'Amy', made it sound a silly, common, out-of-date name. She had to clear her throat twice before she could get out her rehearsed speech. Having said it there was a pause, what to Amy seemed a long, long pause but which was only actually a few seconds, just long enough for Agnes Turner to smooth down the pleat of her skirt. Amy noticed in the lamplight a pretty gold and sparkly bracelet, it was just visible at her cuff, the little stones caught the light, pretty—drew attention to the long, white, rather thin hand and the beautifully manicured nails. Amy hastily put her hands out of sight, she bit her nails and they were horrible.

Agnes Turner looked up at her. 'Sit down. Well, you must realize, Amy, I don't keep so much money in the house. I would have to cash a cheque. Have you a bank account?' She made the question sound as if she were asking her cleaning lady or a child the question. Amy lied and said yes, she had a bank—she hadn't. What little money she had managed to save (London was an expensive place) was in a building society but somehow she felt that wouldn't do, wouldn't impress the elegant woman beside her. 'Well, we must arrange to meet somewhere, Amy.' She smiled a tight smile. 'Not in my flat, it would not do to let my husband see our little transaction, would it?' Amy shook her head. Agnes went on, 'Let me see, you work till about five, don't you, so the evening would probably be better?' Amy nodded, she felt Agnes Turner was taking over, dominating her, Stella again! 'Now where? I'd rather it was not here. Shall I telephone you?'

She looked at Amy, there was no refusal, no 'I'm not paying you any more money', nothing like that. She was cooperative, quite nice really, Amy thought, and the niceness and the cooperation baffled her, made her unable to assess the situation and threw her off her always precarious balance. 'Yes, all right, Mrs Turner.' Agnes got up, Amy followed her out of the gate which Agnes closed and locked. Then Amy stood uncertain. Agnes Turner looked at her as if surprised she was still there. 'Goodbye then, Amy, I'll telephone you.' She turned away from her and said over her shoulder, 'And arrange where I can pay you the money.' She walked away across the road, up the steps to her front door and let herself in.

Amy too walked out of the square towards the bus and home. She felt, although Mrs Turner had agreed to give her the money, she had been the victor. Still, a thousand pounds was wonderful. That cheered Amy as she boarded the bus. All she had to do now was to wait for the telephone call. She wasn't worried about that. They had separate phone numbers, Miss Long and her. Yes, everything would be all right. She was seized with a sudden hatred of Agnes Turner, it came over her like a wave. 'Superior bitch,' she said softly.

The woman sitting beside her turned and said without much interest, 'What?'

'Nothing,' Amy answered. After all, she thought, bitch or not she had got to pay. Only a telephone call stood between her and that next thousand. As the bus sped along, the breath of an idea came into her head. Why not tell Agnes Turner at their next meeting that she wanted so much a month paid into her bank—she'd open a bank account tomorrow, she knew how to do that, that would be no problem. She would just draw it out of the building society, the little bit she'd got, and the money she'd got from Mrs Turner and start a bank account, just pay it in. Barclays, Midland, TSB, it didn't matter which, as long as Mrs Turner knew where to pay it in—she was as rich as all that, she'd pay. Amy felt a warm glow, she smiled widely and the woman next to her looked at her with suspicion but Amy didn't mind what the hell the stupid woman thought about her. She got up at her stop, looked down at the woman, who looked old and grey and poor. 'Cheerio,' she said, the woman didn't answer just turned away, lifting one shoulder in dismissal.

On the stairs going up to her bedsit she met her landlady. 'All right, dear?' she said. 'You look a bit out of sorts.' Amy murmured something and passed her. Upstairs she pushed the door shut, the latch clicked and she was alone. Did she look a bit 'out of sorts'? She looked in the mirror, was she paler than usual? It had rained on the way home and her hair was damp and straight. Suddenly she felt a depression creeping over her, like being in a long black tunnel. Why—she had felt triumphant and hopeful on the bus, now ... She tried to think of the one thousand pounds but all she could visualize was Agnes Turner and the lovely bracelet and the beautiful almond-shaped nails, and she hated herself and suddenly hated what she was doing.

It was Bill who planted the idea in Agnes' mind. Well, hardly the idea but a sort of feeling there might be something in what he said. She had been slow in drawing out money from the bank. She felt she could not just go to the teller and cash a cheque for a thousand pounds, particularly as she normally used her credit card, was punctilious about checking it and paying the amount promptly. She thought it would look a little strange for her to need such a large amount entirely in cash. She couldn't visualize herself pushing such a large amount of money into her handbag and felt sure that the girl behind the counter would be slightly curious. Maybe she was wrong, maybe they didn't care at all, but she felt she would rather not do it. Now she had almost got the required money in notes. She had no fear in making Amy Robertson wait. She knew all the power the girl possessed was in that altered dedication and if she once gave away the secret to anyone her chances of getting any money again from her would be lost—ten days had gone by since the girl's last demand. Agnes had not seen Josephine again and wondered how soon Amy would demand another rise! Josephine Long had little to lose but her joy at having her name in the front of Herbert Shaffer's book. Coupled, of course, with the risk of someone finding out the name should be Agnes in the dedication and she had substituted her own.

Bill gave her this germ of an idea because he was suffering from 'writer's block'; in other words the plot had suddenly become muddled in his head and the part of the story where the character to be highlighted, the villain of the piece who therefore should come to a sticky end or be found out and arrested, could not be manipulated into a situation which would interest the reader—but not give away the whole plot. Bill was not often plagued with this problem nowadays. Agnes remembered when she had first met him as her next-door neighbour in the Isle of Wight, he had been writing detective novels then with small success and even smaller advances. But since their marriage he appeared to find writing and plotting much easier. His drinking too, which had been pretty heavy, had dropped to the normal social level. His chat that evening was about his latest book.

Agnes and he sat after dinner drinking coffee and having a rare kümmel. Bill usually produced a glass of Agnes' favourite liqueur when he wanted to ask her advice about some tangle in his plotting; almost, she thought, smiling to herself, as if he were wanting to soften her up a little. 'Got a problem, darling?' She forestalled him this evening, making her smile wider.

Bill laughed. 'Ah, the kümmel!' he acknowledged. 'Yes, it's this damn black-mailer.' He stopped and gazed at the fire, a log dropped down with a plop and he pushed it back with his foot.

'Jeremy, wasn't it?' Agnes asked.

He looked pleased. 'Clever of you to remember darling. I don't want to bore you with it but the trouble is ...' He paused again.

'You can't find a way to dispose of him?' Agnes asked.

Bill looked up, he was frowning. 'No, it's not quite that, I like the fellow, that's the problem. I feel his blackmailing is in a way—justified.'

Agnes sipped her drink. 'Surely no blackmail is ever justified?' she said.

'Well, the chap he's demanding the money from is such a heel—you know I feel he deserves to pay up, and maybe the reader will feel the same.'

Agnes could not think of any way a blackmailer could be justified and said so.

Bill shrugged. 'Maybe you're right, darling. I suppose he'll have to get his comeuppance but at the moment I can't think how.'

'Maybe you're trying to let him down lightly—so can't think of a violent end for the man?'

'Maybe.' Bill lighted a cigarette.

'Car crash?' Agnes suggested. 'I mean, an engineered car crash?'

'Hmmm. Hmm.' Bill made the noise doubtfully.

In the silence that followed, a companionable silence, Agnes felt her thoughts drifting towards her own problem and realized she would not mind how violent an end Amy Robertson came to. A car crash was pretty unlikely, she hadn't a car and seemed unlikely to be driven by anyone. As far as Agnes knew Amy had no boyfriend. Josephine Long had told her quite a bit about the girl but had never mentioned one. Agnes doubted, too, whether the unattractive girl got asked out much, particularly in other people's cars, and in all truth she didn't want anyone else to come to a violent end, just Amy. Agnes at that moment was unaware that fate, as was so often usual with her, was going to play, at least, a small part into her hands.

The discussion went on around Bill's plot. Agnes, preoccupied with her own thoughts, was not too helpful, or so she thought—when Bill said suddenly, 'There's something about your idea, darling. It needn't be a car crash though—there's "road rage", but who would do it?'

'The victim of the blackmail?' Agnes said.

He shook his head then flung his cigarette end into the fire. 'You're smoking too much, Bill,' Agnes said mildly.

'I know, I know. It's only when I can't work something out, love.' He lighted another cigarette and switched on the *Nine O'clock News*.

Agnes hardly noticed the figures on the screen or heard what they were saying. The thought of Amy Robertson involved in a car crash, killed, was trailing through her mind. Too much of a coincidence for that ever to happen. No such luck, alas. No. Agnes tried to banish that thought but she knew she couldn't. It was so convenient. It would be so far away. Not in any way involved with her or Josephine. She shook her head, thinking.

Amy was a type. A type that Agnes knew so well. She knew and recognized her from her days in hospital—there was always an Amy. One that was not run after by the doctors, or the male nurses, or even the porters. Not whistled at admiringly by the maintenance men, not glanced at with admiration by the consultants, or even had an arm put on the back when it wasn't strictly necessary doing a ward round—the quick kiss in the linen cupboard and more. There was always one who got none of this. She remembered her, this Amy at the hospital dance sitting and waiting for a partner or someone to speak to her. Agnes knew, knew, knew for in hospital she had been that girl. She had been an Amy. She had never been able to flirt, tease—until. What had changed her from the quiet, tired staff nurse with no self-esteem? She knew what had changed her—money. When she had inherited a fortune she had changed. Would money have the same effect on mousy little Amy Robertson? Not as much as she had inherited, but with the rise and her money maybe it would do something for her. It would be interesting to see.

'Do you want any more, dear?' Bill had to ask the question twice. Agnes' thoughts had been so buried in her own past, comparing herself in her early days with what she was now.

'No, no. Nothing exciting, was there?'

Bill switched off, gave her a quick peck on the cheek. 'Thanks, darling. I have an idea for my Jeremy's downfall, comeuppance.' He left the room and Agnes heard him close his 'office' door.

'I wish I had,' she said aloud and went to the telephone and rang Josephine and suggested having lunch together.

She wanted to know how Amy was acting, whether her behaviour had altered at all. What good the information would do she wasn't sure, but she followed, as usual, her own instinct. Josephine seemed pleased to accept her invitation. Agnes suspected that Josephine had not many friends. She put the telephone down, went into the kitchen and washed up and put away the coffee cups and saucers. Took the liqueur glasses through to the dining room and put them in the corner cupboard, a new and beautiful antique that Bill had recently bought.

Agnes felt she must think how to stop this beastly girl, and right at the back of her mind she felt there was a germ of an idea that wasn't really strong enough or clear enough to be realized, even to herself. She felt rather like Bill, wondering what to do, but there was no feeling as Bill had that he was sorry and felt he would like to let his blackmailer off lightly. Oh no, there was no thought like that in Agnes' mind, none at all. She would like her banished—and, she added softly to herself, 'Dead.'

Josephine Long greeted Agnes with warmth and seemed just as delighted to see her as she had sounded on the phone when

Agnes had proposed the meeting. It was obvious she wanted to talk, to tell Agnes about Amy—or as she put it, her 'blasted secretary!' After all, Agnes was the only one she could talk to about their mutual problem. 'She had the effrontery to ask me, no, *tell* me, that a bigger rise would have been more adequate under the circumstances. That's exactly how she put it. I've dictated words like that in letters of mine many times and I suppose she's picked the phrases up and now they're coming in very useful to her.' She picked up a knife, they had not yet been served, and tapped it on the side plate with a little rhythm that aggravated Agnes. She hated people who made unnecessary movements. Economy of movement, she always thought, perhaps it was her training as a nurse that made her so conscious of wasted effort. 'She even told me she had bought a car. Only an old banger, she said but it went quite well.'

'Can she drive?' Agnes managed to ask before the tirade went on.

'Apparently. She got a licence ages ago but has never been able to afford a car.'

Agnes digested this information with some interest. Anything to do with the girl's background, anything that could be used was of interest to her, and a car—shades of last night's talk with Bill!

She told Josephine about the girl's further demand for a thousand pounds. 'How dare she? The little beast. I wonder if you were right, Agnes. Maybe I should have sacked her when I said I would. I've a good mind—'

Agnes stopped her, almost wearily, 'And have her tell the publishers, or even make a magazine article about the poor ageing women who fantasized about going to bed with a famous author—lied about their affair with him, lied about the dedication?'

Josephine nodded slowly, her brow creased in a frown. 'I suppose you're right, Agnes. That sort of thing would sell. Someone would print it and then where would we be? But the whole thing is beginning to frighten me, I'd give anything to get her off my back. Wouldn't you?'

'Wouldn't I just! How do you think I feel about Bill, I couldn't bear him to know! The little bitch! I'd do anything to get rid of her—anything.'

As she said it she remembered again Bill's talking about 'road rage'—had he mentioned it or had it been her? Agnes couldn't quite remember. The blackmailer in his book, she had suggested a car crash and now Amy had a car. She shook herself and sat more upright. An old familiar gesture; straightening her shoulders, she leaned back in her chair, and felt a million miles away from her companion. She was aware that Josephine was still talking. Agnes was thinking. Somewhere in the back of her mind that idea was stirring, swimming to and fro like a fish way down in deep water. She would go and look at the place where Amy lived, not let her know of course, but—

'What kind of car? What make, what year?' she asked so abruptly and out of context of the conversation that Josephine looked startled.

'Oh, a Metro, she told me. A silver one—she was very proud of the silver. Seven years old, I think she said. Why?'

Agnes waved the question away. 'Never mind, I was just curious,' she said. 'Why does she want a car in London anyway? There's nowhere to park it.'

'It's not for coming to work. Her mother lives in Dorking or Guildford or somewhere round there. She goes to see her by train most weekends. She's ill or has a bad hip,

I can't quite remember, but I do remember her talking about it, she seems quite fond of her. This was when I took her on.'

Agnes felt her heart quicken. She was not sure why. 'Well, that's something in her favour, I suppose, if she goes to see her mother.'

Josephine nodded. 'I suppose so,' she said without conviction.

Josephine appeared to enjoy her lunch but Agnes barely tasted hers. She was thinking, thinking, but her thoughts were chaotic, nothing would come up, nothing that made sense, except a car—a crash— and Bill's or her reference to 'road rage'. Josephine shovelled the last piece of lemon meringue pie into her mouth and swallowed. 'I wish she were dead,' she said.

'Yes, so do I,' Agnes replied softly, 'and after all the roads are very dangerous nowadays, particularly for someone who hasn't driven for some time.' She gazed across the room, her eyes narrowed and she was conscious that the woman opposite her had stopped chewing and was looking at her with curiosity, almost anxiety. She countered it. 'Shall we have coffee, Josephine?' she asked and Josephine nodded slowly, not taking her eyes from Agnes' face.

Agnes' next encounter with Amy Robertson was in the gardens of Rutland Square. It was much the same in some ways as her first encounter, she had Mac on a long lead and he was rushing about with excitement. He had a squeaky toy with him which echoed the squeak of the gate. Agnes saw, as Josephine had predicted, the car. Amy drove up, parked rather badly at the side of the square (a good foot and a half from the kerb, Agnes noted), walked across, squeaked open the gate and came through. Agnes was at the far end.

'Oh, I heard the squeak and thought it was the gate and then it went again—he's got a toy.' She sounded nervous.

Agnes did not reply, merely opened her handbag, took out a manila envelope and handed it to the girl, reeled in the dog's lead and started back towards the entrance of the gardens. The girl's confidence had increased and Agnes felt it, though she had half expected it.

'I've got a car!' The girl's voice was light, her face almost smiling.

'So I see,' Agnes replied abruptly.

'I couldn't afford one before. You see ...'

'Before you began your blackmailing, you mean?'

The girl was a little thrown off-balance by the remark but not for long. 'Well, Mrs Turner, why shouldn't I have a car? I work hard, other people have cars.'

Agnes opened the gate, the dog went through first then Agnes. 'And so you think your behaviour merits it?'

Amy was silent, then, 'Well, yes. If you two hadn't been so silly—I mean you having it off with Mr Shaffer and then Miss Long pretending she did—if it wasn't for that I wouldn't have a car, would I?'

Agnes felt her fury mounting. At that moment, had she a weapon, anything, she felt she could kill the girl, there and then in the square, but even so she kept her voice low and composed. 'Well, I believe you haven't driven for some time, I hope you don't meet with an accident.'

Her sarcasm was obvious even to Amy Robertson; the girl's voice shook a little. 'I suppose you hope I do,' she said.

Agnes looked at her, they stood face to face for a moment. 'Well, I suppose

I can say I wouldn't be particularly sorry, Amy,' she said, 'and I hope this is your last request for money.'

Amy, regaining some of her confidence, answered more quietly this time, as a woman entered the square and made her way along the path and up the steps to the house opposite. The door closed behind her. 'Well, we'll have to see, won't we? I had another idea, Mrs Turner really.'

Agnes noted she pronounced the word *r-e-e-l-l-y*. 'And what was that, may I ask?'

Amy half turned on her heel as if to make towards the car. 'I wondered could we sort of—well wouldn't it be easier if you made a sort of little monthly payment, you know, somewhere else—posted it to me perhaps, then—' She seemed a little anxious about her own temerity and looked at Agnes' face.

Agnes did not answer, she was more taken aback by the girl's impudence than she wanted to show. And how much would she demand every month, for perhaps, Josephine Long had said, twelve months before the book came out. 'Well, we'll have to see, won't we?'

Amy did not look at Agnes again but crossed the road and got into the car.

The engine started readily, the gear grated slightly, the car jerked forward and stalled. Amy started again, this time with a little more success. It made a jerky start but the engine kept going and it drove away. Agnes watched it, not moving until Mac let out a small sharp bark, tired of waiting especially on a short lead. Then Agnes locked the gate and went back to her own flat.

'I could have taken him for you, darling,' Bill said as she came into the sitting room. Before she could answer he went on, 'Another old woman killed in her own house in Leicestershire. I don't know!'

'Good for your ideas, though, dear,' Agnes said.

Bill looked quite shocked. 'Darling, what a dreadful remark!' He looked at her in surprise.

'Yes, it was, sorry. I was just a bit cross about something.' Agnes knew her own mood, she had felt it before and acted on it—there was a savage mood there well hidden.

'What made you cross, dear?' Bill asked.

'Oh nothing, just a little thing, not worth bothering about.' Agnes paused and looked down at Bill. He was such a non-violent, sweet person, he wouldn't hurt a fly and

206

yet he wrote about murders. Whereas she ... 'Like a nightcap Bill?' she asked.

'Yes. Wouldn't mind.' He'd obviously forgotten about her remark and smiled at her. 'If you'll join me?' he said.

'Of course I will.' Agnes felt as though she needed a drink or something to calm her nerves after that beastly girl's remark. There was something about Amy that was beginning to be recognized by Agnes. Maybe it was the fact that she saw herself growing in status as her bank balance increased. Was that, she wondered, all that made her or Amy gain confidence, be what she was now? It was a sobering thought. She went into the dining room and mixed the drinks. Coming back she looked down at her shoes, expensive; her slim ankles, at least those were her own, they'd always been slim; her well-cut suit, her expensively cut hair; was that all it was—money? She handed Bill his drink and sat down beside him, he looked at her and put his hand over hers. She knew as she had sat down she had given a long, long sigh and she wished she hadn't.

Bill noticed it. 'That was a big sigh, darling?'

Agnes turned to him. 'It's nothing. Bill.

Well, just a little problem that has to be cleared up, solved.'

'Something I can help with, dearest?'

Agnes shook her head. 'No, not really.'

'Right, but tell me if I can.' That was so like Bill, his respect for her privacy, her space. She took another sip of her drink and thought perhaps it wasn't only money had changed her, made her into what she was today, changed her from that frightened, inadequate young woman with no self-esteem at all, at least, she hoped it wasn't just the money.

Agnes lay in bed beside Bill. He was asleep, his breathing quiet and regular, a sure sign that he had solved his problem, sketched out the plot's progress and so felt more relaxed. Agnes lay on her side, occasionally looking at the luminous hands of her little bedside clock—one thirty, two o'clock. She tried to keep still so as not to disturb Bill. Her mind was racing. Amy's suggestion, monthly payments, had really unnerved her; that she should take such a course, think of it, showed how much her confidence and impudence were growing. Josephine's rise might have also encouraged her to think of such payments from Agnes. Her mind went on and on and she looked at the clock again. Another half-hour had passed and she had come no nearer to a solution. All she was doing was losing sleep. Then she made a sudden decision. Tomorrow she would go and look at Amy's house/flat/bedsit, Clarence Road, Putney. Amy would be at work, she could safely go down the road. It would help. She always needed to know the background of the person she was—how could she put it—waging war against! Josephine had told her the address but no doubt in that part of London, Putney, it would not be easy to find, and she certainly did not want to draw attention to herself by asking the way. Sleep still did not come until she had made another decision; tomorrow her car was going in for service, they always lent her one. She didn't know why but she felt that would be good, things always came to her like that. Having made the decision she felt better and fell asleep.

Agnes drove slowly down Clarence Road, Putney. The address had been given her by Josephine Long, number 21. The street was like so many streets in London nowadays; family houses, red brick and white paint, turned now into flats or bedsits. Brass knockers, brass letter boxes, strips of brass at the edge of the top steps, some polished, some left dull and uncleaned. Agnes could imagine the days when little maids would have polished each one, industrious, afraid of getting the sack if their mistress found fault. Times change.

At number 19 Agnes slowed down even more. Odd numbers on the right side of the street, on the left even. 21. Polished brass, one point in its favour but a Venetian blind let down askew lost the point. Agnes stopped. The silver Metro was parked directly outside, brightly and cleanly shining. Cleaned, no doubt, by Amy—a proud blackmailing Amy. There was grass growing out of the tiled path, losing a point but the path was swept clear of rubbish. Well there it was, what did it tell her about Amy? Not much. It did say though that it was a dismal place to live and an uncared-for street where people lived probably alone in small flats and bedsitters. Trees at regular intervals along the road in square holes in the pavement didn't add much. One had burn marks at its base as if someone had tried to get rid of it. Another had a torn notice nailed to it; long out of date, the words—OR—ALE, a house—a car? Agnes felt depressed by the whole scene, yet at the back of her mind something was forming, so nebulous, so misty but there it was—a plan. Sometimes her plan evolved, taking her along with it, rather like standing on a beach waiting for the tide to come in, engulfing you, deeper and deeper into it, carrying you at the right time to the right place. Agnes gave one last look at 21 and drove home. Next time she would be in her own car.

The picture of that house, 21, lingered in her mind. The maroon door, almost purple, paint chipped, was depressing in itself. No wonder Amy Robertson wanted more. The car must be a great step up for her. She had probably been proud when she drove up to her mother's door or taken her out for her drive. And the mother was probably proud of her daughter. 'My daughter's car,' she could say to her friends. It was unlikely she would know how Amy was able to afford the car. Agnes realized she had fallen into her husband's writing trap, feeling a slight sympathy for her blackmailer but not sympathy enough to wish to continue paying any more money.

Another little piece fell into place in the

jigsaw when Bill came home that evening. Although as yet Agnes had no clue to the picture, the pieces would show when they were all in place. Bill looked slightly worried when he came into the kitchen, Agnes sensed his mood at once, she always did. They kissed.

'Everything all right, darling?' she asked.

'Yes, fine. Better and better. They want to do another film. One of the old books, *Dead Men Talking.*'

Agnes showed her delight. *Dead Men Talking* was one of his earliest books. Agnes also realized why Bill looked slightly worried—his next remark gave the clue. Visiting the States with Bill working each day was not a favourite pastime with Agnes, twice in three years she had been there with him.

'I'll have to go, just for a few days, about five, darling. Would you want to come, it's the week after next?' He looked at Agnes. 'Want to come?' he asked again.

'Not really, Bill, not unless you really want me to.'

He shook his head. 'Up to you, love, just as you like.'

'I'll stay here, dear, and wait for you to come back—longing,' she said.

'I shall be away over a weekend, I think, about Thursday until Tuesday, maybe a bit longer.'

'Right, darling.'

He looked relieved.

'I may go down to the Island, I'll see.' Agnes suddenly knew—even as she uttered the words 'the Island' she knew she wouldn't go there. She would be going somewhere quite different, not Hampshire but Surrey. The idea, or the beginning of the formation of the idea, shocked her a little, but Amy had never seen her car, wouldn't recognize it, that was all right. She would go, go down to Dorking, to Guildford, she must make sure. A plan, the plan was starting to form and she felt the usual small thrill. How it would end, she didn't know; how it would begin, she wasn't quite sure; but she knew the plan was there and a dim outline of the picture the jigsaw would make was beginning to form.

It was about three quarters of an hour after Agnes arrived at Clarence Road that she saw the plump, short figure of Amy Robertson come round the corner. She was carrying two Tesco carriers. Her handbag handle over one shoulder slipped down her arm as she was passing the first house and she put one carrier down, pulled the handbag handle up again onto her shoulder and walked on. Partially hidden by the row of cars on the opposite side of the road, Agnes watched her appear and disappear as she passed each car.

Agnes was parked a little way back from 22, the house almost opposite 21, on the other side of the road. She had her side visor down but the road was pretty wide and she had little or no fear of being seen by the girl. She wondered would Amy put the shopping straight into the car, was it for her mother? But no, the girl walked up the steps of number 21, again put down her carriers onto the top step, opened her handbag, obviously searching for a key. She had no hat on and the breeze blew her rather mousy, greasy hair about her face as she searched. She turned her head a little to get it out of her eyes as she found the key, opened the door, gathered up the bags and went inside. The door banged behind her. Agnes wondered, would she come out and drive the silver Metro away that evening? Or would she go tomorrow morning? Agnes had brought with her Herbert's last book, at least his last published book, *Glass Diamonds*. She had removed the dust cover and left it at home. She did not want to look at his face in the car, the memories came rushing back to her too poignantly. The book itself, without the cover, was black with gold lettering on the spine showing the title at the top and the publisher's name at the bottom of the spine. There was no dedication. Apparently, Josephine had told her, he had not always been in the habit of dedicating his books. If only, Agnes thought, he had not dedicated his last one. If he had not, she would not be sitting here waiting for this beastly girl to either come or go. Guildford or Dorking, she was not sure and on no account could she ask either the girl herself or Josephine Long.

She had, as always, to carry out her plans completely alone. She watched the maroon paint scratched door for another hour, in between reading the book. It was growing dark, surely the girl would not attempt to drive in her near new car and drive it almost as a new driver? Agnes was patient. She read a few more chapters but the ugly painted door remained shut. No lights sprang up in the house; Amy's bedsit might be at the back?

Mac had been a model of patience. He was curled up on the back seat. Only once, as a woman had passed the car leading a large fawn standard poodle, had he shown his disapproval by barking his high, excited bark. Agnes would rather not have brought him but she had not been sure how long her vigil would be and if she had to follow the girl he must be there, she could not leave him alone in the flat, perhaps all day. Now she suddenly decided to give up the vigil, hoping she was right that Amy had decided to go to her mother's tomorrow morning. On the way home Agnes tried to get herself into the girl's mind—Guildford was about twenty miles, a new car and a long time since she had driven. Would she go by quiet side roads or choose the motorway? Agnes had spent a long time last night studying the various routes for both Dorking and Guildford. Whichever way the girl chose Agnes would not be far behind her. What for she was not certain, but she knew she would just leave it to fate as she had sometimes done, or seize the initiative when something happened, or some opportunity arose. She was rather like Mr Micawber, she thought, something would turn up, it always did. Another half-hour and Agnes decided to go home. It was getting darker, lights were springing up and as she again hoped or guessed the girl would not drive in the dark, not choose to. So she would have to come back early in the morning, hope the silver Metro would still be there, after all Guildford or Dorking was not far away, not far to go, not far to follow.

Before she got back to the flat she walked the patient Mac, a good walk in the park, and as she walked she thought of tomorrow. She would wear her dark lavender tweed suit, flat shoes, like she had today, after all you never knew, you might have to walk. And she must change her handbag, she was very particular about such things. Mac frolicked around her, glad of the exercise, barking and rather excited about getting a long walk in the dark. Back at the flat, after making herself supper, feeding Mac, getting out the lavender suit and matching handbag all ready, she had a bath and went to bed. Once there she set her little bedside clock for seven then changed her mind and made it quarter to. She would like to be in Clarence Road by eight, surely the girl wouldn't start out before that? Well, if she did, she did, there would be other weekends. On one thing Agnes was determined: she would not pay Amy Robertson another penny, she would see her dead first. Agnes grimaced a little as she thought about it, after all wasn't that what all this was about?

Agnes did not sleep well. When she did drop off for a short while her dream was the same; she was driving along a dark road, the white line in the middle of the road disappearing and reappearing in front of her. Ahead was the rear of the silver Metro, without lights, disappearing and reappearing. It was disturbing so she got up and made herself a hot drink. She dared not take a sleeping tablet as she sometimes did when sleepless, she was afraid it might make her oversleep.

In the kitchen she made herself a mug of Horlicks, brought it through to the bedroom and put it on the bedside table and as she did so a thought struck her. She sat on the side of the bed, looking at her preparations, suit, stockings, shoes, underclothes, all draped over a chair, ready. Beside the chair on the small table her handbag and beside it her car keys. Mac watched her from his bed. 'Stay,' she had said firmly to him on her way to the kitchen and he had stayed. Her gaze returned to the car keys and handbag—what was missing? What other object was needed besides that bag and keys? She got up, thought better of it, got back into bed to think. She sipped the drink, her eyes still fixed on the table and its contents. She finished the drink, drained the mug, got out of bed once more and took the mug back to the kitchen. Suddenly she had an idea, went to a cupboard low down in the unit, took something from the back with some difficulty, the object was not often used, well, never used. She had to take out an old mincing machine, a pile of pudding basins, a pile of ice trays, cake tins, a rusty grill pan, a wire cake rest before she could the reach the object she wanted. She drew it out, put the oddments back, went back to the bedroom and put the object beside her handbag and got back into bed. She felt she had got the thing whose absence had worried her—a weapon. She fell asleep and the dream of the road and the vanishing Metro did not come back, she slept peacefully until the shrill invasion of the alarm woke her and made

Mac spring out of his bed and rush into the kitchen ready for his breakfast.

Agnes looked out of the kitchen window. The weather had completely changed, there was a misty rain falling, making the morning look foggy. The kettle snapped off but she still stood there looking out, thinking. There was a little mackintosh in the car so that was all right and a towel for Mac. The morning felt humid, muggy, a towel to dry Mac would certainly be needed, she would add another one to her preparations. Her neat, methodical arrangements never let her down. It was now many years since she had retired from nursing but her training seemed to remain with her, even in her housekeeping: when one tin of grapefruit segments remained in the store cupboard in the kitchen, Bill's favourite breakfast starter, she made a note to restock. Bill sometimes laughed at her and said she drilled the grocery cupboard like an army, one row for vegetables, one for tinned fruit, one for condiments, another for soups, she laughed at herself and replied that she never ran out and had to dash to the shops like some people, even Mac had a little shelf now with his tins, boxes of Bonios and munchies, chews and chocolate treats. She had a vague contempt for disorder, untidiness. Mac had fitted into the household, she knew, because of her organization. Sometimes Agnes was not altogether pleased or proud of her neatness, her straight rows of tins. She felt at the back of her mind it smacked of old-maidishness but she knew she was incapable of changing.

Once dressed, Agnes made tea and toast and ate three slices, gave Mac a little more than his usual breakfast, after all she was not sure where or when they would get lunch. She took him out to the gardens. The rain had ceased, but by the look of the sky not for long. Back at the flat she collected Mac's lead, her bag, the car keys, then she checked the flat; stove off, windows locked and shut, she locked the front door with the mortice lock as well as the Yale. She had a curious feeling that she was going on a momentous journey. Outside the rain had started again but the car was parked in their space just outside their flat. Mac jumped in. On the floor of the car, in front of the passenger seat, covering it with the rubber weather mat, Agnes put the object she had fetched from the kitchen in the middle of the night.

A strange thing to put in a car wrapped in brown paper—a steel knife sharpener. The car slid gently away from the kerb, destination Clarence Road, Putney.

Agnes looked at the car clock. It was seven forty-five. Her plan to follow the blackmailer would happen, might not happen today—but it would happen, Agnes was determined to persist until it did.

On the way at some red lights she was conscious of a part feeling of impatience. Mac sat up and looked out of the window as he always did when the car stopped. Agnes stroked his head. 'A strange day we may have today, Mac,' she said. The dog wagged his tail. The light turned to green, the car started up again and Mac lay down, his brown eyes open still fixed on Agnes' face.

As Agnes approached Putney she felt herself becoming anxious. Would the car be there or would it not? As she turned into Clarence Road she could see the silver Metro, she was in time—that is if the girl was going to Surrey that morning. Agnes turned off her engine, pulled the side visor into position, sat back and prepared to wait once again, this time with a good deal more hope. At about twenty past eight Amy Robertson emerged from the purple door, carrying one of the Tesco carriers, a black bin-bag and her handbag. Agnes watched the girl unlock and get into the car. Once in, she did not immediately take off. Inside the car, Agnes could see her quarry arranging her bags, doing up her seat belt. She had a red headscarf and a red sweater. Her rather dumpy legs were encased in black trousers. 'Not a pretty sight,' Agnes murmured to herself. The Metro drew out. Agnes waited a moment then began to follow. At the end of the road the Metro turned left. Agnes followed. She had no fear of Amy recognizing her. Her windscreen was slightly tinted, as were her windows and even so Agnes felt that Amy would be concentrating too much on her driving to bother to even look up at the car following her and anyway she had never seen the Porsche before. Whether it would be better, Agnes debated, to let a car get in between them now and again so that her following was not too obvious she was undecided, but as the journey progressed she would make up her mind about that. As it was, the traffic was fairly light this

Saturday morning; lighter than she had expected, so she drove a fair way behind the car which she hoped she would not lose all the way to Surrey.

The drive through London was not as bad as Agnes feared, the traffic was lighter too. Saturday morning, Agnes had half expected more cars going south. Amy appeared to Agnes to be rather worried by roundabouts. She took one the wrong way round and stalled her engine three times at traffic lights.

Then they left the motorway and struck quieter roads. Dorking was obviously their object. Once there Amy went on driving through the town and just as they were coming to the suburbs a puff of smoke belched out of the Metro's exhaust, the engine gave a couple of bangs and the car stopped. Agnes drew into a lucky parking space behind a small van and watched. There was a garage just opposite where Amy had stopped. She got out of her car, looking left and right to avoid traffic, went over to the garage and had a word with a young man filling a petrol tank. He pointed towards the glass front door of the garage behind the pumps. Amy disappeared through the door.

About five minutes passed, meanwhile traffic was skirting the silver Metro, oncoming traffic behind was hanging back to let it pass. A grey-haired woman driving a white car held up by the blocking Metro leaned out and spoke to Agnes. 'What's the hold-up, do you know?'

'I think someone has broken down—that Metro.'

The woman peered out of the further window. 'Oh dear. I've got a dentist appointment.' She hooted then the cars coming the other way cleared. She smiled at Agnes, waved a hand and drove on. At that moment, Amy and a mechanic came out through the glass door, crossed the road and the bonnet of the car was opened. Agnes waited patiently. Mac sat up, had a look round then settled down again.

After a few minutes the man slammed the bonnet shut, stood talking, gesticulating, as if trying to drive a point home, then as Amy Robertson shook her head he shrugged his shoulders almost up to his ears, turned his hands, palms upward, walked away. As Amy got into the car and he was halfway across the road, he called out, 'Well, don't say I didn't warn you, miss.' Agnes could not see Amy's reaction but the car started and drew away. Agnes was trapped behind two cars. She looked in her mirror, another car was coming by, she would have to let it. She could lose Amy now. She felt the familiar quicken of her heart rate. Her plans might go wrong yet—she smiled to herself, what were her plans? Three cars between her and the Metro, she was still able to see it turn left. More shops, more houses, more shoppers, some old ones dragging trolleys behind them. Agnes even had time to notice an elderly lady trailing a trolley with a dog in it. Front paws and long spaniel ears, looking round it with curiosity. Agnes was glad to see it looked as if it was enjoying itself.

The shops got fewer and disappeared. Houses, rows of semi-detached, gave way to larger but fewer houses standing in large gardens, with, in some cases, sweeping gravel drives. Then Amy turned off the dual carriageway into a narrow road edged with green grass and running through tall trees. Only now and again was a house visible from the road. Agnes felt they were heading countrywards, towards a village perhaps, and would have liked to have been able to consult her map but there was no time and really no need to know.

Traffic on this road was practically nil. Agnes supposed people going to work were already there; in shops, offices, on a Saturday? Well, some did. Agnes glanced at her car clock. Eleven thirty. The time had been taken up in their southern run out of London and, of course, through the busy town of Dorking. Agnes' thoughts were interrupted by two small explosions from the exhaust of the car in front, similar to the ones that had happened in the town. The Metro slowed down, drew into the side of the road and stopped. Agnes stopped her car. Luckily there was a small twist in the road, which must have almost hidden her from Amy. She turned to Mac, who had ensconced himself on the back seat. 'Stay,' she said firmly. She picked up the extending lead in its white plastic container; picked up the knife sharpener: her idea had clarified itself.

'Mrs Turner, what are you doing here?' Agnes had walked along the grass verge and arrived at Amy's passenger door before the girl had even noticed her. The car door was not locked, Agnes got in. The girl was looking at her, her mouth open, her eyes wide. Agnes said nothing. 'The car won't go. The man in Dorking said—'

'I know. Get out of the car, Amy.'

'What for? Are you going to give me a lift?'

'No. I'm not going to do that, Amy, but I think you should check the battery leads.'

'Battery leads, Mrs Turner? What are you doing here? What are the—' Amy's voice was wailing.

'Out you get.' Agnes' voice was sharp, firm.

Amy leant over the battery. A black box enclosed it. It was obvious she hadn't the least idea what she was looking at. As she leaned forward, Agnes acted. She extended the lead, threw it over the girl's head, tightened it. Inserted the knife sharpener into the knot. She knew the way to do it—there had been another time. The knife sharpener twisted the nylon of the dog lead. Twisted and twisted. She did it with a certain amount of expertise. She had seen it done on the television too. Garrotting—a lovely word! As the nylon tightened round the girl's throat she had managed to let out a scream but it sounded just like a bird in the trees, if anyone had heard it. But no one had. The road was still deserted. Agnes' experience told her when the girl was dead. She drew out the rodlike knife sharpener, loosened the dog lead and the girl fell forward. That one scream was all she had managed. Both hands had been occupied in trying to loosen the constriction around her neck. She had hardly struggled, only against the tightening leash. Agnes looked up and down the road. No car had passed. She walked back to her car. Mac sat up as she opened the door. She closed it again; she had another thought. She walked back to Amy's car, opened the door. The girl's handbag was on the passenger seat. Shabby, plastic, half open. Agnes had a momentary thought—should she take money from the bag? No, she decided against it. But what if—She felt another thrill, a compulsion to look into the bag. The girl would never leave those precious dedications behind in the bed-sitting room, never be parted from the very source of her new-found riches. She saw inside the bag and took out with the tips of her fingers a manila envelope. It was thick enough to contain four pages of A4. She pushed it into her suit pocket—they

229

always made mistakes. Had she been a sophisticated girl she would have—Agnes cut off her thoughts. What mattered was she had got them, at least she hoped so. Back in her own car, in her own time, she would check. She put the envelope in her glove compartment.

Agnes drove past the Metro. Amy had fallen slightly to one side and looked as if she was about to fall onto the ground. What if she did? Agnes increased her speed, came to a path leading to a house invisible from the road. She turned her car. As she did so there was a sudden crash of thunder and flash of lightning, the rain started spotting her windscreen with large stormy drops. Seconds later she passed the Metro again. Amy had not fallen but had merely slipped a few inches further sideways. The rain was now coming down as someone had said in Agnes' past, some old patient perhaps, 'Like stair-rods.' Agnes had her wipers going as fast as they would go. The rain bounced off the road, rattled on the roof of the car, poured down the windscreen. As Agnes reached Dorking it was still pouring. People were sheltering in shop doorways. When Agnes reached the motorway the rain let up a little and she was able to let the Porsche speed along at 60 m.p.h. She arrived at Rutland Gate, put her car in the allotted parking space, the sun came out. Sitting there she then had time to examine the lead. She was putting off opening the manila envelope. She was not sure why. The lead was slightly stretched in one place. She snapped the catch on to Mac's collar and took him into the gardens. The ground was wet. Mac splashed about, added his little bit of water to the shrubs.

In the garden she drew the envelope out of her suit pocket; four sheets of paper. One the handwritten dedication to her, and a photocopy of it, one of the typed copy Josephine had typed and a copy of that. She stood for a moment looking at the handwritten dedication to her. He, Herbert had written that himself. His own hand had rested there. She placed the paper against her cheek. She would have loved to have kept that written sheet but that was all over. The tears came to her eyes and Mac, as if influenced by her mood, stopped running about and looked up at her. There was no rain now but her cheeks were wet with tears. She sat down for a moment on the rain-spotted seat and pressed the sheet that Herbert had written against her cheek again. AGNES WHO IS MY FOR EVER. Great sobs shook her. If he had lived—but he hadn't lived. Agnes stood up. Tore the four sheets and the manila envelope into tiny pieces. As she left the garden she dropped them into the big black rubbish bin at the gate of the gardens. It was already half full and the rain had leaked in to the slot at the side and the contents would be wet. That which Herbert had written with his own hand was now rubbish. This thought was again almost too much for her. She locked the gate and went into the flat.

In the flat, for some reason, she suddenly felt hungry. Poured herself a drink, fed Mac then made a mushroom omelette and a salad. Sitting eating she suddenly wished she had checked if Amy had any of her ill-gotten money with her. Wished she had looked and taken it. Then as she enjoyed the crisp lettuce she felt glad she hadn't. As it was it could be diagnosed perhaps as 'road rage' not robbery. She finished her meal. Changed into slacks and a light jumper, opened the mail which revealed nothing of importance then remembered the knife sharpener that had been so useful.

She had left it on the hall table. She took it into the kitchen, washed it and put it back where it had been, in the back of the cupboard. How strange that she had unearthed it. She had, she felt, forgotten it but these things lodged in your mind and when they were useful to you, you remembered them. Was it only last night she had taken it out? It seemed ages ago. As she clicked the cupboard door with a little snap she felt a certain wonderful feeling of achievement. 'I have done it,' she said to Mac who wagged his tail vigorously as he always did when spoken to. 'We have saved Bill from ever knowing.' She wondered if the body had been found yet. But she wondered it without anxiety or apprehension. Tomorrow the papers would probably tell her, she would wait until they arrived. They would be interesting. It was good too, that the torrential rain, which had started at the right time, would probably obliterate any other tyre marks or any evidence that there had been another car. And she thought of the one man in the red car that had passed her, his long hair, she had seen that but she felt no fear of him, he had not even glanced towards them, he had been driving fast.

She cleared the table and washed up. Monday's papers and Josephine's reaction would make an exciting day. How would she take the death of her secretary? With great relief, if she had any sense. After a rest Agnes felt she deserved, after all the day had been fairly nerve-racking and tiring, Agnes took Mac to the park.

Once there she let out the lead to its full length and as Mac tugged and twisted it, it did much to straighten and smooth out the piece that had been round Amy Robertson's neck. The twisting steel had been the perfect implement to turn the nylon ribbon into a garrotte. How useful ordinary, innocent objects could be in the right hands. The rain had left the grass of the park wet and the macadam roads and paths shiny in the sun. The walk was pleasant and soothing. Agnes stayed longer than usual. The birds sang, the bright droplets of rainwater dripped from the leaves, ridding them of the London dust and making the earth and greenery smell sweet and new and springlike, bright and washed. Agnes drew a deep breath, called Mac back to her before reeling him in to a shorter lead. 'All's right with the world, Mac,' she said and she really meant it.

Josephine Long was wakened by the newspapers plopping through her letter box, she took *The Times* and the *Daily Mail*. This morning she had a headache and had not slept well. The worry of the book, the dedication, Amy's knowledge of her deception all swam about in her mind. Also, she had been out to dinner with one of her authors the night before. A very good meal and good wine, but for some reason wine, even one glass, gave Josephine a headache. Another plop through the letter box, her mail had come. She looked at her watch, eight o'clock—no, her watch was losing she remembered, it needed a new battery. She got up. The kitchen clock said quarter past eight. She had missed the news. She made herself a pot of tea and took it through to her sitting room; it was sunny there and the kitchen was cool and faced north so never caught the early-morning sun. Her head throbbed.

Still in her dressing gown and slippers, she put the tray down on the little coffee table in the sitting room by her armchair. Then she went through to the bathroom and got two Codis from the cupboard, collected the newspapers and the thin catalogue, Selfridges, and a letter from the hall mat and took them into the sitting room. She tossed the catalogue to one side. Opened the letter it was from a friend who usually only wrote to her when she wanted a bed for the night, a glance through it confirmed this was the same. Then she picked up the *Daily Mail*. There were two headlines, one above the other about some political move but the smaller one, a little lower down, arrested her. ANOTHER ROAD RAGE VICTIM? She read the smaller print beneath the headline.

'The next of kin of the murdered girl had been informed so we can reveal she was a Miss Amy Robertson.' The short piece went on to disclose: 'The girl had been strangled, she had not been sexually assaulted and her handbag and money were untouched. So apparently robbery or sexual attack had not been—' Josephine could not read any more. Her secretary, Amy, dead! She was shaking. She felt the paper rustling in her hands, she felt faint as if she were going to pass out. She pulled herself together, poured the tea, took the two Codis and the faintness wore off a little. She sat back in the chair, staring out of the sunny window at the houses opposite, the bricks made pink and attractive by the light. She said aloud, 'I killed her.' She lifted the cup with both hands. They were still shaking, but not quite as much. Her mind went on accusing herself. If she hadn't switched the dedication, Amy would never have been able to force money out of Agnes or herself nor would she have been able to get a car and the fact she had got a car had meant her death. What had happened? Had she been going too fast, too slow, driving badly? What had made some maniac attack and kill her? Josephine felt the tears running down her face remembering the girl, small, fat and mousy. A blackmailer, yes, but did she deserve strangling? She forced herself to read more.

Apparently the car had broken down. A man had come forward from a garage in Dorking. The girl had had trouble with the car, practically opposite his garage. His assistant had been serving petrol and had come in and told him about the car and he had gone across the road. He had said that her petrol pump was not letting the petrol through properly but she had said she didn't want anything done, she would risk it. So she had probably broken down again. He had warned her. There was a small picture of Amy and another of her mother's cottage in Gradley Magnum near Dorking.

Murdered. Josephine tried to imagine what it would mean. She would have the police call at her office she was sure. Why had she given her the rise—two rises? And what about the car? Agnes Turner's money? She realized because of her deception she was losing her nerve. She began to wonder, had any other agent ever changed a dedication, made it to herself rather than to anyone else? Could they sue her, the publishers? No, the author—but he was dead. Still, there was his wife. Could his wife—no, she didn't know. She couldn't tell because she knew nothing, no one who had done such a thing before and she dare not ask.

Had Agnes Turner seen the papers? She must telephone her. Then an explosion in her mind. The copies of the dedication. Oh God the police would find them in her digs or somewhere, maybe Amy had taken them down to her mother's place for safety, or could they be hidden in the wretched girl's workplace, in other words, in Josephine's own outer office? She had searched the desk in the girl's absence but she might have missed it. It might be somewhere else in the office. She reasoned with herself that if it was there, now that the girl was dead at least it would be safer, she would comb the whole office not just the desk, as she had already.

She got up, still feeling shaky, wobbly. She went to the telephone and dialled Agnes' number. It was early, but if Agnes had seen the newspapers she would hardly be— Still, if she had read the article, seen the newspaper, why hadn't she already rung her? The phone rang for some time before the receiver was picked up. Then Agnes' voice, calm—sounding completely in control—answered, 'Yes, who is it?' Agnes Turner, Josephine had noticed, never gave her number, always just asked who it was phoning her.

'Have you seen the newspapers, Agnes?' Josephine felt her voice was hoarse, weak, she could hardly get the words out and the hand that held the phone was sweating.

There was a little pause before Agnes replied. 'Yes, I've seen them, Josephine,' she said. Josephine marvelled at the way she spoke. It was as if she had been

239

answering a question about the weather.

Agnes Turner had read the papers and was expecting Josephine's call. When it came she had already imagined what the agent's reaction would be and she was not surprised. 'Yes, I have seen the papers. I understand that Amy's car had broken down, maybe she had been driving erratically and enraged a following driver? They do mention road rage in the *Mail*.'

'But, Agnes, it's terrible. I feel it's my fault the girl is dead, absolutely my fault.'

'Your fault, what do you mean, Josephine?' Agnes was genuinely puzzled by this reaction.

'If I hadn't changed the dedication it would have been— She wouldn't have been able to blackmail us and she wouldn't have managed to buy the car.'

'Oh, come now,' Agnes almost laughed, 'if I hadn't had an affair with Herbert you wouldn't have had to. We could go on going back and back, Josephine.'

'You sound so relaxed, Agnes. Poor girl, she was strangled, it must have been terrible. And another thing—'

Agnes interrupted her again. 'Josephine,

the girl is dead, it's nothing to do with us, just fate. But as it's turned out, we won't have to worry about the wretched little blackmailer any more.'

The remark did little to pacify Josephine. 'I must talk to you, Agnes, somewhere where we aren't known.'

'That would be almost anywhere,' Agnes replied, laughing with genuine amusement as she said it. They named a time and place.

'I need to talk to you, Agnes, I really do.'

'All right, we'll talk.'

Agnes put the telephone down. She was due at her hairdressers at eleven. She went through to her bedroom, opened the door of her large wardrobe. The green linen suit, she took it out and smoothed it fondly. Bill liked her in green. Also from way back, when she had what she regarded as 'Righted a Wrong', she always liked to wear green. She made up carefully after her shower. She felt good, as if a great big worry had been lifted from her shoulders, as indeed it had—no Amy any more and therefore no threat to her dear Bill. Perhaps Josephine was a slight threat, particularly if she became hysterical, but

Agnes held a card in her hand. She knew something that Josephine did not know and that always meant 'power'. Josephine did not know that the dedication copies were safely disposed of. Whilst she sat under the drier at the hairdresser she could not help smiling once or twice but she pretended to read and that it was something in the magazine, *Cosmopolitan,* that was making her smile.

She took a taxi to Bournos in Goodge Street. It was always impossible to find a parking place there and anyway her Porsche was at her garage being cleaned. The wheels had got a little muddy on Saturday's trip and Agnes hated the Porsche to be anything but as pristine as possible. Anyway, of course, it would have got wet in yesterday's London rain but standing in Rutland Gate even in pouring rain would hardly account for the wheels being slightly muddy. So she felt happier to know by the time the car was returned to her the wheels would look as they always looked.

Bill had telephoned her last night, as he did every night he was away from her. 'Are you all right, my darling?' he had asked.

'Perfectly, but missing you so much Bill,'

she had said. It had been true, now Amy was dead and gone Herbert seemed to be fading too and she hoped it would stay that way. Even when she put back the dust cover on *Glass Diamonds* and saw Herbert's eyes looking at her, they did not have quite the effect they had before when she had removed the cover and Amy had still been alive and a danger to her and, in a way, to Herbert's memory.

Josephine Long was waiting for her, sitting at a table halfway down on the left side, facing the door. The restaurant was dark and although it was sunny a small orange-shaded lamp lit up each table. The light reflected in the wood panels that ran the whole way down the restaurant.

'Agnes, I'm so glad to see you.'

Agnes smiled, trying to look reassuring. There were only two other couples in the whole place and those well away from the table Josephine had chosen.

A waiter appeared almost at once. 'An aperitif, madam?'

Agnes nodded. 'A gin and tonic, please. And you, Josephine?'

Her companion glanced up at the waiter. She looked anxious, tense. 'Oh yes, thanks,

I'll have another, a double, please.'

The waiter removed her empty glass and looked again at Agnes. 'Ice and lemon, madam?'

'Please.'

He moved away from the table.

'You look so relaxed, Agnes.'

Agnes put her handbag on the chair beside her. 'Why not, Josephine?' she asked.

'I can't get over it, poor girl, to be strangled.' She had brought *The Times* with her and was about to open it and show Agnes the piece which she had already read. Agnes felt completely bored with the whole scene.

'Please, Josephine, I don't honestly want to see any more about it, let's enjoy our lunch.'

'Enjoy lunch, Agnes, how can I?' Josephine Long looked distracted. 'I'm much too worried, where are the copies, Herbert's handwritten copy, the others she made? I searched her desk. I mean the desk in my outer office, not a sign of them. She must have hidden them somewhere, in her digs or even at her mother's. How do we know?'

Agnes thanked the waiter as he put down

their ordered drinks, sipped hers and as she did so she felt again the feeling she had had pressing the piece of paper where Herbert's hand had rested to write the dedication to her, AGNES WHO IS MY FOR EVER. Then she felt again the tearing paper, the tiny pieces, like confetti disappearing into the rubbish bin, gone. All the stupid copies gone, all gone. She looked down into the glass, the sparkling bubbles, the little crescent of lemon, she shook the glass and the ice clicked against the side. For some reason the small sound had brought Herbert Shaffer back to her. For a second the feel of his arms, his body was so close to her—would it always be like that? She could look at his face on the cover of the book but would it be always some little sound, some little half-noticed object and there he would be? And was she glad of it, glad of the sudden almost-presence—would it last? So that now and again just for a second, he would be there—yes, she was glad, if that was so she was glad. It wouldn't hurt Bill, it couldn't.

'Agnes, did you hear what I was saying?' Josephine's voice was high and full of stress.

'Of course I did, and I know it's a worrying problem for you.'

'For me! What about you, it's a problem for you too.'

Agnes looked at her over the rim of her glass. 'Well, you altered it, Josephine, I didn't.'

'But your name was on it.'

Agnes nodded. 'I know, but let's not worry. Maybe the papers will never be found, and if they are they won't mean anything to anyone.'

Josephine looked incredulous. 'I can't feel like that about it, Agnes, I will always worry, particularly when the book is published and feel that perhaps someone will come forward and say that the dedication was to you and not me because the papers will be found, perhaps by her mother?'

The waiter appeared. 'Would you like to order now, madam?' They ordered and the man, almost a boy, went away.

'He looks tired,' Agnes said. Again her tablemate looked at her as if she could not believe her ears.

'Agnes, don't you realize the danger we just might be in, or I might be in? God knows what. Supposing the publishers—'

Agnes felt her patience ebbing. 'Josephine, the girl is dead, the mother knows nothing about it, or so we presume, and the matter will probably end there. If the publishers ever find out after the book is published, well they won't be able to do anything about it.' Agnes was enjoying the meeting.

The food arrived. Josephine did not even pick up her knife and fork, Agnes started to eat. She looked up, suddenly she knew just why she was acting as she was, keeping the woman in ignorance of the fact that the evidence of their duplicity was gone, destroyed. It was because she was jealous; jealous of the fact that Josephine's name would appear in that false dedication, her name should have been there. She, for a moment, wished she had not changed it but there was Bill and Herbert was dead. She took the roll on her side plate. 'Oh, it's nice and hot,' she said and smiled again at Josephine

Josephine stood up. 'I can't understand your attitude, Agnes.' Her eyes were reddened as if she was about to cry. 'That poor girl dead. Oh, I know she was blackmailing us, but to die like that. I'm going back to the office.'

Agnes put another curl of butter on her bread roll. 'The police will probably come and see where Amy worked, you know.' Agnes' voice was not comforting.

'And what am I going to say to them?'

Agnes looked up at her. 'I suggest you tell them what a good secretary she was, that was why you had recently given her a rise.'

Josephine turned, picked up her scarf from the back of her chair and did not look at Agnes again and walked out of the restaurant.

The waiter came up to the table. 'Is there something wrong, madam?' he asked.

'My friend isn't feeling very well,' Agnes replied. He looked rather helplessly at the full plate. 'Shall I?' he said.

'Oh yes, take it away, don't worry, I'll pay the whole bill.' He looked relieved and removed the plate and glass. 'Will you be wanting a sweet, madam?' he asked. Agnes put her knife and fork carefully together on her empty plate. 'Yes, I think I will,' she said. He moved off.

Agnes finished the rest of her drink. She rather wished she had had a glass of wine but the meeting had been so tense she hadn't had time to think about that. As she thought this Josephine, who had come back into the restaurant, spoke to her. 'Agnes, I do admire you. I do admire the way you are handling this and I know I should be doing the same and I will do my best but I do want your support. May I ring you if the police do come, may I ring you?'

Agnes looked up at her, she felt she had complete power over this woman, it was so easy. She wondered, would she cause any trouble? Would her over-anxiety be a nuisance. But she answered kindly enough. 'Yes, of course you may, get in touch with me whenever you want to, Josephine.'

'Thank you, Agnes. I can't stay, though, I really don't think I can stay.'

'Of course not, just get in touch with me when you want to.' She watched Josephine walk towards the door and disappear into the street and then looked with appreciation at the sweet trolley.

Bill returned from the US, Agnes met him at the airport. He looked round for her, searching the crowd. When he saw her his face lit up. 'Darling, I've missed you so much,' he said as he kissed her. Agnes was conscious of the sheer delight of being reunited with him, it gave her a feeling of security. How could she ever have been unfaithful to him? She felt unable to understand herself but she remembered, even as they walked to the car, that feeling she had had in the restaurant when lunching with Josephine. She imagined it was like a flashback after giving up a drug. She had heard patients talk of a flashback long after they had given up LSD. It felt, they had said, as if they were still on it. Perhaps in time it would go away and Herbert would become just a memory but no longer able to make her heart lurch and bring on that longing for him.

In the car and when they arrived home after a rapturous welcome from Mac, Bill told her how the trip had gone. How much the scriptwriters had altered small pieces of the plot of his book. 'They're tough customers, darling. But you know me, I have no passionate feelings about slight differences that they make. I know some authors lose sleep and rant and rave to try and get the film presented exactly as the book was written. They don't even like them to change a name.' Agnes felt that described Bill so well; comfortable to live with, warm, easy-tempered, perhaps not thrilling, not full of ups and downs, moods and changes, but comfortable.

They went to bed early that night and made love and Agnes found it easy to respond to him. He was such a gentle lover. She tried, even as he lay beside her afterwards and had kissed her as if thanking her, she tried not to think of Herbert and she was pleased that she found it easier. She longed to talk to other women who had had lovers. Helen perhaps? But she knew she never would, never could.

The next day Bill had a rest and they drove out into the country and had lunch in a lovely manor house in Sussex. The weather was cooler but a perfect day. They drank wine and motored back through the leafy lanes that Sussex could still boast of. Agnes had no idea tomorrow was to be slightly less peaceful and she was to be disturbed in a fashion she had never thought of. When she saw Bill off to the station the next day she would have a visitor, the very last person she ever expected to call on her.

The next morning started routinely, Bill was an early riser. At breakfast in the kitchen with Agnes, Mac consumed his

251

customary small bowl of cornflakes.

'What are you doing today, dear?' Bill asked.

'Nothing really, Bill. I'll give Mac a good walk this morning. Helen may call me, if she does she can come here to lunch.' Bill nodded. 'What time will you be home?' she asked.

'I'm not sure but it won't be late. It's only an indoor run-through, but with Max Chilton being ill the new member of the cast, Evert, nice fellow, will have to feel his way in.' Agnes nodded. 'Michael's calling for me.' Bill looked at his watch. The front door bell rang. 'That will be him, he's always punctual. He doesn't seem to give a damn about the traffic.' He looked out of the window to the street below. 'Yes, it's him. *Mercedes Benz* written in silver letters on the spare—trust Michael!' He laughed, kissed Agnes and was gone.

Agnes took Mac to the park. Mrs Mason, her daily help, had a key and would get on with things until Agnes returned. The help had been a legacy from the last tenant, a Lady Rouse and was a boon and a blessing. Never late, never ill, never rattled. She would come in each day, had made her own routine and stuck to it. For dinner parties Agnes hired a cook who brought a washer-up and preparer with her—another legacy from Lady Rouse, who had retired to a house in the country.

The park had dried up again after a few days of rain. Agnes let the lead run out to its full length and Mac took advantage of it. The part of the lead that had been round Amy's neck now showed no trace of it. The reference to 'The Road Rage Murder', as it was still called in some of the papers, had given way to another murder in a country cottage somewhere in the south involving a whole family. That had overshadowed poor Amy.

How had that been done? Agnes wondered. A woman and two teenage children had been killed, the woman stabbed and the two children, one stabbed and one suffocated. Why hadn't one of them been able to get away, run screaming from the house? Agnes sat for some moments on a park bench, enjoying the sunshine. She had walked at least a mile and a half. Mac sat at her feet. He was a short-legged little creature and, for the moment, had had enough. Agnes looked at her watch; half past ten, she would walk home now and have coffee with Mrs Mason. As she neared her flat she glanced at the gardens in the middle of the square. Dusty now and shady but no longer any Amy to make an appointment for her to pay out more money. Agnes felt a wave of satisfaction as she put her key in the front door.

Coffee with Mrs Mason was as pleasant as always. Mrs Mason would talk about her family but usually brought good rather than bad news. They seemed to be doing well, there was never any drama, her two teenage children were studying as they should ready to pass their GCSEs, no drugs or pregnancy or problems. Her relaxed cheerfulness was always a joy to Agnes as were her nurselike methods of cleaning and tidying. They had finished the coffee and Mrs Mason collected the cups and saucers with her usual, 'Well, must get on.' Agnes left the kitchen and went into her bedroom, intending to tidy her dressing table drawers. She had just got started when she heard the front door bell ringing. She left it for Mrs Mason to answer.

A few seconds passed and she came into the bedroom. 'There's a Mrs Sylvia Shaffer, Mrs Turner. Shall I let her come up?'

Agnes turned, a handful of lipsticks in one hand. 'Mrs Shaffer? Of course.'

Mrs Mason left the room to press the front door release catch. Agnes put the lipsticks back in the drawer; looked at herself in the mirror, took a lipstick out of the drawer again and applied it to her mouth, took a tissue and blotted her lips, picked up a comb and ran it through her hair. She heard Mrs Mason open the flat door, walked out of the bedroom just as Sylvia Shaffer appeared. 'Thank you Mrs Mason.' The woman smiled, went back to the kitchen and the two, Mrs Shaffer and Agnes, were left facing each other in the rather small hall.

'I'm sure you're surprised at my calling on you Mrs Turner.'

They had moved through into the sitting room. Mrs Shaffer had seated herself in one of the two winged chairs near the window. Her back was to the light but Agnes could see her complexion well enough to note how beautifully she was made up. Her well-cut black jacket just revealed an immaculate white silk shirt. The short black skirt was short enough to show her well-shaped legs and slim ankles. Her feet, in patent court shoes, were placed neatly side by side. 'Well, yes I am a little.' Agnes tried to make the remark sound as pleasant as possible.

'I'm sure you are. Well, I'm afraid you will be almost as surprised at what I want to talk to you about.'

'What is that, Mrs Shaffer?'

Sylvia Shaffer paused, plucked a tiny piece of lint from her skirt with a long-nailed hand. 'Mrs Shaffer? Do call me Sylvia, didn't we agree to that in Harrods when we met?'

Agnes felt herself getting impatient. 'Yes, perhaps, I really don't remember. What is it you want to talk to me about?'

'Your bracelet.'

The answer was so unexpected, so strange, Agnes could only repeat the words. 'My bracelet?'

'Yes. There's one or two things—please forgive me. I saw it on your wrist in Harrods.'

'Yes.' Agnes felt totally out of her depth.

'I found it in the flat with Herbert. I took it back to Josephine Long's office. She was having an affair with my husband, you know.'

At that moment Mrs Mason put her head round the door. 'I've finished, Mrs Turner.'

Agnes got up. 'Excuse me one moment, Mrs Shaffer.' She found her handbag, it was Mrs Mason's pay day. She paid her. Her mind was racing—the woman in the sitting room was about to accuse her of being in Herbert's bed, was that it? But wait, why had she said Josephine was having the affair? Agnes leaned for a moment by the kitchen table—a story, what she had to say, slotted into her mind with amazing clarity. She was going to assume that because of the dedication and Josephine's assertion about her affair, Sylvia Shaffer believed no one else was involved, only the bracelet was puzzling her. She, Agnes, must do her best to unravel the puzzle—'But go carefully,' she whispered to herself. She took time to put two glasses and a decanter of sherry on a silver salver. She went back into the sitting room.

'I'm sorry, I had to pay—'

'Did Josephine Long take the bracelet? Steal it, borrow it, or what? Oh thank you.' She took the proffered sherry and sipped it daintily. 'Please tell me, she's not worth protecting. She had had an affair with my husband some time ago, I thought it was a short affair, now I understand she had seduced him again, this time with more success apparently.' She put the glass down on the small table beside her. 'Do tell me, about the bracelet I mean. Did she steal it, borrow it?'

Agnes sipped her sherry and put the glass down with the same deliberate slowness before she answered. 'Mrs Shaffer—Sylvia,' a slight smile followed the use of her visitor's Christian name, 'I'm only telling you this because you have ...' she paused again. 'My husband, Bill and I, we were at a book launch, he had just given me the bracelet you saw me wearing. It was very expensive.' Agnes looked very serious now. 'I met Josephine Long there for the first time, we went to the ladies' room together. I took off the bracelet to wash my hands, we had been eating the usual snippets and my hands felt sticky. I, foolishly, left the bracelet on the shelf above the washbasin. Outside I noticed it almost immediately. Only Miss Long and I had been in there so I was not particularly apprehensive.' She stopped again, this time she noticed Sylvia was sitting rather more upright. 'Josephine

Long had left and my bracelet was not there.'

'Did you?'

'Oh yes, I asked her. I rang her up straight away but she denied seeing it. I was devastated.'

The rest of the story was told with apparent reluctance by Agnes, indeed she managed to look quite distressed. 'My husband is not particularly observant. But he was proud of finding something I liked so much and the next time we went out he asked me why I wasn't wearing it.

'The next time I saw it was on Josephine Long's desk. I called to face her again with the fact and to take her one of my husband's books that she had asked him if she could borrow.' Here Agnes stopped and looked squarely at her visitor.

'She took it, stole it. How like her!' Sylvia's voice was full of contempt and malice.

'I took it off her desk, Mrs Shaffer, I don't know why it was there and I don't think she saw me take it.'

'Sylvia, please, Agnes.'

'I took it. Perhaps I should not have, but it was mine and I was so pleased to have it back.'

Sylvia finished her sherry and Agnes got up, refilled her glass. 'I put it there, Agnes. She left it in Herbert's bed, my husband's bed.'

Agnes sighed a long sigh. 'How awful for you, Sylvia.'

'Oh, it wasn't that bad. We had grown apart but such a woman. Such bad taste on Herbert's part.' She saw the refilled glass. 'Oh, thank you Agnes. I love a good sherry and this is a good one.'

'Thank you.' There was a long silence. 'Are you going to confront her, Sylvia? I would much rather you didn't.' Agnes spoke softly, her voice friendly.

'Oh, no, that's not necessary. It merely shows what kind of woman Herbert was sleeping with. I don't admire his taste. It was the bracelet appearing on your wrist again in Harrods that interested me.' She finished the sherry and got up. Agnes accompanied her across the outer hall to the lift. 'We must meet again if you would like to. I will send you an invitation to the launching of *A Hot Night in a Cold Country*—ridiculous title.' She laughed a rather shrill, trilling laugh. As the lift doors opened she turned to Agnes. 'You don't think she killed that secretary girl, do you?' Agnes did not have to put on a shocked expression, it was quite natural. 'Sylvia, what a dreadful thing to say.'

Sylvia shrugged. 'No, I suppose not.'

She got into the lift and the doors closed on her. Agnes went back into her flat, conscious that she was sweating a little. She picked up her glass and swallowed the rest of her sherry. Had Sylvia Shaffer believed her story? As she crossed the room to pick up her guest's sherry glass she caught a whiff of perfume, it was recognizable at once to Agnes, it was Joy, Patou's Joy. The fact filled Agnes with a sudden flash of resentment—so Herbert must have known that scent yet he had said several times how he loved her perfume. He had been conning her, obviously, and she resented that even more. Maybe he said that to every woman he slept with.

That last remark Sylvia had made about Josephine and Amy had really shocked her and scared her a little. Anyone making any connection between Amy and— She hoped Sylvia would not confront Josephine with the story about the bracelet—but she felt almost sure she wouldn't. She must tell Bill of the visit, he would be thrilled to go to Herbert Shaffer's book launch and she felt she must keep in Sylvia Shaffer's good books, she disliked the feeling but she knew it was the right approach. One thing, though, she realized, it would not do, not do at all, for Sylvia Shaffer ever to see her with Josephine Long. What Josephine had said which had made her laugh was now true, they must go somewhere where nobody would recognize them. She washed up the glasses and polished them long and carefully and as she did so she was going over her story again. It fitted. It had been very quickly made up and it worried her a little in case there were any mistakes in it but she did not think so and after a time the worry wore off and she started to get herself some lunch.

Bill was delighted to hear that Sylvia Shaffer had called and that the reason for her visit, according to Agnes, was to invite them both to the launch of Herbert's latest book *Hot Night in a Cold Country*. He was a little surprised. 'Are they publishing it already, such a short time after his death?'

Agnes shrugged. 'I don't know, darling. She wouldn't say when the publication was to be, but she wanted us to be there.'

'Great, I shall really look forward to that.'

Agnes touched his arm affectionately. 'Darling, you're not getting a bit snobbish about authors, are you?' She waited while Bill shuffled his feet and grimaced a little.

'Yes and no. I admired Herbert Shaffer's work. You got me interested in it and when I started to read his books, I enjoyed them immensely. Of course, I know I'm small fry compared with him.'

They were breakfasting in the kitchen the day after Sylvia's visit. 'Oh, come on darling, lots more people read your books than read his, I expect.'

Bill shook his head. 'Doubt it,' he said, but nevertheless he looked pleased. 'I'm going to take Mac for a good walk in the park then I'm going to shut myself in the office and work. No telephone calls, no lunch, no visitors.'

'Not even a coffee midmorning?' Agnes asked. Bill shook his head.

Once Bill and an excited and delighted Mac had departed, Agnes went straight to the telephone to ring Josephine. After yesterday's bracelet story to Sylvia Shaffer, Agnes felt that the story must, in some way, be justified to Josephine in case Sylvia did confront the agent with it. It was, Agnes felt, rather like a jigsaw puzzle and each piece must fit but the subsequent picture must make the most perfect falsehood—a challenge indeed. Nothing to Agnes was more stimulating, more an antidote to boredom, than such a challenge.

Josephine sounded disturbed. The police had been to see her, asked her questions about Amy and her work. Agnes tried to reassure her, get over to her the fact that of course the police would be bound to ask questions about the secretary's working background—after all, she had been murdered. Josephine was still, to Agnes, singing the same old song. 'It was all my fault. If I hadn't altered the dedication she would still be alive.' Agnes was tired of listening to her.

Agnes suggested that they drive out to the country the next day and have lunch somewhere and a long talk. Josephine eagerly accepted this idea. Agnes decided not to mention Sylvia's visit, all that could be coped with, would have to be coped with, tomorrow. Agnes had already made her mind up where to lunch—at a rather nice-looking hotel she had seen.

After about an hour Bill came back with

Mac. He brought him into the kitchen to dry him as it had started raining when he had been on the way home. There was a special large towel for drying Mac, he loved it. It pleased Agnes to hear Bill laughing as he enveloped the little dog in the towel and tried to dry him. Mac's one object was to get the fabric between his teeth and drag it round the kitchen. 'Now to work, Agnes,' he said abandoning the towel. 'Don't worry about lunch, will you, I don't want to be distracted until I've got the next bit of the plot worked out. Then I'll emerge.'

Agnes was used to this and always stuck to the rules, no matter who called or telephoned. She usually prepared a very good meal in the evening and Bill would come out of the office as he smelled the inviting smell of a roast.

Mac got another good walk that day after her solitary lunch. The rain stopped and the sun came out. Agnes felt she needed to wander over the grass, under the trees, along by the river. She had to think out the conversation; the story that she would tell Josephine Long tomorrow. It had to be right. It had to justify accusing Josephine of taking the bracelet without unduly upsetting her. By the time she got back to Rutland Gate and was entering the lift up to her flat she had planned it all out. The thought of the lies she had had to tell Sylvia had left her a little tense, a little anxious. Now, as she closed the lift door behind her and the soft sound of the lift took her upstairs, she felt relaxed and well-rehearsed and knew what she must do and what she must say tomorrow.

Bill's door was now firmly shut, she could hear the clicking of the processor. Agnes decided to make herself a cup of tea but, true to her promise to Bill not to disturb him, she took the tray into the sitting room with Mac trotting along beside her and sat down by herself. She gazed at the blank television screen. 'I simply had to say you had taken it, Josephine. If he was in love with you, how else could Sylvia have found the bracelet in Herbert's bed or room or wherever she found it unless it had come off your wrist?' She sipped her tea, it tasted good; a mixture she made herself of Assam and Lapsang—delicious. Agnes loved tea. The explanation she had just whispered to herself seemed perfect to her but how would Josephine Long take it? Well, tomorrow would show and, as usual, Agnes felt that familiar thrill of the prospect of telling her and watching her face to see if she was believed.

The next morning was an ideal one weather-wise for a run in the country— sunny and warm. Agnes was feeling pleased they had decided on a country run. She did not get out of her car as Josephine had said she would meet her outside her office. When she did appear, after Agnes had been double parked for only about five minutes, her appearance was a little unnerving. Josephine looked ill. The make-up she had obviously put on to try and hide her paleness looked glaring. She looked too as if she had lost weight, which Agnes felt was impossible to put down in such a short time entirely to Amy's murder. Was it Herbert's death? Perhaps it affected her far more than Agnes had realized. She was dressed in black and for a moment Agnes wondered if she was in mourning for that blackmailing little nothing Amy Robertson, or perhaps for Herbert. She suggested this as Josephine settled herself in the passenger seat and snapped on her seat belt. Agnes made the remark with a laugh but her companion did not laugh or even make a light reply. She looked at Agnes with serious eyes.

'I don't know how you can make remarks like that Agnes with Amy—' She broke off, shut her lips tightly together and gazed at the road in front of her. She did not speak again until they were well out of the worst of the London traffic, then, 'You know, I do blame myself for all this, Agnes—if ever a person was responsible for another's death, I am that person.'

Agnes tried not to lose patience and show her irritation by a snappy reply. 'What about the person who strangled her, Josephine Isn't he really to blame, as well as you, and the fact that you'd altered the dedication?'

'No, I don't think that. No.'

Agnes gave up the argument. After a few more miles she spoke again. 'Let's enjoy the drive, Josephine and let's hope we manage to get a good lunch.'

'I can't understand you, Agnes,' Josephine almost wailed. 'I can't understand you at all. I know she was blackmailing you but even so, I can't begin to understand your attitude.'

Agnes glanced at her and smiled. 'Few people can, Josephine,' she said.

At last Agnes recognized the hotel. The inside was as nice as the outside. Old-fashioned shining wood, brasses, white tablecloths. A dining room, Agnes thought, like a dining room used to be before chicken in the basket and bar lunches—chips with everything.

The waiter looked after them. Josephine had a glass of red wine, Agnes a tonic water; she always abstained when she was driving. She felt a trace nervous. The rehearsed speech had to be made after she had told Josephine what had been said on Sylvia's visit to Rutland Gate. She waited until Josephine had finished her almond-covered filleted plaice, which she had not eaten with much appetite. Then Agnes told her what had happened between her and Herbert's wife.

Josephine listened, her expression one of disbelief. 'You didn't, you couldn't have said this about me, Agnes—made me into a thief. I could never, never steal anything. Do anything like that. You know I couldn't, Agnes!' Her cheeks were red, her lips trembling.

Agnes launched into her rehearsed

speech. 'I simply had to say you had taken it, Josephine. If he was in love with you, how else could Sylvia have found the bracelet in Herbert's bed or room or wherever she found it? It had to have come off your wrist. You told her you were having an affair with him.' Agnes finished the long explanation, her eyes fixed earnestly on Josephine.

It worked. Josephine suddenly realized how Agnes had got it back. 'Of course, it was on the desk, on my desk. Sylvia threw it there and you took it. I didn't see you, I was so upset.'

'Yes, I took it, I had to, I'm sorry about it, sorry I had to take it and I hope you will forgive me, after all it was a present from Bill and he was already asking me where it was.' Agnes genuinely felt a bit sorry for Josephine. How much she had changed since the book-launch party where Herbert and she had met. Then she had looked so elegant, so composed, now she looked shattered, thinner, older. 'You must miss Herbert, Josephine,' she said with, for Agnes, a hint of compassion.

Her companion looked at her for some seconds before she spoke. 'I feel you have no idea how much, Agnes,' she said.

Agnes touched her hand, just a touch, but Josephine snatched the hand away as if it had been burnt. 'Sylvia Shaffer invited Bill and me to the launch of his book. Does that mean it will be published soon?'

'Yes, they're trying to get it on the market within a month. Miles Evert, the editorial director, thought it the best work Herbert had done.'

'Bill was pleased. We shall go.' Agnes gestured to the waiter for the bill, paid it and left a generous tip—she felt in a generous mood.

They drove home. Agnes dropped the agent at her office. Before she got out of the car Josephine turned to her. 'I feel those copies will turn up. I've searched for them again. They're not in the office, they must be somewhere.'

'True, they must be somewhere, but the girl is dead and the book will soon be published, that will end it all, won't it?' Josephine got out of the car and hardly said goodbye, did not even thank her for the lunch, which, Agnes knew, was not in character.

As she drove away Agnes was not quite

sure how she felt about Josephine Long. She bored her but, in a way, boosted Agnes' feeling of power. If she had decided to put her out of her misery, tell her the truth that those threatening pieces of paper had been destroyed, that she herself had killed Amy for the sake of both of them, how would Josephine have behaved? Of course, Agnes had no intention of telling her anything but it was amusing to imagine how she would react. Relief on one count and total panic on the other. Josephine had little capacity for conspiracy, Agnes thought.

As she drove up to her own flat she was annoyed to see their space, their parking space, was occupied by a light-blue Mercedes. She had to go round the square and find somewhere else to park until the Mercedes departed. 'Damn them,' she muttered to herself. As she walked back to the flat Helen and a grey-haired, rather handsome man were just walking down the steps of Agnes' block of flats—Helen looking vastly pleased with herself, particularly when she saw Agnes.

'Agnes, I've been to call on you but there was no answer.' She looked at the man and then looked back at Agnes. 'I suppose Bill is out or working?'

'I'm sorry, Helen.' She glanced enquiringly at Helen's companion.

'Oh, Agnes, this is Horace Winterbourne. He's just joined the golf club. He comes from Australia so I'm just showing him around London.' She finished the introduction, the man shook hands then smiled rather vaguely.

'I'm sorry I can't ask you in, Helen, Bill is working. Working hard at the moment.'

'Oh that's all right. I did explain to Horace that Bill was a famous crime writer.' She put a proprietary hand on the man's arm, they got into the Mercedes. 'We'll ring and make a dinner date, Agnes, OK?'

'Yes, fine, Helen, let's do that.'

The car drew away. Ghastly car and probably ghastly man, Agnes thought watching the almost baby-blue car out of the square.

She retraced her steps to her own Porsche, drove it back to its correct place. 'Road rage,' she said to herself, and the leafy road where Amy had died flashed, for a moment, across her mind and she shivered.

Bill greeted her just coming out of his office. 'Someone rang, I looked out, it was a Merc—awful colour. I didn't answer.'

'It was Helen with a new boyfriend, darling. You were wise. She is going to ring us up and make a dinner date to meet him!'

'Hmm, hmm.' Bill went into the kitchen. 'Could do with a cup of tea.'

Agnes joined him. 'I'll make it, Bill.' She filled the kettle. 'That woman, Miss Long's secretary—saw it on the news while I was having a sherry. Some bloke saw another car parked near it and a man walking towards the Metro.'

Agnes tried to appear disinterested. 'Did they give a description of the man or the car?' she asked, feeling her heart quicken a little.

'No, couldn't describe the man, even his clothes or the car. The chap who saw them was going too fast.' Agnes thanked goodness for her dark suit, if it had been her that the man had seen. She wondered was it the man in the red sports car? 'We'll look at the *Nine O'clock News*,' Bill said, putting two lumps of sugar in his tea with a little grimace towards his wife; Agnes tried to keep Bill's weight down, he loved sweet things and it was a task. 'They won't find that man. Road rage is a new thing, isn't it? Though some drivers nearly drive me to murder, especially when they hog the middle lane on the motorway.'

Agnes permitted herself no reply, after all, what was there to say?

Agnes, with Bill, watched the later news. The road where the body of the girl hanging over her car had been was of course vacant but the road itself was shown. Amy's mother's cottage was also pictured, another quick flash of the Metro, parked, presumably, outside the police station, and that was it. The man walking towards the car was also mentioned again and the fact that another car had been seen some way away from the Metro. Very little description of either the car or the man was given and the whole incident was quickly over to give way to a minibus accident involving the death of three old-age pensioners, and injury to ten others. This was given far more time than Amy's murder.

Bill shrugged his shoulders. 'Not much to go on. This road rage business is going to grow, I think.'

Agnes looked at him. 'Why do you think

that? And why do you think it started so suddenly, darling?'

'Cars and drivers are like battery chickens now—too many cars packed into too little space. I believe hens peck each other's eyes out in sheer frustration. The motorist is doing the same, feeling the same.'

'Perhaps so,' Agnes said.

She became rapt in her own thoughts, thinking of Amy. If Amy had been anything but a human animal, say a cat, a dog, a pony, she could not have hurt her. She looked down at Mac—she could never hurt him, even shout at him. Why was she like this? She could not remember ever being different, even as far back as she could remember when she was about four. The nuns in the orphanage where she had been brought up, they were cold, heartless in their punishment, in their discipline. She had hated them all. Never been able to please them. She had never been attractive; sometimes they would take to a little girl with golden hair and blue eyes. But their rattling rosaries, their musty smell had meant a sort of hell to her and she meant nothing to them. She remembered the birds, a stray dog that had once come into the orphanage and a cat—she had saved her food for them. Any starving, stray creature tore at her heart. Not Amy—the human animal never made her feel love—only Bill she felt sure of. Only the human animal was devious, twisted. She had watched the short piece of news about the murdered girl without any feeling of regret or remorse and she didn't feel that she was wrong, it had always been like that.

'Had enough, dear?' Bill had to ask her twice before she came back from where her mind had been wandering to where she sat.

'Yes, thank you, Bill. Do you want to see the play later?' He nodded. Mac padded out into the kitchen, giving one short, sharp bark when he got there. 'Biscuit time,' Bill said laughing.

They watched the play, a murder mystery. But Agnes found it difficult to follow, there was so much chasing, so many cars, so much blood, so much noise. Murder need not be like that, it could be quiet, secret and neat. Some of the plays, admittedly, had murders that were quieter, neater, a body found in a river, but usually they were stabbed, bleeding, mutilated—why did murder fascinate so many people? Play after play, documentary after documentary was about killing. 'Must see that—good murder mystery on tonight. Mustn't miss that.' Agnes did not particularly like this type of drama, she liked Jane Austen, where words and romantic glances were important. She supposed, as she sat there listening to Mac in the kitchen crunching up his biscuit, that she knew too much about murder—was better at it than anyone on that stupid little box. But then she had never done harm, only good—dispatched people who deserved what they got, not innocent children and old ladies. Mac followed Bill back into the sitting room. On the television men were chasing the suspect through a dark factory.

'Don't want to see any more of this, darling, unless you want to. It's all noise and shooting, very contrived.'

Agnes shook her head. 'No, Bill. I like something more subtle.'

'Me too.' Bill picked up the remote control and the screen went black. Agnes thought of Amy slumped across the car. 'Something more subtle,' she repeated.

'Well, there will be no blood, shooting, stabbing or car crashing in my film, darling.

I'm glad, really. There's so much to learn about what the public want.'

Agnes nodded. 'Your books are not violent, Bill, just quietly murderous.' They both laughed. Agnes felt how very little Bill knew about her past but they loved and understood each other and that was all that mattered.

The ten thirty news showed a picture of Amy Robertson. The face suddenly appearing on the screen startled Agnes. It was obviously taken from a snap and did not flatter the girl at all. Bill did not even see it. He had left the room to give Mac his last run before bedtime. Nothing more was revealed about the man or the car. Agnes switched off the set and began to get ready for bed.

In the bedroom, creaming her face, Agnes heard Bill shut and lock the front door, heard the patter of Mac's claws across the polished floor of the hall. She felt very safe, secure in the knowledge that she had been so sensible in that Surrey road. Had she not stopped to withdraw the dedication from, that beastly girl's handbag, the names, hers and Josephine's, would have involved them both—that had been clever, astute. Agnes wiped away the

279

cream; but then she was always thoughtful, when she did a thing she did it properly.

'There's a full moon, it's lovely out,' Bill said, coming into the bedroom.

'Good,' Agnes said, 'good.'

Helen, true to her word and, Agnes thought, with an obvious wish to show off the new man in her life, telephoned. The dinner invitation was accepted, rather reluctantly by Bill who was not a lover of dining out. Helen, or her new man, had chosen to take them to dinner at the Hilton and Agnes pointed out to Bill it was bound to be a good meal. 'Dressed up, though,' Bill grumbled. But on the evening he was his usual good-tempered self and looking quite handsome, Agnes thought, as he came up to her to have his black tie adjusted.

Helen had certainly moved up a notch or two from the golf pro. Horace Winterbourne was rather a surprise to both Bill and Agnes. He talked well, chose a very good claret and was a criminal lawyer. The last fact, of course, interested Bill and by the time the first course was finished, crime, murder, domestic abuse, robbery were colouring the conversation between the two men. Helen, strangely enough, mentioned 'The Road Rage Murder', meaning Amy Robertson. Agnes listened with interest to Horace's remarks about the killing. 'I don't think it was road rage, I think it was a revenge killing.'

'Do you suspect the man they saw walking up the road?' Agnes felt the question forced out of her.

'Don't know,' Horace answered. 'Could have been a woman—something womanish about the strangling, I feel.' Agnes looked at him with even greater interest. 'Why do you say that, Horace, would a woman be strong enough to strangle another woman like that?'

'Yes, easily. I had a case once. I defended a woman who strangled her father, a big man, she used a wooden spoon to twist the picture cord.'

'Even so,' Agnes interrupted, 'surely he could have fought her off, a woman against a big man?'

Horace ordered another bottle of the excellent claret as the roast beef arrived, then answered Agnes. 'In such a combat the man would be too busy clawing at his throat to try and loosen the garrotte to fight back, especially if, as in this case, the woman was behind him.'

Bill looked interested too. 'Did you get her off?'

Horace looked down modestly. 'As a matter of fact I did. It's years ago.'

'For goodness' sake, let's talk about something else,' Helen broke in. 'It's all one hears about these days, radio, television, newspapers, they can't talk about anything else.'

Horace put out a hand and took Helen's, held it for a moment. A look of affection passed between them, Agnes was glad to see it. Helen was rather a butterfly-minded girl, she thought, well, not a girl exactly but— She was right, though. Before she switched her mind away from the talk of murder she had to agree with Horace, Amy had done exactly that, as Horace had described. It was interesting but she felt her mind wandering to animals again and she hoped that no one reading the description of the murder of Amy in the papers would ever try it on a pet or any animal. She could not bear to think of it and was glad when Bill and Horace determinedly started to talk in a lighter vein. But Agnes was aware that this tall, good-looking man had quite unwittingly comforted her. His matter-of-fact attitude, the case of the girl who had murdered her father; he had given the impression that the girl had been justified in her action though he had not said why she did it. Just as she, Agnes, felt she had been justified.

Agnes enjoyed the rest of the meal and the fact that Bill was enjoying the outing too. Her only anxiety now was Josephine, would she crack one day and reveal the whole sordid little secret of the changed dedication? But that would mean Bill might get to know of her affair. Agnes knew she would not allow that. There was Bill to consider and even, in a way, Herbert's name to protect, at least from the fact that she and he had had that passionate affair.

The dinner party broke up at eleven thirty with promises that they must all meet again. 'Isn't he a doll, Agnes?' were Helen's words as they donned their coats and the two men where out of earshot.

'Yes, he is, I like him very much. Now don't do anything to lose him, Helen.'

Helen smiled. 'No, he's so much cleverer than I am, that's why he likes being with me. I think I shall marry him, Agnes.'

Just like that, Agnes thought, and she

realized that Helen was right and probably a good deal wiser than one would imagine.

As they reached Rutland Gate Agnes noticed that Horace and Bill were again talking about what was to Horace his profession and to Bill plots. 'It's very often the case, it's not the murderer necessarily who gives the game away but some chance remark of someone on the fringe of the case, an unknowing, unthinking witness.'

Bill nodded. 'Yes. Useful to me, that approach.'

It was not useful to Agnes but rather chilling, and it brought back the problem of Josephine sharply to her mind. As they parted and the taxi drew away from Rutland Gate the red lights of its brakes flashed as it paused at the corner of the gardens and turned round—red for danger, she thought, red for danger.

'Pleasant evening,' Bill said as they reached their flat and let themselves in to a rapturous barking.

'I thought you'd enjoy it,' Agnes said, but she was preoccupied and Bill could sense it.

'Didn't you like him very much, dear?' he asked.

'Oh, yes, very much, and I think he's

good for Helen. Somehow they make a couple, don't they?'

'Hmm.' Bill didn't contribute much to that remark but Agnes, as she slipped out of her shoes which were pinching a little bit and the heels tired her, thought, I must telephone Josephine in the morning—we must meet, I must see that she's calming down. And if she isn't—well, something will have to be done. At the moment, Agnes didn't know what but she knew she would come to some conclusion—she always did.

After a second visit from the police, Josephine was devastated. Why had they come a second time? In a way it was not so much by the fact they had questioned her, that she knew was inevitable, Agnes had told her that they would try to find out more about the girl's background, what upset her was as they asked the things she had realized how little she knew about the girl whose death, she felt, was her fault. She had not been talkative or confiding—or, Josephine wondered, was it she herself who had been cold and silent with the girl? When she had asked her to make coffee midmorning she had never, as far back as she could remember, encouraged the girl to stay, drink with her and maybe talk. Now as the girl's life unfolded, in the tabloids particularly, Josephine's feeling of guilt deepened.

During the questioning it was revealed that Amy's mother was disabled with arthritis, would not even think of going into a home and this surely would have been a great worry to the girl. When Amy did get home at weekends apparently she had done all the week's washing and ironing, taken her mother out in a wheelchair. Indeed, by the sound if it, had been a wonderful daughter. What a boon the car would have been for the girl and the crippled woman. Josephine began to feel totally different about the whole affair. Agnes could afford a thousand pounds or so, wouldn't miss it. Maybe the salary she had paid the girl had not been generous. The thoughts went round and round in Josephine's mind like a little caged animal on a wheel, she could not sleep, eat or concentrate on the mail. She opened it but couldn't take it in and several novels had been delivered to her ready to be read or to be passed on to a reader but they remained unopened. All her thoughts were geared to the fact that the girl's death had been due entirely to her. It became an obsession. Something that filled her days and nights—it made her feel ill. The case seemed to be at a complete standstill. So many more murders and robberies had filled the space that had been occupied by The Road Rage Murder.

The police had been kind and polite. The CID man, called Houseman, and a woman, good-looking and very sympathetic, asked her questions.

'Was Miss Robertson happy at her job, Miss Long?'

'Yes, very.'

'Was she efficient?'

'I would say so, yes. I had recently given her a rise because she confided in me that her mother was getting more disabled and she wanted to spend each weekend with her and getting down there cost money.' A lie but she said it because she had to.

'Did you know she was getting a car?' More lies. 'Yes, I asked her to have a few lessons because it was some years since she had driven.' Josephine felt the lies slipping off her tongue. She'd never suggested Amy had refresher lessons, the girl had not been particularly efficient at her work, she knew nothing about the mother. The papers had told her all that, pictured the little garden, the small house.

When the police had gone she could not remember exactly how she had answered the questions, what she had said. She tried to reconstruct the scene in her mind but couldn't. All she could think was that changing that dedication had killed Amy Robertson as if she herself had been there and killed her. Would they suspect her? Yes, of course they could, and would. Almost frantically she wanted to talk to Agnes Turner. She gave her confidence. She must talk to someone and Agnes was the only one that she dared utter a word to about the whole dreadful affair. She did not know that Agnes, at that moment, was equally anxious to talk to her.

Two mornings later the phone rang in Josephine's office as she was trying to cope with her mail. She had opened two heavy parcels of typescript but had not yet read the covering letters. She threw the brown paper that had wrapped them onto the floor and tried to concentrate on the first letter when the phone rang. She was so pleased to hear Agnes' voice, it was like someone on a desert island sighting a craft. 'Yes,' she said, her voice trembling with eagerness, 'I would love to meet you—at the Waterside Café, where we met before, yes.'

Agnes sounded crisp, businesslike but she was so pleased to hear her voice. Josephine dumped everything, it didn't matter, work could wait, she must talk to Agnes.

She arrived at the café, it was raining, she went inside and chose a dark corner. There was no sign of Agnes. She came, after Josephine had been waiting for about a quarter of an hour, and did not apologize.

Agnes' meeting with Josephine, she felt, was rather like a replay at a football match except it was more intense.

'I miss Herbert so much, Agnes, even though he had tired of me he was still there.'

She even felt a slight touch of sympathy. She too missed Herbert but she could bear it, perhaps better than Josephine, because he had died still loving her and there was Bill to go back to. She had been in love with Herbert but she loved Bill. What was the difference? One stormy, one tranquil—she was not sure.

Josephine was also very worried about the second visit she had had from the police. She was almost hysterical when she mentioned it.

'What did they ask you, this second time they came?'

'I can't remember but it made me think, almost, that they thought I'd killed her.'

'Oh, rubbish, Josephine! What did they say to make you think that?'

'Oh, asking about her mother and did I know where she lived and had I ever talked to Amy about her.'

Agnes began to feel impatient. 'Well, surely that was just to get a better slant on the girl's character and motives in life?'

Josephine shook her head and covered her eyes with her hand. 'I still feel as if I killed her anyway, Agnes.'

After more talk Agnes got up. 'Josephine, for goodness' sake, it's all over. Soon the book will be published, the dedication will be seen, Sylvia will be furious with you but she knows already what the dedication will be because she saw it after you had changed it from mine.'

Josephine looked up at her. 'You help me, Agnes, you really do,' she said.

Agnes wanted out. 'Maybe, but don't

call me again. Just think of it as being past tense, get on with your agency, your work, get another secretary.'

'I can't do that. Not yet.'

Agnes was firm. 'We shouldn't meet until the launching of the book, whenever that is. Goodbye, Josephine.'

The agent half rose then sank back in her chair. Agnes left the café conscious that her small trace of sympathy for the woman had evaporated. She got into her car and made for Knightsbridge and Harrods. When she was irritated she always felt the urge to shop. The perfect place at the moment, she felt, was Harrods Food Halls. Its cool surroundings, perfectly arranged merchandise, slightly echoing the sounds of footsteps, made her feel relaxed. As if to help her mood even more she found a space to put the car in Lancelot Place almost opposite the store.

Josephine Long was a strange mixture, she thought as she waited to cross the road. A career woman, self-possessed, assured, she seemed to be cracking. Perhaps her type of woman, independent, alone, relying on their own initiative and knowledge to make a living, perhaps they were the most vulnerable because of their loneliness and lack of support. Perhaps that was it. Agnes walked through the store into the Food Halls and started to walk round and look at the more luxurious offerings. She did not even blame Josephine for the fact that she had caused her to come here and probably to spend quite a lot of money, though the woman rose to the surface every time she took her mind off buying. She bought two fillet steaks, some game pie, almost but not quite oblivious to the cost. Some smooth and some rough paté. She drifted from counter to counter revelling in the good, polite and helpful service. What a wonderful thing, she thought, remembering long-past days, what a wonderful thing money was. At the sweet counter on the way out she paused just to enjoy the luxurious smell of chocolate and look at the pretty boxes ready to be packed expertly with the Harrods special range, anything you fancied. The trays of boxes of fondants, gentle, plastic colours, marrons glacés. She stopped, she was not particularly fond of chocolate and anyway sweets were bad for Bill but she bought just a tiny box of fondants for him and she was about to turn away when a voice she knew said, 'Not spoiling yourself with chocolates today, Agnes?'

She turned. There, standing almost beside and slightly behind her, was Sylvia Shaffer. In her hands she held an oval rose-coloured box, a pink ribbon swathed round it and tied in a flat bow at the top.

Agnes switched on a smile. 'Not today, Sylvia.' She indicated the carrier she was holding in her hand. 'More mundane things, I'm afraid.'

Sylvia laughed, her now-familiar tinkling laugh. 'I think I saw you buying game pie, that's not very mundane. Very expensive, isn't it? Every time I come into the store it seems to have gone up a little but it's worth it. Herbert used to love it. I'm sorry I saw you buying it, I didn't mean to pry—rude of me, even to comment.'

Agnes answered, 'Not at all.'

Sylvia went on, 'I'm getting this for Miss Long's secretary's mother. I must go down and see her. I met Amy quite a few times latterly.'

'How nice of you.' Sylvia shrugged. 'Not really. I'm leaving for the States after the book launching. Oh, by the way, I asked the publicity department to send you and,

of course, your husband, an invitation.'
She took the box of chocolates, now in the
white carrier of the Food Halls, and moved
away from the counter. 'I'm thirsty, Agnes.
Would you join me?' Agnes felt her mouth
was dry, maybe due to the air conditioning.
She agreed and they made their way to the
Fruit Bar, found a place at a vacant table
and sat down.

Agnes looked at Sylvia with interest. She
was well dressed. Her pale-blue suit was
well cut. She had on a plain thin gold
necklace and small earrings. Her handbag,
also small, leather, had a cord drawing
the top together. This did not meet with
Agnes' approval, she liked straight lines in
her accessories and there was something
Dolly Vardanish, young about the bag
placed on the table. She flicked open
the small menu listing the fruit drinks.
'Passion fruit?' she asked. Agnes nodded
agreement and they ordered the drinks.

Sylvia leaned back in her chair and
surveyed Agnes, her eyes quizzical. 'As
I said, they've posted you the invitation,
the launch invitation. Sounds like a ship,
doesn't it?' She laughed. The fruit juice
was placed in front of them. 'I see you're
wearing the bracelet—that bracelet that

puzzled me so.' Agnes raised her cuff a little and exposed the gold and diamonds. 'There are people who will steal anything, they're like magpies. By the way, I saw your husband, Bill, isn't it?'

'I didn't know you knew him, or really would recognize him?'

'Oh, yes, Herbert bought a couple of his books. I read them, they interested me. His photograph was in the back of the books.'

'I must tell him, he'll be flattered they interested you.' Agnes was a little surprised.

'Oh, it wasn't meant to flatter, I just like murders.'

'When did you see him?'

Sylvia twisted the glass gently, her well-manicured' nails catching the light, pale-pink varnish this time. 'Just before I came in. He was in his car—was it his? A Mercedes?'

'Yes, he took the car this morning. I believe he was going to Elstree.'

Sylvia twisted the glass a little more. 'Was that your daughter with him, Agnes? What a lovely girl, so tall and graceful.' There was a pause. 'Oh, sorry, have I made a gaffe? It was just that she kissed him as he opened the car door for her, I thought—'

Agnes forced a smile. 'Oh, that will be Greta. She's a lovely girl, isn't she, she's working with Bill.'

'Really, I see.' Sylvia drank her juice and got up. 'Nice to see you again, Agnes. So we'll meet again at the launch. I shall not enjoy it.' She stood looking straight at Agnes. 'I loved Herbert for quite a long time but unfaithfulness wears you out and certainly you can't care about someone unfaithful, not quite as much.' She left the small Fruit Bar, the scent of her perfume lingering behind her for a few seconds. Agnes could not at first get up. Was it the same girl? The tall girl who had posed as a Swedish banker but according to Bill was really only an out-of-work actor? The one she and Helen had seen that day in Bond Street and Agnes had been ashamed of her mistrust. Had she been wrong?

At last she picked up her purchases, left the store and drove home. Bill was not in, but then she was not expecting him until later. Hating herself, she rang the Elstree studio; they were not filming today or rehearsing—no, Bill Turner was not there. She put the telephone down.

'Mac,' she called. He came out of the kitchen, his pink tongue out. 'Walkies?' she said and picked up the lead, snapped the catch onto his collar and left the flat. She must get out, walk, think. Mac approved. They stayed in the park, walking and walking for far longer than usual, about an hour and a half. Bill—Bill, her dear, gentle, reliable Bill, it couldn't be. When he came back tonight he'd tell her about the girl, whoever she was he had picked up to take to wherever they were working. Sylvia hadn't said much but she had said enough. She must not judge, she must not judge, she must not jump to conclusions. If he was having an affair how could she condemn him after Herbert? She felt sick, confused, uncertain. When she got back, she groomed and fed Mac, she changed, put on a particularly attractive housecoat, got the fillet steaks ready for cooking and the asparagus, uncorked a bottle of red wine. She would not believe—could not believe. She remembered Sylvia's words, 'I loved Herbert.' Probably she had. But did she, Agnes, love Bill enough to take his unfaithfulness? Should she tell him about Herbert? No, that had been something so special it could never happen again. But did Bill feel the same? Oh God, how we mess our lives up she thought.

Bill got home about eight thirty. He called out as he came in, 'It's me, darling.'

'Special dinner, Bill. I hope you haven't eaten,' Agnes called back.

'No, I haven't. But why a special?' Bill came into the kitchen and Agnes offered her cheek to be kissed.

'Oh, I don't know. I went to Harrods and felt expensive. Avocado and prawns, fillet steak, asparagus and new potatoes, wine, Brie and biscuits and coffee.'

'Great, what have I done to deserve this?'

Agnes turned and looked at him. 'Being a sweet and faithful husband for three years, well, nearly three years,' she said, and waited for his reaction. He merely kissed her again on the other cheek. Agnes turned on the grill but did not put the steaks under, they would have the avocados then she would pop the steaks under the grill for about three minutes. The asparagus was cooked and bathed in sauce and in the keep-warm oven with the potatoes. Beautifully organized, she thought with a little grimace. Beautifully organized as she always did everything.

The dinner was a tremendous success. Agnes could not analyse her own feelings. Sylvia, Herbert, the girl with Bill, Josephine Long, the dedication, the lies. After coffee Bill put the washing-up in the machine then they went and sat side by side on the settee.

'Did you have a good day, Bill?' Agnes asked suddenly as the television switched to advertisements.

'Not too bad.' Bill did not justify his remark. The advertisements stopped and the documentary resumed. Agnes saw and learned nothing from the screen. She was arguing, arguing with herself in her head. What right had she to object to Bill if he was having an affair and it was going on now. If Herbert had lived she would still be having her affair with him, wouldn't she? How could she blame him? If Sylvia had meant the information in malicious vein, told it because she knew of Herbert's affair or affairs ... Agnes had married late. She was fifty when she married Bill. She looked sideward at her husband; men didn't age as woman aged, she thought. Sylvia, beautifully turned out, well preserved; terrible words, nevertheless she looked brittle, stiff, youth was beautiful.

'Do you remember the girl at the last book party, the Swedish banker she called herself?'

He glanced at her. 'The Swedish banker, the out-of-work actress? Yes, I got her a small part, picked her up this morning.'

Agnes felt a jolt, believe him or not believe him? 'To take her to Elstree?' she said.

Bill lit a cigarette; a sign of stress to help him with a lie, she wondered?

'No, we went to the studio in Ealing to do an interior shot, the only part she appears in, poor kid. It's not much but someone may notice her.'

'Do you see her often, Bill?' Agnes tried to make the question sound easy, casual but Bill drew heavily on the cigarette.

'Now and again,' he said. Did he look uncomfortable? She couldn't tell. Perhaps he did a little. 'I could do with a drink.' He got up and left the room. Agnes was left alone, sitting on the settee. What was best, to know or not to know? She suddenly got a sharp memory picture of Herbert face down as if asleep but dead. Maybe, had he lived he would have tired of her. Maybe Bill would tire of the girl. When he came with a drink he handed her one as well.

'Oh, by the way, darling, I met Sylvia Shaffer in Harrods. She said she had just organized our invitation to the book party. *Cold Night in a Hot Country*, wasn't it?'

'Good, you're getting quite friendly with her, aren't you?'

'Yes, she's not bad when you get past the rather icy exterior.'

Bill smiled at her. 'You liked him too, didn't you?'

'Yes, I did.'

Their eyes locked for a moment then Bill leaned forward and kissed her on the lips. Was that because he knew that she knew about the girl, if there was anything to know, did he guess about Herbert? She looked back at him after the kiss. 'What was that for, Bill?' she asked.

'Oh, a silly cliché ran through my mind—from a play or a picture wasn't it. Love doesn't have to say I'm sorry.'

Agnes wasn't at all sure what he meant or how he meant her to take the words but she knew how it applied to the two of them (at least she thought she knew) and was for a moment reassured.

The next day brought the invitation to Herbert Shaffer's book launch. It was at the Dorchester, which as Bill said, without malice, indicated the difference between himself and Herbert Shaffer. Even seeing Herbert's name on the invitation made Agnes' heart contract a little. But there it was and alas there he was not, only his name and his book remained.

Sylvia Shaffer drove down the road, past the place where Amy had met her death, but not knowing it, although the photographs had appeared in the paper, the road was much the same and the spot was not particularly picked out. She was on her way to the little village where Amy's mother lived. She was not quite sure why she was motivated to call on Amy's mother but something she felt was wrong, something did not fit. Josephine Long's story did not ring true. Sylvia knew her husband, once he had had a lover he did not go back to her and Josephine was not particularly attractive in the first place. The dedication—yes, she had seen it but could not believe it; that Herbert had been having an affair with her, with the agent, and died during it. But the bracelet was an expensive one, surely Josephine Long made enough money to buy herself such a trinket if she really coveted it—somehow she could not envisage her pocketing it in the ladies' lavatory. Still she had, look where it had turned up! But she still felt something was wrong somewhere. Was the plain little Amy in any way involved? That question, Sylvia supposed, was why she was on her way to visit Amy's mother. She had seen the pictures of the cottage, knew the name of the village and judged the village was small enough for her to find the cottage. The chocolates she had bought in Harrods were on the passenger seat beside her. She now thought they were slightly inappropriate for a woman who had recently had a daughter murdered. She didn't know if Amy had any brothers or sisters but she thought she had read somewhere that she was an only child.

The car entered the rather pretty village. Sylvia drove slowly down the main street, and almost at once there was the cottage; small, its front door on the pavement, no front garden, no picket fence, a rather ugly cottage. The newspapers had certainly managed to make it look better than it was. Two doors from a small, rather tacky village shop with a Wall's Ice Cream sign swinging to and fro on the pavement outside. A pushchair with a struggling, red-faced toddler straining against the straps that held it fast and it was bawling loudly, its mouth wide open, its woolly cap ridden up onto the top of its head. As Sylvia drew up a young woman came out of the shop, calling to the baby, 'All right, all right. I'm coming.' She put a carrier bag on the pushchair and wheeled it away. She looked harassed, ill-kempt and cross, the child went on crying.

Sylvia rapped the knocker on the door then noticed a bell on the lintel with a glow of light behind it—a recent addition by the look of it because the paint around was scratched where it had been installed. Nothing happened—then at last she heard movement inside and a voice called out, 'I'm coming, I'm coming. If it's bread, I don't want any.' The door opened and Amy's mother stood looking at Sylvia. She looked about fifty, her face and eyes were young, unexpectedly young. Her fair hair, streaked with grey, was long, untidy, almost to her shoulders and tied back with a piece of ribbon. It had a natural wave and curl at the ends. Sylvia looked downwards. She held a stick in one hand, a deformed hand, and she leaned heavily on it. Dung-coloured cardigan and sheepskin slippers.

'Yes?' Her voice was surprisingly harsh.

'I'm Mrs Shaffer, Sylvia Shaffer, your daughter worked in my husband's agent's office. I was terribly sorry to hear about her death.'

The woman pursed her lips. 'Come in.' She turned and limped away up the small passage, supposedly called the hall, turned left into a rather dark room. The window did not let in much light but Sylvia could see the little general shop, at least the side wall of it and a small part of the front.

'Sit down, Mrs—er ...' The woman hesitated.

'Shaffer.'

'What did you say you were?'

Sylvia repeated the information she had given on the doorstep. The woman's stick clattered to the floor, Sylvia picked it up and leant it against the armchair into which the woman had lowered herself and, at her request, sat down opposite her.

'Thank you. Would you like a cup of tea Mrs Chaffer?' Sylvia shook her head.

The woman looked relieved. 'I can't move much. Now Amy's gone it's ...' She paused. Sylvia thought she was going to cry and prayed not but she only closed her eyes for a moment then opened them, those very young, blue eyes. 'She was really silly to buy that car but she was a good girl. She got a rise, two rises, and of course she thought it would be good, easier to drive down, take me out, she said on the telephone. She was a good girl. What's that?'

Sylvia had just put the chocolates on the table, the pretty decorated box stood uneasily beside a lace mat on which was a vase of plastic flowers.

'Chocolates. I'm so sorry, I didn't know what to bring you.'

Amy's mother did not smile but she looked at Sylvia. 'It was good of you, well, nice of you to come. Did you say Miss Long sent you?'

Sylvia tried again, raising her voice a little, realizing the woman, among all her other afflictions, was a little deaf.

'Oh, well, it was nice of you, thank you for that.' She motioned towards the table and Sylvia noticed again how deformed her hand was.

'So Amy told you that she was buying a car?'

Amy's mother nodded. 'Oh, yes, she

was very pleased, very excited. Well, she deserved it, I think.' She shifted in her chair and made a little grimace as she moved her hip. 'She was a good daughter with more spirit than I gave her credit for.'

'To drive again after such a long time, you mean?'

Mrs Robertson nodded. 'That too. But she tackled Miss Long, said the rise wasn't enough, and got another one.' Sylvia tried to look interested but the next remark made her looking interested no effort. 'Yes. Amy knew something that she shouldn't have.'

'What do you mean, Mrs Robertson?'

There was a bang on the door, a key turned and a woman, elderly, white-haired, came in. 'Oh, I'm sorry I didn't know you had a visitor. I thought I'd make a cup of tea for you.'

'This is Mrs Hudson, my next-door neighbour. She thinks I'll scald myself so she makes me tea. Do have one with me, Mrs Chaffer.'

Sylvia agreed, almost absent-mindedly. The remark the woman had made, 'she knew something she shouldn't have', stopped her hearing what was said, made her preoccupied, curious, anxious to hear more.

Mrs Hudson made the tea and brought in a tray with pretty china, one of the saucers was slightly dusty; the teaset had probably been brought out specially when the neighbour had seen the visitor. 'There now—"enjoy" as my American son-in-law says.' She went out, closing the door quietly behind her.

'She is so good, I don't know what I'd do without her.' Mrs Robertson put her hand towards the teapot.

'No, let me.' Sylvia was about the grasp the handle of the teapot.

'Stir it first, I like it strong,' Amy's mother said.

The tea poured, the biscuits passed, four chocolate Digestives on a paper doily on a matching plate, Sylvia asked, 'What do you think your daughter knew that she shouldn't have, Mrs Robertson?' Sylvia tried to make her question sound casual.

'Well, the book wasn't dedicated to Miss Long, Josephine Long, at all, it was dedicated to someone else. She said I shouldn't tell anyone but it doesn't matter now, does it? Not now she's dead, I mean.'

Suddenly she got out a handkerchief from her cardigan pocket and wiped her eyes. 'I miss her coming, Mrs Chaffer, I really do.'

Sylvia waited a moment before she pressed the woman to go on. 'And you don't know who the book was really dedicated to?'

'No, but it wasn't Miss Long. She was very keen to have it dedicated to her and she altered it to her name and gave it to Amy to post to the publishers.'

Sylvia nodded slowly. 'And why do you suppose Miss Long was so anxious to have her name on it, the dedication I mean?'

'Suppose it was an honour, you know, having a book dedicated to you and she wanted it. Amy said she was like that.'

Sylvia nodded again. 'I see.'

The woman picked up a book from the chair beside her. 'I mean look.' She opened the book at the fifth page and handed it to Sylvia. In the middle of the page it read, *To Patricia Highsmith in admiration.* That's an honour, I think.'

Sylvia handed the book back to her. 'But you don't know who the book was really dedicated to?'

Amy's mother put down the cup with

a slight rattle into the saucer. Sylvia wondered how she could ever hold the cup in a hand that was so deformed, but she managed it. 'No, she wouldn't tell me that. Just that Miss Long altered it. More tea?'

Sylvia got up. 'No, I must go Mrs Robertson. I really came just to say how very sorry I am about Amy. Thank you for the tea, it was so nice.' The woman put both hands on the arms of her chair as if she wanted to get up and see her visitor off. 'Please don't get up.'

'Thank you for the chocolates, Mrs Chaffer.' Sylvia did no more to correct the name. She was not even sure that Mrs Robertson realized that she was the wife of the man who had written the book, but it didn't matter, it didn't matter at all.

As she closed the front door behind her and walked to her car, Sylvia thought of Amy. The only times she had seen the girl had been when she went to the agent's office. Once, twice, she had dropped in a manuscript for Herbert one day, she had called in again, she couldn't remember what for, probably at Herbert's request. Yet now, having seen a little of the girl's background and seen the picture

310

flashed on the television screen and in the newspapers—she seemed more real. That 'she knew something that she shouldn't have' seemed to make the girl more alive now she was dead. Whose name was on the dedication that Josephine Long had discarded and substituted with her own? Silly woman. What did it matter now? Should she go to see her, demand that she tell her the original name, was it worth it? She didn't owe much to Herbert, only his money and certainly not a faithful marriage.

Sylvia was a little surprised that Amy's mother had not mentioned the police or how many visits they had made. Obviously, as mother of the murdered girl, police and reporters had visited her, but either she was reticent about these visits or did not think they were worth mentioning. Maybe police visits to call on such a lonely and disabled woman might be, in that little village, something not to be talked about. Her grief too, was low key, just the almost furtive wiping of the eyes. She had not spoken of any other children or any other relatives. Sylvia's mind still came back to that remark, it wouldn't leave her, 'she knew something that she shouldn't have'. Josephine, by the sound of it, was an adulteress, a thief and a liar and she supposed if she had changed the dedication she was also a type of forger, not someone to try and question.

Josephine Long had read one and a half chapters of a new novel her chief reader had recommended. The reader was a youngish woman of about thirty-two, whose opinion Josephine respected, and the beginning of the book was certainly worth reading. She had lately, she felt, been rather lax with her work, so many things, emotions seemed to be surrounding her like high waves, heavy seas. Josephine Long was proud of the literary agency she had built, authors trusted her, felt she was doing her best for them but lately there had been so much to disturb her concentration, occupy her thoughts. Herbert Shaffer's death had hit her hard, foolish really. Herbert had, it was sadly true, finished with their affair, drifted on to someone else, but she hadn't changed, she had gone on loving him. Then the bracelet story that she simply had to back up, agree had happened, changing the dedication. To his contract for his last book, dear dear Herbert, she had given her whole undivided attention, every bit of her had gone in to make as much money for him as she could, as if it were a homage. That was stupid really because his wife would get it all, but perhaps— She felt that was all she could do for him now. What the dedication might do, what effect it might have on Mrs Shaffer she did not care about at all.

As she read the second chapter the telephone rang. She picked it up, her eyes still on the manuscript in front of her, it was the police. Could they come and see her, just a few more questions, or would she rather come to the station? Josephine felt panic, that ending, 'would she rather come to the station?'—it sounded threatening, but what more could she tell them? They had asked so many questions, they had been twice to question her, why again? She had told them about the girl's work, her rise—both rises, the car; there was so little she could tell them about the girl's private life.

'Why more questions? I've told you all I can.'

'Oh, just a few more routine questions, Miss Long. We can call in, chat, won't take long. In your office perhaps?'

'Very well, but I really don't understand.' The phone went off and Josephine replaced her receiver, got up, went to a cupboard, got out a bottle and poured herself a brandy, she felt alone and frightened. She walked to and fro behind her desk. Why hadn't she talked to Amy more? She'd never really liked the girl, perhaps that was the reason. But if she had talked to the girl more, heard all about her mother, her home, what good would it have done?

The police, a Detective Inspector Henderson by name and a new younger man with him, fair-haired and fresh-faced, looking as if he were there to learn. Josephine put two chairs for them and sat down in her own swivel chair behind her desk. Once seated she felt a little less fearful, after all how many timid authors had sat opposite her, asking advice and listening to her suggestions for changes in the books? New writers who would take her advice, do almost anything to get their work accepted and she, Josephine Long, was to them a magic key that might open the door to a publishing house.

'Am I right in understanding you gave

Amy Robertson two rises, Miss Long, why was that?'

'I told you, I thought the first was inadequate.'

'I see.' Detective Inspector Henderson had an irritating habit of leaning forward in his chair, putting one hand on the desk and drumming gently with his fingertips; his nails were bitten. He seemed quite unconscious of the finger tapping. More questions, all of which she had answered before, and then one she hadn't.

'Amy's mother, Miss Long, you had not met her, I believe?' He stopped drumming.

'No I never met her, I've told you that already.'

'Yes, I believe you did. But she told us something, the girl's mother I mean, said something, I wonder if you could explain to us—tell us what she might have meant.'

Josephine felt and was aware she looked puzzled. 'What did she say?'

'That Amy knew something she shouldn't have.' The younger man said those words, the older one just looked at her, no doubt to get her reaction. Josephine fought hard not to show any reaction at all.

'What could she have meant by that?'

315

She was aware that her voice trembled a little and she coughed midsentence to try and hide it.

'Well, her mother, Mrs Robertson, felt her daughter could have been killed because of this something she knew, Miss Long.'

Josephine had given up smoking years ago but suddenly she longed for a cigarette.

The questioning went on. 'Something about the dedication of a book Miss Long—being changed?'

'Changed? The book was dedicated to me, I would hardly want to change it.'

The Inspector answered, with a patient, persistent look, 'Well, Miss Long, why should the deceased say it was changed, what possible motive could she have had?'

'I don't know, I simply don't know.' Josephine felt she was raising her voice too much but could not stop herself.

Then an even more disturbing question. 'Well, just as a routine, Miss Long, where were you on the morning of Miss Robertson's death?'

'Are you suggesting—do you think I killed her?' Her voice rose even more in spite of her efforts to stay calm.

'No, just a routine question Miss Long,

we're not suggesting anything at all.'

'Well, I was in my flat, I spent the weekend at home.'

Henderson looked at his shoes. 'Anyone staying with you that weekend, Miss Long, or did anyone call that morning?'

'The milkman, the paper boy.'

'Ah, that would be earlier, wouldn't it? Well, that's all for now, I think.' Both men got up. 'Thank you for being so cooperative, Miss Long.'

Josephine saw them through the outer office and locked the door behind them. She felt sick, almost faint, she was convinced they thought she had killed the girl. She was sure from the way the questions had come out, why else would they want to know where she was that morning, why else? She'd got to talk to Agnes Turner, she'd just got to, no matter what Agnes had said about not getting in touch with her. What about road rage, what had happened to that? She poured and drank a little more brandy, sat down at her desk, put out a shaking hand, picked up the telephone and dialled Agnes Turner's number. As the telephone buzzed its intermittent note she hoped Agnes' husband would not answer

the phone. She was lucky, it was Agnes'
voice that answered as she always did,
not giving the number. Josephine drew
a long breath before she answered. She
knew Agnes would not be pleased and
she certainly was not.

'Josephine, what is it now?'

Josephine decided to take the bull by the
horns. 'I think they feel I might be the one
who killed Amy.'

There was a pause. 'Whatever makes you
think that?'

Agnes' voice was a trace less abrupt.
'They asked me what I was doing, where
I was the morning she was killed.'

'How ridiculous, what did you say?'

Josephine broke down. 'I feel so frightened, Agnes, I can't talk to anyone but
you, please let's meet somewhere.'

Another pause, then, 'Very well, the
same place, the café by the Serpentine
tomorrow morning at eleven o'clock.' The
telephone was replaced by Agnes none too
gently, Josephine put her receiver down
and noticed that her hand was still shaking.
Well, she was meeting Agnes, but what
could Agnes do for her? Nothing but
talk to her, the only person she could
talk to who would perhaps relieve some

of her fears. Was she overreacting to what might, after all, be as they said 'a routine question'? Perhaps others were being asked where they were, where they had been that morning, but who? Whom else could they ask?

Agnes meanwhile was having her own problems. She had not been able to forget being told Bill had been seen kissing that lovely girl. Well, why shouldn't he? His wife was fifty-odd, for God's sake men did this! It was proving themselves, that's what they said, that's what people told her—her friends. But she would have to accept it, say nothing, allow the affair to go on, perhaps that was the way to handle it, let it go on for a while then Gerta, or whatever the name was, would get out of the affair, get tired of being with an older man, look for a younger one. 'Please God, please God,' she said aloud to herself, alone in the bedroom putting the moisturizing cream on she felt would do no good. Jealousy—something new to her, she had never suffered from jealousy before, never loved anyone enough but suffer was the right word for the feeling, suffering it was. Her own affair with Herbert, had Bill ever found out what would he have felt? Jealousy like she was feeling now?

Bill came home latish that evening, he was tired but triumphant. 'It's going well, darling, really well. For the first time I feel, as the kids say, I'm getting my head round it.' He laughed. He looked young, well, younger. Was it because of—?

Suddenly she couldn't bear the uncertainty any longer. She went up to him, put her hands on his shoulders. 'Do you sometimes feel you would like ...' She stopped, gripped his shoulders a little tighter.

'Would like what?' He looked at her, his face serious.

'Would like a younger woman, to go to bed with, I mean?'

Bill put his arms round her. 'Who has been saying what, darling?' He said it with humour.

'Oh, nothing, Bill. I just thought—'

'Well, don't think, not about things like that. We have a good marriage, darling, we love each other, you must know how I feel about you. I'm as likely to want someone else as I hope you are, right, darling?'

That was that. Was it a strange avoiding strategic answer or was it the truth? Agnes retained her grip on Bill's shoulders, his eyes looked into hers, honest eyes, true eyes? Yet hers that looked back into his, did they look the same, was that what kept her marriage together, accepting no matter what?

'Right, sweetheart,' she said, and kissed his lips. It was then the telephone rang, Agnes went to answer it. It was Josephine Long. When she came back into the sitting room Bill was reading *The Times*, he didn't even ask her who it was, just looked at her and smiled, and she smiled back at him.

She did not feel very much like smiling, Josephine's almost hysterical phone call had shaken her a little. Why had the police gone back to her, why had they asked her where she was on the morning Amy was murdered? She needed to think and think alone, but after the little scene, almost a love scene with Bill, she felt the need to stay with him. They sat very close together on the settee; there was something unspoken between them, an atmosphere both warm and enveloping. Agnes had never felt so close to Bill and she wondered, was Bill feeling the same? As if in answer to her feelings he put out a hand and covered hers. She thrust thoughts of Josephine Long and Amy Robertson out of her mind, she would give her whole thoughts to this new problem Josephine was facing after Bill and she were in bed and he was asleep, then she would think. She always did her best planning in the dark. They watched television and Agnes was able to give her whole attention to the play on the screen.

'Another murder mystery?' Bill said lightly.

'Good for business, our business darling,' Agnes replied.

Sylvia Shaffer was determined to make the launch of her husband's book as well presented and memorable as she possibly could, rather for the benefit of herself than her dead husband. The publishers had chosen the Dorchester and the invitations were at that moment being sent out. Sylvia remembered only too well how much Herbert had detested his own book launches, but strangely enough had quite enjoyed other people's. This time, however, he would not be there to suffer the launching of his last book.

When long ago he and Sylvia had met he had swept her off her feet. He had been handsome, slim, ambitious; she had been pretty, longing for parties, pretty clothes, expensive perfume and with an ambition to attain these things that matched his for attaining fame and fortune. As the years had gone by, no children had arrived, which did not worry either of them, neither were particularly child-lovers. Sex had dwindled away. His affairs had been numerous and it hardly bothered her and it hardly bothered him to keep them from her. He became, in her opinion, gross, unattractive. They learned to tolerate each other, spending much of their time apart and leading their own lives.

As to this dedication, her friends would find it unremarkable. She was determined to deliver the invitation to Josephine Long herself, she was curious to see if it was true that Josephine Long had loved him so much, how his death, particularly under such circumstances, had affected her. Sylvia felt Herbert's agent was a strange woman; stiff, rather old-maidish in some ways, a trifle bossy perhaps? But Herbert, as he had grown older, may have liked a more dominating woman, maybe in bed as well as in the office. A change in him could have happened and she herself would have been totally unaware of it.

Sylvia went by taxi to the agent's office. The door was locked—unusual. The few times Sylvia had visited the place the outer door had been unlocked and she had gone in and been greeted by the secretary. Now Sylvia rapped on the door; there was a pause, then it opened and Josephine Long stood in the doorway then backed away to let her enter.

'Mrs Shaffer?'

Sylvia was taken aback by the appearance of the woman. She looked much thinner, her face was very pale and the make-up had done little to help, the blusher certainly didn't help at all. 'I thought I would bring the invitation to you myself, Miss Long.' She held out the white envelope.

'Oh, the invitation to the book launch, thank you.' She took the envelope. 'Do come through.' They walked through to the inner office.

'You have not got a new secretary yet, even a temporary one?' Sylvia asked.

'Secretary? No, I haven't bothered, not yet. I can't. I'm being so harassed by the police.' Almost by habit she sat down in her swivel chair.

Sylvia did not sit down, she looked at

the untidy desk littered with manuscripts and torn-open envelopes. 'Harassed by the police, Miss Long, why's that?'

Josephine shook her head. 'I don't know, I don't know. Please sit down, Mrs Shaffer.'

Sylvia remained standing. 'No, I must go.'

'I think they imagine I killed Amy Robertson, Mrs Shaffer.' The words were blurted out, she did not raise her eyes to Sylvia's.

'Oh, nonsense, of course they don't. The papers and television attributed it to "road rage", I'm sure you heard that yourself.'

Josephine almost jumped to her feet then sank back into her chair. 'Then why are they asking where I was the day Amy was murdered?'

Sylvia was surprised herself that such a question had been asked but she did her best to minimize the importance of the question. 'Well, I expect—that's ridiculous—I expect they're asking everyone that.'

'Who is everyone, Mrs Shaffer?'

Sylvia thought of her visit to Amy Robertson's mother and she decided to say nothing about it. If Miss Long decided to visit Mrs Robertson and found out that Herbert's wife had been there, well so what! Sylvia thought of the words heard in that little cottage, 'She knew something that she shouldn't have', thought she understood them better, or maybe she did. Perhaps Herbert had dedicated the book to his wife? She thought it very unlikely, but if he had and Josephine Long had put her own name there instead she could understand how Amy and her mother would feel and she felt that the woman sitting at the desk in front of her deserved all she was getting. 'I shouldn't worry, Miss Long, I'm sure it will all blow over.' She pushed the white envelope containing the invitation further across the desk. 'Anyway, I hope we shall see you at the launch, I'm sure Herbert would have wanted you to be there.'

Josephine Long looked up. 'Do you think he would have, Mrs Shaffer? He was a wonderful man. It's very nice and understanding of you to say so, I did love him, really I did.'

'I'm sure you did.' Sylvia felt she was speaking as if to a backward child or an imbecile. 'Well, goodbye, Miss Long.'

The agent did not attempt to see her out. Sylvia's high heels tapped across the floor of the outer office, she gave a brief glance at the desk where the dead girl used to sit. She sensed Josephine Long standing motionless at her desk, watching her. As she closed the door of the outer office behind her, Sylvia was aware of a fleeting thought: Did Josephine Long kill the girl, was the car, seen nearby in the lane, hers? Good God, the thought startled her and all just for the dedication in a book! Could she have done such a thing?

Once in the taxi on her way home she felt glad she had delivered the invitation herself and seen Josephine Long. The circumstances of her lover's death in bed beside her must have been pretty horrific, but she deserved it, in Sylvia's opinion. She deserved anything she was getting, after all she had proved herself an adulteress, a thief, a liar and even, Sylvia thought again with a slight, malicious smile, a forger. Perhaps the police might have taken the woman into custody before the party. Whatever happened Sylvia was very determined not to get involved in any way. There was something so sordid, so tacky about the whole affair and now she was left, left with Herbert's money and her own. She could travel as much as she wanted. She wondered, should she settle in the States, she really preferred it there and had many friends there too? But then England was nice, she loved London—perhaps it would run to two houses; a small apartment in New York and keep the flat in London. It was comfortable surmising such things, much better than thinking of a frustrated literary agent, much better. She got out of the taxi when she arrived at her flat and gave the man such a large tip that he leant out of the cab and said, 'Thanks, miss—have a nice day!'

Detective Inspector Henderson looked round his team, one or two nodded, some looked blank. He focused on a young, blonde, pretty policewoman who was looking at him with large eyes and he realized probably thinking of something totally different.

'Now I want door-to-door in Albion Square. It's not easy, it's not going to be easy at all. Posh houses never are—right?' Detective Inspector Henderson coughed and waited and the blonde young policewoman said, 'Oh, I don't know sir.'

'Well maybe not.' Henderson looked at

his watch. 'I want to know if anyone, anyone saw Miss Long go out on the morning Amy Robertson was murdered, from say eight in the morning onward.'

Young Hill, sitting next to the policewoman looked knowing.

The young policewoman leaned near to him and whispered, 'What's his bag?'

'Well, motive and opportunity, that's what she's got, this Miss Long.'

'It's only a dedication in a book, for God's sake.'

Hill nodded. 'Yes, but as the guv says, if he'd sort of passed her up, you know, made the book a tribute to his wife instead of to her, Miss Long changes it, the secretary twigs it and puts the bite on—wants more and more.'

'Even so,' the policewoman persisted.

'Oh, there's more. She's been through it a bit, this Josephine Long, after all this lover, Herbert, dies beside her in bed, perhaps while he was on the job or maybe he was doing the "back to the wife" speech—who knows?'

Henderson was waving them off. 'I think, and the guv thinks, she's anxious, frightened. She could have done it, desperate.' They filed out.

'So there goes your "road rage",' someone said.

DI Henderson stayed where he was, standing at the desk at the end of the room. He went over to the map, traced his finger over the route from Albion Square (where Josephine Long lived) on, on through London to the town where the garage was where the mechanic had looked at the car, advised the girl, then on towards the village and there—bingo! The car stops—another car stops not far behind, a few minutes later, maybe longer, a car is seen by a householder turning—was that the same car that the witness in the passing vehicle had seen parked? He rubbed his forehead, strangling, garrotting—womanlike? He had a gut feeling about the woman's guilt, the whole thing seemed to speak to him, say to him, 'It's a woman's crime'. The wife, worth going back to? But not keen to have our Herbert back when he had talked to her, had only met the agent a few times, Mrs Shaffer, aware hubby was playing around—couldn't care less. Cold bitch, was the DCI's diagnosis of Sylvia Shaffer.

Josephine Long might see the police moving around Albion Square, he judged her frightened. She could be at the office most of the time, so she might not see much of the door-to-door, but if she did, well, she did. There was nothing to go on, nothing, but someone had killed the girl. No sexual assault, no robbery, he didn't buy the road rage theory, not at all, never had. Jealousy, hate, malice, revenge, robbery, sex—all these motivated killing. If he could get jealousy, hate and revenge all on a line on the fruit machine he'd get the jackpot. Miss Long was a likely suspect. Henderson was a cautious man, he moved slowly. He had a lot of collars to his credit, today or tomorrow Albion Square door-to-door might turn up something, maybe he could afford to let Miss Josephine Long stew. The door-to-door enquiries might produce nothing. People who lived in such respectable, wealthy environments usually kept themselves to themselves. The best source of information in such a place often came from the gardener or the dailies. It would be a boring and painstaking task. No one relished the job, he could see, and it took up valuable time.

Another thing on his mind; a witness had come forward two days after the murder, just a telephone call, to say a car had backed into his driveway to turn. This always annoyed the owner of the rather attractive private house and he had gone out to remonstrate with the driver, but it had gone, with, as he put it, a rather jerky start, which had raised a little flurry of gravel; another cause for annoyance. The description of the car had been vague. He had hardly been able to see it for the shrubbery around the entrance to his drive, just the top of it. Hill had journeyed down to see the man, a Mr Sebastian Mellor. He had got almost no description of the car and certainly not even a glimpse of the number plate or the driver. He had thought the car had been brown or maybe maroon, Mr Mellor could not say any more than that.

Henderson had decided to call on Josephine Long again and asked to look at her car. It was a dull copper colour, certainly not maroon and certainly not brown; though I suppose the copper, he thought, could be confused with brown. It had an upper brake light which the man had described, so many cars had that now. Henderson had noticed though, and so had Hill, that there were a few sharp pieces of gravel embedded in her tyres. Miss Long had not taken the further visit at all well, had spoken hotly of 'police harassment' and why didn't they understand her fondness for her dead secretary and the shock it had been to her. She had also appeared completely baffled as to why they wanted to examine her car, let alone the tyres. Little or nothing had appeared in the papers about a car that had turned in someone's drive.

DI Henderson had ended up feeling rather sorry for the woman. If she was innocent so many things were falling into place to make her look guilty. Had she gone out that morning, or had she, as she persisted in saying, not left her flat all day? Well, if someone had seen her leave or come home, things would not look good for her and she would have to be asked to come to the station for more questioning.

Meanwhile the murder of Amy Robertson had stopped being front-page news. 'Enquiries are being followed up.' Henderson sighed, so little to go on, an ageing Metro, an unattractive girl choked to death; no blood, no sex, no robbery and an open handbag on the passenger seat containing a purse with sixty pounds and loose change untouched. Road rage, he didn't think so, had never thought so. The car had broken down at the garage and had done again exactly what the man had said it would, broken down again. No leads at all, except the tenuous one that led to Miss Josephine Long. Did she go out that morning, or did she not? If she did go out in her car and was out during the time of the killing, it boded ill for her. Was she lying or wasn't she? Albion Square might tell him, but it might not. Meanwhile he had to do what was so often an annoying part of his job—wait and see.

Agnes sat waiting for Josephine. From where she sat she could see the Serpentine. Two swans, sailing across the water against the green background of shrubs, raised their graceful necks then dipped them down to the water to sweep up pieces of bread a few people standing on the bank were throwing to them. There was also a small cluster of ducks, noisy, disturbing the glassy water with sudden flapping, wild wings and landing quacking where the bread was thrown.

Josephine was late but Agnes felt in a particularly relaxed and peaceful mood. She sat watching the birds, thinking of nothing, her mind already prepared for any eventuality the conversation might bring up. The agent's hysterical outburst on the telephone was still in her mind and she had prepared her answers, she felt, for almost anything that Josephine could accuse the police of saying to her or accusing her of. She hoped things had not progressed so far as that and she hoped that Josephine was not being followed, she doubted it and hoped not. She did not particularly want to be seen with her and get involved with her troubles.

She thought as she watched the feeding birds that if Josephine was right and the police did suspect her of killing Amy it would not mean a great deal, even if she were imprisoned she felt away from it, it did not matter to her. After all Josephine had no husband to worry about, no one who would be hurt or heartbroken by her being in prison, no children, no relations that she had ever mentioned. Agnes recognized the coldness in herself but she knew that's how she was.

At last Josephine arrived, she looked much the same. Agnes was bored by the change in her looks, her fear, her eternal clutching for reassurance. This time, however, Josephine was quieter. She recounted the visit of the police, the examination of her tyres, which she couldn't understand, though she did realize and had read about the car backing into a gravel drive. There was about her a quiet resignation.

'They think I did it, Agnes, and in a way they're right. If I—'

She was about to start on the old rigmarole of the car again. Agnes stopped her, 'Could you give them a straight answer about the Saturday morning, Josephine, did you go out?'

'No, I didn't go out all that day. On Sunday I went out to dinner, that was the only time during the whole weekend.'

'Didn't anyone see you, call, telephone during the Saturday morning?' Agnes tapped the table a trace impatiently. 'They must have, Josephine, surely.'

But she shook her head. 'The postman came and the milkman and the paper boy, they say that was all too early. They want to know about later.' She ordered mineral water and drank the whole contents of the glass at a gulp as if she were thirsty. 'The police, two of them, have been in Albion Square this morning. I saw them early knocking on doors, asking about me, I suppose. I don't really care, Agnes. It seems since Herbert's gone it really doesn't matter all that much.' She ordered another mineral water. 'It could have been me, the man in the dark suit walking towards the car; I have a black trouser suit, I could have worn it.'

'But if you can prove you didn't leave the house, I mean your flat ...'

Josephine shook her head. 'I can't.'

Agnes felt the conversation was getting nowhere. 'Do you know, if he, if Herbert had loved me, none of this would have happened. We could have lived together, worked together—why didn't he stay with me? I would have done anything in the world for him, Agnes.'

'He might still have died, Josephine.'

Josephine shook her head. 'No, I don't think he would, I think he would have lived, we would have been together.'

Agnes watched her. There was something so real about what Josephine was saying and the realness got to Agnes, this was no infatuation, no hero-worship, she had really loved Herbert and he didn't deserve such love any more than she herself did. Agnes sighed, he would have probably left her,

Agnes, in the end for someone else even though the dedication had said 'for ever'. She saw in front of her eyes the written dedication, his signature, as if she had it in her hand at the moment, she could have written it, copied it exactly, just from memory, as if she had photographed it, not Amy, not on paper but in her head.

She looked across at the quiet yet distraught woman opposite. 'Well, I don't know what to say to comfort you. I don't believe Herbert was a faithful man, I don't believe he would have been faithful to anyone, he certainly wasn't to Sylvia and I doubt he would have been to me.'

Josephine put her head down onto her hand for a moment. 'He would have to be to me, I believe, in the end he must have realized how I felt.'

Agnes had nothing more to say. She knew that she was not capable of feeling as Josephine Long did. She had known it long ago but she could recognize it in the other woman—the constancy. 'Well, I'll see you at the launch of Herbert's book, Josephine.'

'Oh of course, I couldn't let him down. People know I am—was—his agent, they would think it strange if I wasn't there.

Of course but with the dedication—but I can't help that.' She drank the rest of her mineral water then with her lips twisted in a little smile she added, 'That is, of course, if I'm not in prison.'

'Of course you won't be, don't even think such a thing.'

Josephine shrugged, stood up. Agnes thought how much she had changed, she was not thinking of the loss of weight, the loss of colour, no, she seemed to have acquired a new dignity and maybe a quiet acceptance of Herbert's and perhaps Amy's death. Possibly in a way she blamed herself for both. 'Thank you for seeing me, Agnes, bearing with me. I'll see you at the launch.' She walked away and did not look back. Agnes wondered what she was being thanked for. She got up and strolled slowly along the waterside, the swans had gone away and the ducks, the water was still for the moment. They would come back when more people gathered on the bank to feed them.

Agnes was with Bill at the launch of Herbert Shaffer's last book. She looked round her and thought to herself: This is where it all started. She sipped the white wine, it was light, slightly fruity and delicious. Everything else around her was the same as that other book launch which seemed now so long ago, so much had happened. The atmosphere was the same; the publishers, the agents, the writers. The difference, there was no Herbert. A large photograph of him stared down from the wall and several of his books were carefully or was it carelessly laid on tables for people to pick up and riffle through. There was the dedication—TO JOSEPHINE WHO IS MY FOR EVER. Some people must have noticed it but Agnes did not hear any reaction from anyone.

Sylvia came up to Agnes and Bill. She kissed Agnes, air-kissed and pressed Bill's arm. 'Sad Herbert's not here,' she said, 'but he wouldn't have enjoyed it, he hated launches, particularly his own.'

'He came to mine,' Bill said with his usual pleasant smile.

'Good, I'm glad he did.' Sylvia drew on her cigarette then stubbed it out in a nearby ashtray. She did not mention the dedication either, neither did Agnes. Agnes had glimpsed Josephine Long across the crowded room but decided not to go over to her.

Bill wandered off but there seemed no young and beautiful girls around. Agnes saw him join up with a good-looking grey-haired man who looked and sounded like an American. A woman with rather too golden hair joined her. 'This smoke gets my contact lenses,' she said, dabbing her mascara delicately with a tissue.

Agnes sympathized. 'More writers smoke than other people, do you think?' she said.

'Yes, funny that, I suppose it's the tension.' The woman put the tissue away. 'I write historical romances, by the way. Marion Hunter.' Agnes put on an interested expression. 'Wine gives me a headache,' the woman went on but emptied her glass nevertheless.

A man joined them. 'Hello, darling. How's tricks?'

'Bloody advance decreased again.'

'No, really?' Agnes melted away.

After a time she contacted Bill to see if that little message might pass between them that meant he was ready to leave, but he only smiled and waved to her and went on chatting animatedly with an elderly lady smoking a cigarette. Agnes was pleased to see Bill was not smoking. She felt she wanted a rest from the noise and chattering people and made her way to the ladies' room.

Inside it was a haven of quiet. The soft pink lights and the pink mirrors were soothing if a little inadequate for checking one's make-up. Apparently it was empty. Agnes crossed the pink carpet and looked at herself in the mirror, took out a lipstick and repaired the colour on her lower lip, patted her hair, sat down for a moment on a seat, she felt tired.

After a few minutes there was a sudden noise behind her and from a separate room which housed the lavatories Josephine emerged. She was clutching a glass in her hand with a little fizzy water still in it. It flashed across Agnes' mind, her nurse's mind, thinking of the two glasses of mineral water Josephine had drunk at the waterside café—was she diabetic? The next moment she knew this was not the case.

'Agnes, I'm glad I've met you in here, I'm leaving, I can't stay.' She put the glass down on the little make-up table. 'I brought this in to finish off.' She smiled at Agnes and picked up a glass of wine standing beside the other glass, she had obviously put it there. She drank it.

'Did anyone say anything to you about the dedication, Josephine?'

Josephine shook her head and answered almost vaguely, 'Some people said—made remarks. One said it was a great compliment, things like that, I didn't listen, Agnes, it's over now.'

'Over?'

Josephine drew a small plastic bottle from her pocket, it was empty. Agnes could read the label, smudged and old, she could still see 'Nembutal gms 1.5, take one or two at night'. Above it was printed, 'Mrs C. Long'. 'They were my mother's, I've always saved them, just in case. Now I've taken them all, Agnes.'

Agnes could not believe her. 'Why have you done that, how many were there, how many have you taken, Josephine?' She was already, in her mind, telephoning the nearest hospital, stomach wash-outs, saving life.

Josephine finished the wine. 'I've rung for a taxi, I trust you, Agnes, to say nothing, tell nobody.' Agnes backed away from her, for a moment she felt unable to decide anything and Josephine went on, 'You had more than I did of him, of his love, but maybe he and I will meet up somewhere.' She laughed a rather shaking laugh and opened the door then she turned once more. 'Goodbye, Agnes. As I told you I trust you to honour my privacy, I can't live without him.' The door swung to behind her. Agnes opened it, she watched Josephine cross the room—did she stagger a little at the door? Agnes followed her, watched her go across the front hall of the hotel, through the front doors, the concierge opened the door of the taxi and slammed it to, saluted and it drove away from the kerb and mixed in with the other traffic.

Agnes went back into the powder room and sat down again. Would the police take the suicide as a confession of the murder of Amy? With Josephine's death all danger to Bill and herself and her marriage was wiped out. So be it. Had there been enough capsules in that bottle? A lot of questions poured through Agnes' mind. Would Josephine get to Albion Square or end up being taken by the taxi driver to the nearest casualty department and have her life saved? Or would she get to her own bed, sleep and still be alive in the morning? Time would tell and time only.

Agnes got up, went back into the

crowded room, where people were still chatting, smoking, kissing each other goodbye, drinking. She went and stood by a long table, looked up at Herbert's face—those yellow eyes looked down at her, the lips were slightly parted just showing the gleam of his white teeth. She felt his arms round her, perhaps she thought for the last time. TO AGNES WHO IS MY FOR EVER.

'Ready for off, darling?' Bill stood beside her.

'Yes, Bill, quite ready.'

Bill looked up at the picture of Herbert Shaffer. 'Pity he died, probably had a lot more to write about—to say.'

'Maybe he'd said it all,' Agnes answered but Bill didn't hear her, he was busy saying goodnight to one or two people behind them, nor did he hear the words as she left the room; she had to say it once more but this time it was different—

'TO JOSEPHINE WHO IS MY FOR EVER.'

This Large Print Book for the Partially sighted, who cannot read normal print, is published under the auspices of

THE ULVERSCROFT FOUNDATION

Other DALES Mystery Titles In Large Print